THE MERCY BOYS

John Burnside was born in 1955 and now lives in Fife. He has published six collections of poetry and has won a number of awards, including the Geoffrey Faber Memorial Prize. He was selected as one of the twenty Best of Young British Poets in 1994. His first novel, *The Dumb House*, was published in 1997.

THE MERCY BOYS

JOHN BURNSIDE

Jonathan Cape
London

Published by Jonathan Cape 1999

2 4 6 8 10 9 7 5 3 1

First published in Great Britain in 1999 by Jonathan Cape
Random House, 20 Vauxhall Bridge Road, London SW1V 2SA

Random House Australia (Pty) Limited
20 Alfred Street, Milsons Point, Sydney,
New South Wales 2061, Australia

Random House New Zealand Limited
18 Poland Road, Glenfield,
Auckland 10, New Zealand

Random House South Africa (Pty) Limited
Endulini, 5A Jubilee Road, Parktown 2193, South Africa

Random House UK Limited Reg. No. 954009

A CIP catalogue record for this book
is available from the British Library

ISBN 0-224-05009-5

Papers used by Random House UK Limited are natural,
recyclable products made from wood grown in sustainable forests.
The manufacturing processes conform to the environmental
regulations of the country of origin.

Typeset by Deltatype Ltd, Birkenhead, Merseyside

Printed and bound in Great Britain by
Creative Print and Design (Wales), Ebbw Vale

Then said *Mercie* the Wife of *Mathew* to *Christiana* her Mother, Mother, I would, if it might be, see the Hole in the Hill; or that, commonly called, the *By-way* to Hell.

John Bunyan, *The Pilgrim's Progress*

part one

dundee

Some time around the middle of the morning, Alan was wakened by the noise of someone banging somewhere, though he couldn't tell where the noise was coming from, whether it was outside, or in one of the other flats. It must have been around ten, maybe earlier, maybe a little bit later; he'd lost his watch, so he couldn't tell what time it was, but there was a cool gold light flickering on the ceiling over his bed, and it was quiet, like that hour-long quiet of mid-morning when people are away at work or the shops. It was usually a good time, this hour when he struggled awake and found the world again, like some toy or game he had abandoned the night before, endlessly puzzling, yet strangely beautiful and, in his half-waking state, the moment would have been perfect, with the warm thrill of the alcohol still ringing in his blood and the watery light of Magdalen Green playing across the wall and ceiling – perfect, except for the noise, a loud banging that he'd thought at first was only a part of his dream. He must have been hearing it in his sleep – that was what happened sometimes, when there were noises outside, or when he turned awkwardly in the night, so his arm would be trapped and aching, and his mind would build the noise or the pain into whatever he was dreaming. Once he'd had a nightmare where someone had come up to him out of nowhere and stabbed him through the shoulder with a sword – the long steel blade passing right through the flesh – and when he woke up the pain was still there. It had taken him a while to realise where he was. He'd even put his hand up, to feel if there was blood. He could still see the stranger's face: the gleeful look in his eyes, the almost friendly smile as he raised the sword – like the sword Errol Flynn used at the pictures – then thrust it into Alan's body with all his strength. He'd had dreams like that more than once – dreams where someone came and tried to kill him, with a gun or a knife, and the strangest thing, what disturbed him most and stayed with him afterwards, when he started awake, was the way the killer would always be smiling, as if he thought he was doing him a kindness.

He didn't want to get up. He wanted to kick off the covers and lie on the bed, with his arms and legs straight out, letting the hangover-feeling seep away, bleeding by degrees out of his body and into the cool air. Most of the time – when there wasn't any noise – he didn't really mind the hangovers. He was used to them by now – and besides, it seemed right, somehow, to lie in the warm, alone, acutely aware of his body, of the exchanges of heat and cold that were happening all the time, without his noticing, the tiny movements and perturbations of blood in the inner ear, the ripples of acid or bile in his stomach. To begin with, when he'd first started having these vivid hangovers, he would get desperate and panicky; he would even feel suicidal sometimes, with the ache of shame and fear in his whole body, like a huge, invisible bruise. It was as if he had been held down and crushed, like that king in the play he'd read about in school, the one who had been trampled under a door, so that no wounds would show. It wasn't so much a pain as an ache, a dullness in which tiny, electrical sensations sparked and crackled across his skin, like cellophane when you crumple it up in a ball and it unfolds again by itself, in tiny shuddering movements. That had bothered him for a long time, but he didn't mind it now. He knew what was happening, and how long it would last, and it was a good feeling, sometimes, to shift very slightly, or push back the covers, and feel the long rippling shivers running up along his spine. If he could just lie still, in the quiet, he was fine. Maybe it would bother him, that he couldn't remember much of what had happened the night before, or how he'd got home, and sometimes he had a vague feeling of guilt, with half-memories of something terrible that had happened in the night. Sometimes he woke with the conviction that he had committed some terrible act, an assault, or a murder. It was a ridiculous idea – one part of his mind knew that – but it wouldn't go away, and he kept seeing flashes of violence in his mind's eye, things that he had done and blanked out, so he wouldn't have to face his crimes. Usually, though, he put everything out of his mind and lay still, with his eyes half-closed, listening to the quiet, or the sparrows yammering in the bushes outside his window. Usually he could lie like that for what felt like hours and when he looked over at his watch maybe only two or three minutes had passed. That was the best of it, the way time stretched or folded in on itself. Sometimes it would come to a halt altogether, and that was the best feeling of all, to imagine his life had been suspended, not finished, but held in abeyance, kept in reserve forever, like a soul in limbo. But now, he had lost his watch, and he didn't know what time it was. It made him feel strangely uncomfortable, as if, by losing the watch, he had lost some sense of himself, some notion of how things were.

He didn't want to even move, never mind get up, but the banging kept on and on, insistent and dull, somewhere above him. Somebody hammering was what it sounded like. He couldn't understand why there was always noise around him, in a place like this. There was always somebody hammering, or people shouting, or traffic noise, and it seemed so ridiculous, so absurd, somehow, a whole lot of fuss about nothing, as his mother used to say. He didn't see the point. People had to keep themselves busy, for no good reason, doing, doing, doing, as if their lives depended on it. Alan swung out of bed and set his feet on the cool floor. He could feel all the bones in his feet, and he was aware of how fragile they were, like fine splints of polished chalk, or bone china. He stood up. He felt light-headed, and it was as if he would never stop rising, as if he was growing taller and taller, into something light, something almost gaseous. Immediately, as if it was connected in some way with his movement, a knock came at the door.

'Alan?'

He stood very still and listened. It was a woman's voice, a voice he knew, but he couldn't place it. It sounded middle-aged, and he had an idea that the woman who owned it was tall and heavy, a little overweight, but good-natured, and pretty in her way, with dark curly hair and tiny dimples when she smiled. The knock came again, longer and louder this time.

'Alan? Are you there, Alan?'

He lay down and pulled the covers over his face. If he waited, she would go away, and then he could work out who she was. There was a long pause, and he was sure he could hear her listening, even though there was no sound. He could tell that she knew he was in. He could feel her thinking it through, whether to knock again or go away, or maybe just stand there and wait, to see what happened. He tried thinking about something else. He thought, if he forgot about her, if he could

6

prevent himself from thinking about her standing there at his door, she would disappear. He thought about the dream he had had: how he had been walking on Magdalen Green, only it wasn't really Magdalen Green, because there were tall trees all along one side, and he couldn't see Riverside, just the light off the firth, and green fields all around him for miles. He had been much younger in the dream, maybe twelve or thirteen. The grass had been very green, with little pockets of blackness here and there, like the darkness of fairy rings. He had been looking for something in the dream: he had his head down, and he was walking slowly, turning from side to side, scanning the ground. He had the idea that it was a key, or maybe some money, definitely something small and hard and metallic, but what he found was nothing like that. When he saw it first, it was just a white shape lying in the shadow of the trees, at the far end of the green. At first it looked like a bird, but after a moment, he realised it was an angel. It was very small, not life-sized at all, like the ones you see in picture books; its wings were spread out on the grass and the feathers were damaged or missing in places. It had little pearl-white hands, with surprisingly long fingernails, more talons than nails, really, like the long nails threaded with blood he remembered from his little brother's budgerigar. When he saw the hands, he remembered what the teacher had said in class once, how you couldn't clip a bird's nails, because there was blood flowing through them, right to the tips. The angel's hands were like that, soft and white and delicate and full of blood. He couldn't see the feet, but he imagined they were the same.

The face was half-concealed but he could see enough to know that the angel was unconscious. The face was simple and flat, like the faces of the spirits carved on the gravestones in churchyards. Its mouth looked hungry, the way a new baby looks hungry, and it was making small sucking motions in its sleep. It looked cold, too. He was afraid to pick it up – it bothered him that it was naked – but eventually he summoned his courage and half-carried, half-dragged the fallen body out of the shadow of the tree and into the sunlight. It looked even stranger in the full light. It looked so white and smooth, it reminded him of the time they'd gone to a mushroom farm, on a school visit. He had thought the mushrooms were some kind of trick: they looked too clean, too white to exist, but that was just how the angel looked. Now, in the broad daylight, it seemed unbearably vulnerable, and he knew, if he left it there, it wouldn't be long before a cat or a dog would get it. He winced at the thought of the claws tearing its soft, lightly fledged skin. He decided he had no choice but to take it home and find somewhere safe to hide it. Then, if it woke up, he could talk to it, and find out where it came from, and maybe it would tell him things, like the future, or what God was like. It was about then the banging had started, and he had looked up, across the green, to see what the noise was. There was nobody there. He had the idea that the noise was coming from the sky, and it had something to do with the angel, and then he thought, if the banging continued, the angel would die. That was the last thought he'd had before he woke: that, and the knowledge that the banging wouldn't end, and a feeling of helplessness, that he couldn't do anything about it. As he thought back over the dream, he began to drift. He noticed the banging outside had stopped. Then he was dreaming again and the woman at the door went away, in the dream and in real life, and when he woke up again it was the afternoon.

From where he was lying on the floor, Rob could see the legs of the television stand. They were black, with chips here and there in the paint showing the metal underneath, and they were very thin – too thin, Rob thought, to support the weight of the TV. Slowly, tenderly, aware of his body as a mass of pain and fatigue, he pulled himself up into a sitting position. He didn't know how he had come to be lying on the floor – he must have fallen asleep there last night, when he came in from the Mercy, so that meant Cathy would have walked around him as she was getting ready for work, and she hadn't even tried to get him up, or made him a cup of tea, or even bothered to check to see if he was all right before she'd gone out. She would have seen the half-empty whisky bottle and the glass on the floor beside him, the ash-tray full of crushed cigarette butts, his shoes at the other side of the room, where he'd kicked them off, and she had just left him there, as if he was just a piece of the furniture. Which, of course, he was, as far as she was concerned.

After a moment's pause, and with some difficulty, he stood up. He felt a bit dizzy – he'd felt like that the day before, he remembered – and he went out into the kitchen to see if there was anything to drink. There wasn't. Outside, Malcolm's dogs were barking and it felt like the noise was inside him, inside his brain, pushing against his skull, trying to break out. He felt a slight panic, then a stillness at the back of his head that, for a moment, he thought was just another blackout waiting to happen. He needed something. He needed energy. He got a glass out of the cupboard, then turned on the cold water tap and let it run. He still felt dizzy, and there was an empty feeling in his stomach, a kind of butterflies thing, from no food, maybe, and he looked at the clock on the cooker to see what time it was. Twenty past twelve: no wonder he was hungry. He put the glass under the tap, so it filled quickly and flowed down over the sides, then he drank it, gulping it down like a baby. The water was cold and unimaginably soothing, a miracle in his mouth and throat, and he didn't stop drinking till the glass was empty. He could feel himself thinking, turning things over in his mind, trying to get a hold on his situation. He was grasping at something, trying to recapture a sense of himself as an orderly being, but whatever it was that joined one moment to the next, whatever it was that created the illusion of a logical, manageable existence, was missing. He tried to remember the night before: he had no memory of coming in, or of lying or falling down on the floor; he didn't even remember leaving the pub. He didn't remember if Cathy was there when he got in; now, as he looked around him, he was beginning to notice what a mess the place was – things lying on the kitchen floor, knives and spoons and pieces of a broken cup, bits of food and little spillages of whisky and water, dirty dishes scattered all over the units; even the plant pot from the window-sill, Cathy's sick little spider plant, had toppled over, leaving a heap of dry compost at the rim of the sink – and he couldn't remember any of it.

As soon as it hit his stomach, the water set off the usual chain reaction: a small tightness, then a ripple of cramps, like tiny waves of teeth, gnawing at the inner tube of his gut. It wasn't the first time – Rob was almost used to it by now – but the pain was sharper than usual, and that cold feeling came in his head again, till he was scared he would pass out. He walked through to the bathroom quickly and got there just in time: dropping to his knees, he gripped hold of the sides of the bowl and threw up – not food, not even last night's beer, just a bitter, watery fluid, with tiny, bright spots of red in it, like blood. It didn't last more than a couple of seconds, and then he was breathing, his eyes closed, fighting off the dizziness and panic. It was strange how this worked now: there were phases in the day, times like this, when he could barely stand, and he vomited bile and blood, or whatever that red stuff was, and then, just half an hour later, he would be okay, sitting in the Mercy, getting down his first nip. He wouldn't feel great, but he'd be calm, and he'd know things would be better, with the second, or the third drink. That was how it was now. When he was younger, he'd never had any problem: no hangover, never sick, nothing like that. Now, though, what with everything, what with money and Malcolm's dogs and Cathy nagging at him all the time, he wasn't as resilient as he used to be.

He threw up again, and this time it was just that bitter fluid, a froth of gas and acid from his empty stomach. He waited a while, but it seemed to be over and, after a minute or two, he walked back through to the kitchen, filled the glass again, and drank more water, taking it in slow sips this time, and pausing between each mouthful, to breathe. That was what it was all about, he thought. It was all in the breathing. He finished the glass and, suddenly, all he wanted was to be out of there, out of the house and into the light of day, to go somewhere and be alone, where nobody could find him. Or he could go to the Mercy. The boys would probably be there by now, wondering what had happened to him. He noticed the sugar bowl, sitting there amongst the plates and cups, and he scooped up a handful of the sticky white cubes, and ate them, washing them down with more water. He was feeling better now. All he really needed was a drink and a cigarette, and maybe some fresh air to clear his head. He walked through to the hall quickly and put on his jacket.

As soon as he got outside and tasted the cool air, he felt dizzy again, and he stood for a moment, leaning against the door-frame, while his head cleared. Some kids were playing up along the street, a couple of girls with a rope, and one fat, sad-looking boy, sitting on the edge of the kerb, watching them. The girls were singing an old-fashioned skipping song – he didn't think they did that any more, for some reason – a sweet, slightly plaintive song that made him feel sad all of a sudden, though it was a pleasant sadness, like the sadness of summer nights, when you had nowhere to go and you sat out by the river, with a couple of cans of beer, watching the water flow. Like when he'd been with Helen. For the time being, at least, Malcolm's dogs had stopped barking next door. Rob looked up at the sky; it was a soft grey, like smoky gauze, or the beginning of a mist.

He was closing the door behind him, taking care to turn the key in the lock so it clicked shut properly, when the boy who stayed at Malcolm's came out, banging the door behind him and setting the dogs off again – a hard, insistent noise that he felt as soft steady blows beneath the skin, definitely beneath the scalp, a physical sensation against the skull. The boy looked at him as he went past, but he didn't say anything; then, a few yards further on, as he passed the wall of the flats, he stopped, hawked up some phlegm, and spat it out, spattering the wall with a thick, dark line of slime, a knot of mucus, wet and grey, with a life of its own, almost, like the slow creeping life of some mollusc out of the sea, some mussel, or water-snail. The kids all stopped playing to watch the boy pass, but he didn't take any notice of them. He crossed the road at an angle, then moved up the path to the Perth Road, lighting a cigarette as he went, on his way to the bookies, or the pub. Rob wondered where Malcolm found them all. For as long as he had been living in this house, there had been boys like this one coming and going, boys almost identical to Malcolm, in their black waxed jackets and motorcycle boots, (they never had bikes, they just had the clothes, and the hair), coming in and out at all hours, tormenting the dogs in the night till Rob got up and banged on the walls, shrieking threats at them, while Cathy lay in bed, not saying a word. Malcolm was supposed to be her cousin, though it was a bit of a mystery what side of the family he was on. But then, everything was a mystery as far as Malcolm was concerned. Where his money came from, for example. Some people thought he was dealing drugs, or receiving stolen goods, but Rob figured he didn't have the basic intelligence even for that.

They had been living next to Malcolm for over two years. According to Cathy, they had been lucky to get the place – she went on about that all the time, how they had been lucky to get it, and how they wouldn't have done, if Malcolm hadn't helped out – but Rob didn't think much of it, especially when Malcolm and his latest wee pal came home late from the pub and sat next door, playing crap music and watching television till the small hours, while the dogs went berserk outside. Of course, even though she went on and on about how nice this place was, and how they could do a lot with it, if they only put a bit of money and time in, Cathy still wasn't satisfied. What she really wanted was a flat of their own; that was why she kept going on at him to get a regular job, so they could start a mortgage – as if any bank manager was going to give him a mortgage – and buy a nice wee flat, and do it up really neat, with new furniture and pictures on the walls, and nice matching colour schemes, paint work and fabric and carpets, all in soft peach tones, and maybe blues and sea-greens in the bathroom, only not too cold, even if it was the bathroom, you'd still want the colours to be warm, with a bit of red in them. Though as far as mortgages were concerned, she had another think coming. Rob wasn't about to get trapped in that kind of debt, and he wasn't going to spend half his life doing up some flat, so she could nag him about keeping it clean and tidy. She wasn't going to get him into any of that. Anyway, if their current accommodation wasn't too wonderful, it was only because of the dogs. As he'd reminded himself a thousand times, if Malcolm's dogs were gone, his problems would all be over. The only problem was getting rid of them. That, and the fact that, if anything happened to these mutts, Malcolm would just go out and get another two.

The dogs were only puppies, according to Malcolm. They were Rottweilers, naturally. Malcolm wouldn't have been seen dead with anything normal, like a golden retriever, or a Labrador, or something like that – not that it was normal keeping any dog in the town, where it wouldn't get any proper exercise and would just sit around barking all day. The thing was with Malcolm, he had those dogs because they were the biggest, ugliest breed he could think of – it was a surprise he hadn't got pit bulls – but whenever he talked about them, he would go on about how gentle they really were, how they used to be sheep-dogs in the mountains somewhere, and how

they were great with kids. From time to time, usually when
Rob was out, he would come over and see Cathy, and they'd
sit there talking about animals and cars, which was all either of
them was really interested in. Sometimes Rob would come
back for his tea about five o'clock and find Malcolm there,
sitting over a cup of coffee and a plate of biscuits like some old
wifie, telling Cathy she should really get herself a dog, and
how he knew some boy whose bitch just had puppies, or he
would be encouraging her to go out and buy a car, as if they
had that kind of money, saying he knew somebody who
would give her a good deal, if she wanted him to enquire. A
couple of times Rob had been on the point of telling Malcolm
to keep his nose where it belonged, and out of their business.
But he hadn't said anything, out of consideration for the fact
that the boy was Cathy's cousin. All he wanted, really, was a
bit peace.

He waited till the boy from Malcolm's got to the top of the
street and disappeared then, slowly, he made his way up the
road, past the kids, who stopped to watch him pass, but didn't
say anything, past the row of tiny gardens, with their patio
roses in pots and clumps of lupins, past the piece of waste
ground where they were supposed to be developing some
new flats. By the time he got to the Mercy, he'd stopped
feeling sick, and it was showing signs of rain.

It was late in the afternoon, almost evening. The window was still open; Alan could see the sky, pale-blue and grey, with streaks of ivory in places, like the sky in a Chinese painting, half-present, half-erased. The air was cool and soft and damp, pressed against the window, and seeping through the gap, a cool, sweet grass smell, mingled with the coming night, with its dark thread of water and charcoal. He had just come out of the shower, with only a towel around his waist, and he could smell himself, warm and damp, with the hint of Old Spice deodorant and that after-scent everywhere of Imperial Leather soap, and all of a sudden, he was staring it in the face: the cold line of the horizon, the darkening sky, the quiet, banal certainty of death that came from time to time, on evenings like this. It was absurd. He pictured himself, dead; he thought of his body, perfumed with soap and Old Spice, carried into an ambulance, or laid out on an autopsy table, and he saw the utter absurdity of his existence. It was something that happened from time to time, but it didn't bother him, now. He was almost used to it. As long as it wasn't too painful, he wanted to know he was dying, when the time came, so he could pay attention, and know what it was like. There was that book he had read, about how it was never easy to die, there was always going to be some pain, unless maybe you died in a coma, or in your sleep, so you didn't know about it. Yet he had a faint suspicion that, at the last moment, the pain wouldn't matter, and it would be good, to feel yourself dissolve and slip away. He didn't believe in life after death. He'd read all those books in the library, about how people came out of their bodies, and maybe walked into a cool, pleasing light, or maybe had visions of Jesus, or their Auntie Jessie, coming to meet them. He was pretty certain it was just like dreaming, that last moment, and maybe people saw those things because that was what they expected to see. Still, it happened, one way or another: you saw something. Or maybe your whole life flashed before you – your whole life, including that last moment, when your whole life flashed in front of you, so everything was repeated, again and again, in miniature, into eternity, like the tiny images in facing mirrors. Maybe there was an afterlife of a kind, but it wouldn't be what the teachers had told him in school. For one thing, they had always said that animals don't have souls. That seemed funny to him, because most of his teachers had pets: middle-aged women who had lived all their lives with sly cats, or bristling, affectionate terriers, would deny them a full existence in eternity because of what the man in Rome said. It had been one of the surprising moments of his school years, to recognise this small triumph of dogma over love. According to the Church, the afterlife was for humans: no dogs, no monkeys, no geese, no hedgehogs. It didn't matter that some people – plenty of people – liked animals more than humans, or that humans were as much animals as anything else. He could imagine old Joe Muir, who had a smallholding at the edge of one of the towns where Alan had gone to one of his many schools, asking for some time off from heaven so he could go back for a day's work on his land, just to stand amongst his chickens, or step out of the lambing shed at first light, and breathe the cold March air. Old Joe only ever really talked to his animals; whenever he met another human, he clammed up and got all shamefaced. At school, the teachers said heaven would be a place of eternal bliss, because the souls would know God, for all eternity, which made it sound a bit boring, to say the least, and Alan couldn't help thinking he'd want to smuggle in a coyote, or an armadillo, or even just a couple of goldfish. And when they said there would be no animals in heaven, he wanted to ask if there would be plants, or wire fences, or turnip crops, or weather. Would there be rain, or first snow, or that moment when you came home from the baths and sat down at the table, and your mum dished you up leek and potato soup, and asked you how hungry you were? For years, he could only imagine the afterlife as an infinite cool fog, with islands of thought and movement here and there, where the glad souls shivered with the knowing of God, enduring all eternity like patient jellyfish floating in a lukewarm ocean. Finally he decided, if that was all there was, they could forget it. Maybe there was life after death, but he didn't see why you had to be the same as you were before. If there really was an afterlife, he thought, let it be the curve of a dry-stane wall as it crosses a field and rises to the summit of a hill, or the smell and feel of a cinema, when the last of the audience has left, and the dust settles in the pale glow of the house lights. Better still, if the soul moves on, let it be reborn, as an armadillo, or a snow bunting, or a pond in the public park, thick with water weeds and frogs' spawn.

He couldn't see it though. The only life after death he could imagine was someone else's life, or maybe a kind of limbo, where some remnant of the soul, a thin tatter of being, persisted, like a difficult stain, or the smell of garlic. He remembered one afternoon, in chemistry, when he was supposed to be investigating the properties of water glass. He was dropping pieces of cobalt and copper salts into the mixture, and watching those wet, animate strings of crystal climb towards the surface when, all of a sudden, he came to a dead stop, and sat down by the window, in the bright sunshine, while Mr Kennedy, the demented science teacher, had descended upon him. For a moment, he had just felt dizzy, sick to his gut; then, while Kennedy stood over him, asking him what was wrong, he felt he'd just caught a glimpse of something, Hell maybe, or eternity, or the ghostly other-world he'd been reading about, in *Tales of Mystery and Imagination*. It wasn't the phantom of Ligeia that had crossed his mind, though. It wasn't that tangible; it wasn't that susceptible to exorcism. Instead, he had a vague sense of himself as lost – not yet, not then, but eternally, and inevitably, wandering the streets, a danger to himself and others, abandoned by everyone, even his mother, and left to wander the streets, damned to spend his summers camping out along the railway lines, to walk up and down those arteries of grass and buddleia, through cities and junctions, hunting for small animals or picnic scraps thrown from passing cars and trains. And all the time Kennedy was talking: first he'd been annoyed, but now he was really worried – maybe he thought Alan had eaten or drunk something poisonous, or inhaled some dangerous gas, because he took him by the arm and started walking him over to the door. Alan didn't really know what was going on: he remembered sitting down, in the cool darkness of the corridor now, and the feeling began to go. Mr Kennedy was still standing over him, looking properly concerned, and for a moment Alan felt sorry for him – he didn't know why, he just felt sorry, for Mr Kennedy, for the whole class, for his mother, for everyone. Somebody came with a glass of water – he seemed to remember it was Theresa McDermott – and he drank it quickly, tasting the hint of something mineral, a hint of iron or copper, mixed with the cold. For a moment, he knew something – even now, years later, he felt that – though, try as he might, he couldn't remember what it was. Maybe – probably – it was something you couldn't say in words, so it couldn't be remembered either, and somewhere in that memory there was a sense that anything that mattered, anything that really mattered, couldn't be talked about in words, or told to someone else, or even remembered. It was beautiful and sad at the same time. Everybody was going around talking to each other, and maybe even loving each other, and wanting to say how life really felt to them, and they couldn't, even though they could see and smell and taste it. It was like that, too, with moments like this, when he thought about death, and it didn't really bother him, he just wanted to know about it, when it came, and have no expectations of heaven or hell, or any kind of afterlife. Other people had those moments too, moments of sudden fore-knowledge or insight, but they never talked about them, and Alan felt cheated somehow, because he couldn't talk about them either. For some reason, he didn't know why, it wasn't done. So much wasn't done, and he had no idea why, and he felt sorry for people, because they decided on this, and they probably didn't even know why themselves.

It was later than he'd thought. Out on the street, a gang of boys were going by, talking loudly, probably students on their way to the pub. Alan remembered he had told Rob he would be in the Mercy by the afternoon. He knew why Rob had asked him, checking a dozen times in the course of the evening, to make sure he'd got it right – no doubt about it, he would want to borrow some money again. Still, Alan didn't really mind. You had to help your friends, was how he saw it, just like you had to be loyal to your family, and look after people who couldn't look after themselves. That was what his mother always said. Only now he was late, and Rob would be sitting there, too ashamed to ask for a sub from Sconnie or Junior, and waiting for Alan to show, so he could get a round in. Quickly, Alan finished drying himself; then he put on a clean white shirt and black Levis. The shirt was a bit creased, but the jeans were all right. He pulled at his collar a couple of times, in front of the bathroom mirror: a surprise, as always, when he looked at himself and saw how thin his face was, how dark around the eyes he looked, how strangely red his lips were against the pale skin. He'd wet his hair in the shower and combed it, but it had already started to spike up, and he ran his hand over the top of his head in a vain attempt to flatten it. He looked like the nervy boy in the children's story, the boy with the scissors. Struwelpeter. Yet whenever he was away from a mirror, he forgot how he looked; he just thought of himself as being like the others. He stared at himself and the thought passed through his mind that this wasn't really him. You could never see yourself as you looked to others, or as you really were, in a mirror, because you always put on a face, you always adopted a pose. He kept the stare up for a while, half-smiling at the absurdity of it all, then he turned away, slipped on his shoes and walked out, through the close, to the dark, grass-scented street. He was in such a hurry, now, that he didn't even look to see if Jennifer was there.

This was the point where the evening started – when the grass on Magdalen Green began to soften and melt into the dusk. Alan liked walking around then – being the outsider, catching glimpses through the windows of people at their tea, or sitting in their front rooms, watching television, or listening to music. His neighbours were strangers to him: in all the time he had lived on Magdalen Yard Road, he had never understood how they existed, what it was they wanted from life, why they would put such an effort into raising their kids and getting on at work. He would watch them, on winter mornings, going outside and starting their cars to warm them up, then going back in, while the exhaust fumes darkened the air, and he wondered what it was that kept them going. There was no feeling of superiority in any of this – if anything, he felt a soft, detached pity for them, and for himself, and a sense of the coldness, the neutrality of the world they inhabited. He remembered reading, once, how some philosopher would take his afternoon walk every day at exactly three o'clock, so regular in his habits that the townspeople would set their clocks by him. It was an interesting idea: to reduce life to the barest routine, to do the same thing, day after day, with no real purpose other than to neutralise the power of chance, or fear, or whatever capacity for damage lived inside his soul. It would have been the habit that mattered, to begin with, the fact of acceding to the monotony of life that he must have felt would somehow protect him; but then, gradually, things would have altered. Instead of a dull ramble around the usual streets, he would have found that every walk was different. Every day, there would be some change in the quality of the light, some new colour, the smell of fresh bread from the bakery, or a gust of wind from the river. Naturally, his route would never have varied. Nor would his pace. Alan admired that: a life full of landmarks, a life of endless detail. It was something to believe in, this life of observed moments – an escape, somehow, from time.

22

By the time he got to the Mercy, the others were already there. They were in their usual places, Sconnie and Junior sitting in close, leaning their elbows on the table, Rob set back slightly, looking uncomfortable and out of place. As soon as he saw him, Alan knew he'd guessed right: Rob was short of money and, eventually, would tap Alan for a sub – a tenner, or a twenty, maybe. He'd done it four or five times already and Alan had no expectation of seeing the money again. Someone had just got a round in, so Alan bought himself a pint and a wee one, and sat down.

Sconnie and Junior were in full flow. They had accumulated a whole flotilla of glasses on the table in front of them, and they were telling stories back and forth, while Rob sat listening, holding his pint glass in one hand and sipping at it, his chair pulled away from the table, as if he wanted to make it clear that, on this occasion, he was just the audience. At times like this, Sconnie and Junior had a way of talking as if they were repeating well-rehearsed lines; their stories had the sound of something that has been told a thousand times before – if not by the present teller, then by somebody – even when they were events that had only just happened, snippets of news from the television or the papers that they had gleaned during the course of the day. Alan could never tell what Sconnie or

Junior felt about what they were saying – there was no trace of scepticism in their recitations, yet they didn't seem to attach any significance, other than a vague curiosity value, to these bizarre tales. Nevertheless, telling stories was their favourite pastime – that, and arguing about country music, or playing word games with terms they had come across in newspapers, or specialist dictionaries – outmoded scientific terms, words from Scots, folk words, odd curiosities from *Brewer's Dictionary of Phrase and Fable,* or *Old Moore's Almanac.*

When Alan sat down, Sconnie was just beginning the recitation of a story he'd read in a magazine somewhere. It was always part of the routine that whoever was telling the story couldn't – or pretended he couldn't – remember where it was he had heard it. Sconnie's story concerned a man who had come home and surprised his wife and her lover in bed; as far as Alan could make out, the events had happened in a foreign country, maybe Spain, or somewhere in South America. The man's name was José, and the woman's was Antonia; Sconnie didn't seem to know what the lover was called. He sat there as he always did, self-aware, his heavy, plastic-framed glasses perched precariously halfway down his nose, as if they were about to fall off at any moment. It was part of the suspense – maybe the biggest part – whenever Sconnie was telling one of his stories. Meanwhile, Junior was listening with his usual bemused, half-incredulous look, smart as always in his pressed black jacket and white shirt, his hair neatly parted. Sconnie and Junior were the same age, and they liked much the same things, but they were as different to look at as you could imagine. It was odd to think of them as friends, but that was what they were – as much friends as any two men could be, who sat in the same pub every day and drank together for six or seven hours.

'So in walks José,' Sconnie was saying. 'And he hears a noise, like somebody's being murdered somewhere. It's a couple of minutes before he realises this noise is coming from the bedroom – and then a bit more after that before he realises it's his wife. Only she's not being murdered.'

As always, in the course of one of his stories, Sconnie paused for effect, while he took a swig of beer and, as always, Junior pretended to get annoyed at this, shifting in his chair and telling him to get on with it.

'So,' Sconnie continued, wiping a smudge of foam from his upper lip, 'he goes through. And there's this boy with his wife, giving her a good seeing to. They're completely away – they don't even notice José to start with, not until he starts shouting at them to stop. It's only then, when the other boy gets up that José sees he's a big bastard, with a body like a weight-lifter, all hair and muscles, and balls the size of a bull.'

Junior snorted. Sconnie ignored him.

'So the other boy gets up out of the bed and the two of them – Antonia and the lover – get José down on the floor and they kick the shit out of him. By the time they're finished, he's pretty well unconscious. Then they carry him into this old store room and lock him in there.' Sconnie puffed happily on his cigarette. 'This is in 1984, mind. The boy is in there for over thirteen years. So because she's a bit of a softie, Antonia feeds him through a little hatch in the door, and the other boy, the lover, goes in now and again and throws a bucket of cold water over him, to keep him from smelling. Thirteen years, he's living like this; then the wife and the other boy go off somewhere on holiday and he gets discovered. So what do you think he says to the police when they go in to rescue him?'

Alan and Junior shook their heads and leaned forward in

anticipation. Rob was still sitting slightly apart, holding his beer in his hand like he was performing some kind of balancing act. Alan noticed he looked a bit pale, like he'd been sick again.

'At first I cried a lot, but after a while I got used to it.' Sconnie shook his head. 'That's all he says. He doesn't even want to press charges. He's just glad to be out.'

'Well,' said Junior. 'Just shows you.'

'Just shows you what?' asked Sconnie, incredulously.

'It just shows you,' replied Junior. 'You can get used to anything, if you have to put up with it long enough.'

Sconnie let out a low, scornful grunt.

'It just shows you,' he said, 'that you can never trust anybody. Especially not women.'

'That's true enough,' Rob murmured, from his place at the edge of the circle.

Sconnie turned.

'Are you all right, son?' he said.

'Yeah.'

'Only you're sitting there like you're at a funeral.'

'Aye,' Junior added. 'Your own.'

'I'm all right,' Rob said quietly, looking away.

'Did you read that thing in the papers?' Alan put in. 'About that woman in Forfar?'

He paused to get their interest. Sconnie and Junior had turned to listen, with odd, fixed expressions on their faces, as if they were bemused by his sudden intrusion on to their territory. Rob wasn't really paying attention, though. He was looking at his empty glass now, waiting for the next round, glad that the spotlight was off him. Alan could see that he would have to slip him some money, some time soon.

'So?' Sconnie asked.

26

'So what?'

'So what about her?'

'It was in the paper,' Alan continued, satisfied that Sconnie and Junior were letting him in on their game. 'There was this woman in Forfar. And these two boys kidnapped her. They were just wee boys, about twelve or something. They kept her in a flat, it belonged to one of the boys' mothers, but she was away visiting her sister.'

He glanced at Sconnie to see if he was still listening. He was.

'Anyway, these two wee boys did all kinds of stuff to her. They cut her hair off. One of them raped her. The other one tried to cut her fingers off with a pair of scissors. They had her in there for three days. She only escaped when they stole some of the boy's mother's drink and passed out.'

Junior made his sceptical face.

'This was in Forfar?' he said, doubtfully.

'Yes. I think it was Forfar. Or maybe Arbroath.'

Junior nodded.

'Arbroath more likely,' he said.

Sconnie looked at him. 'Why's that?' he asked.

'Well come on, Sconnie, son,' Junior said, picking up his empty glass. 'You know what Arbroath's like. Whose turn is it?'

'Mine,' said Alan quickly, with a glance at Rob.

'All right,' Junior said. 'I'll not argue.'

Alan went to the bar to get the drinks. Halfway through the order, Rob joined him.

'Want a hand?'

'Thanks.' Alan slid a couple of pint glasses along the bar to him. 'Are you all right?'

'Fine.' Rob looked anything but fine. 'It's just that I'm a bit short right now, is all.'

Alan reached into his pocket and pulled out a couple of notes. He paid for the round, then turned to Rob. 'I can lend you some, if you want,' he said.

Rob nodded. He looked at the money in Alan's hand like a hungry man seeing food for the first time in days. 'Just till I get sorted,' he said.

'Sure. Will a tenner do?'

'Thanks.' When the money had exchanged hands, Rob seemed to relax. He took the pints over to the table, then came back for the whiskies.

'Thanks, Alan,' he said again. He was still embarrassed. He hadn't paid back the money Alan had given him the day before, and he knew that Alan would never ask for it.

'No problem,' Alan said, and they took the drinks back to the table.

Alan didn't get home till after midnight. When he did, he was still thinking about the last story Sconnie had told, about a ghost he'd seen, over near Errol, when he was still working. He'd been driving back from some job he'd been on, and he must have been tired, because he'd had a couple of moments when he'd drifted off, and he'd realised that he'd lost time, that he couldn't remember the last few seconds. But he'd been completely awake when he saw the girl – a thin, blonde-haired girl in a night-dress, picked out in the headlights suddenly, as she ran out of the woods and across the road in front of him. He'd said it was all slow motion and really clear, the way things sometimes are in dreams: he'd seen the girl at the last minute, and it was too late to stop; she had seen him too, and she'd reached out one hand – he'd seen how thin her fingers were, before the van struck her and she flew up into the air, hitting the roof and rolling over the back, so that, when he finally stopped, he knew she would be somewhere on the road behind him, dead maybe, or badly hurt, at the least. He sat a moment, watching the rear-view mirror, hoping she would appear, as if by some miracle, shaken, but basically unharmed. But she hadn't – so he'd got out and started walking back along the road to find her.

Except that he hadn't found her. It had been cold and dark

29

along the road: the woods were completely still, with just the odd call, somewhere in the distance, where a couple of tawny owls were out hunting mice. Now that he was out of the car, he didn't feel tired at all – in fact, he felt very calm and logical, going over in his mind what he would have to do, if the girl was badly injured. Then he'd started to wonder where she had come from: there were no houses that he could see along that stretch of road and, considering the clothes she'd been wearing, it hardly seemed likely that she'd been out for a walk. He was running through all this in his head when he realised that he'd been walking too long – or too long, now, for the girl to have fallen on to the road. He stopped and looked up and down both ways: it was dark, but not so much so that he wouldn't have seen her in that light-coloured night-dress. Finally, he decided that she must have gone sideways and rolled down the verge and he went back to the car to get a torch. He had gone up and down that stretch of road again and again, searching for that girl's body, and he hadn't been able to find her. He hadn't even found any sign of a collision – no blood on the road, no marks on the front of the car. It had been a good half-hour, probably longer, since he'd hit the girl; at last, when he couldn't find her, he'd driven in to the police station in Errol, and explained to them what had happened. The policeman had listened patiently to his story, but he didn't seem unduly concerned by it. Finally, when Sconnie had finished, he'd spoken, in a quiet, calming voice.

'Thanks for coming in,' he'd said. 'But I wouldn't worry about it. We'll take it from here.'

Sconnie had been dismayed by this. The police boy had listened to his story, he hadn't interrupted him once, and now he wasn't even taking it seriously. He'd tried again, he said, to make the policeman understand that there was a girl out there, somebody he'd hit, who might still be alive, lying in a ditch somewhere, with the life slowly bleeding out of her. He'd even admitted that he'd been tired at the wheel of the car, that it was probably his fault.

'Well, sir,' the policeman said, 'it's very honest of you to point that out. But the fact is, we've had about twenty reports of this girl over the last year or so. The story's always the same: late at night, a girl runs out, a girl in a white night-dress. She stops when she sees the car coming, but it's too late. The car hits her. Then she's gone. Nobody has ever found a body.'

And that was that. The policeman had told Sconnie to get off home, that the sooner he forgot the whole thing, the better. Only Sconnie wasn't tired at all now and he'd driven back the way he'd come, just to see what would happen. He'd half expected to find the girl in the road – though he hadn't been sure if he'd find a body, or a ghost.

Alan couldn't get that story out of his mind. For some reason, the girl Sconnie had described seemed real to him, real in a way other women could never be, more beautiful, more desirable than any woman he had ever met. He could see her in his mind's eye: she would be slender, blue-eyed, with fair hair and a very red mouth. He thought he knew who she was: one part of him thought it was someone he had dreamed, but elsewhere, in some dim corner of his mind, he couldn't help knowing that it was Jennifer.

Meanwhile, Junior was going home to his own ghost.

As far as the boys at the Mercy were concerned, he was a widower. His wife, Estelle, had died some years before any of them knew him, and if anyone had told them she was still alive, they wouldn't have believed it. Junior didn't say much about his dead wife; just once, in fact, when Rob had been talking about marriage, and someone had asked him, Junior, if he had ever been married, he'd answered, quite simply, that he had been, once. It was Sconnie, of course, who had pursued the matter, and found out that Estelle was dead, that she had died after a long illness, and that Junior considered it a merciful release. Nobody from the pub had ever been to his house – it was an agreement they had reached by some secret process, that Junior's life outside the pub was his own – just as nobody ever enquired where Sconnie had been, when he disappeared for days at a time; everybody knew what he was up to, he would even talk about it now and again, how he just couldn't stand being there any more, how he couldn't walk along the Perth Road and see all the same faces, the same buildings, the same dog shit, and he would take off, catching the first train to wherever he felt like going and staying there, or just wandering from place to place till his money ran out. Junior envied that. There were times when Sconnie came back exhausted, with a ghostly look on his face, as if he had witnessed or suffered something terrible, but nothing he could have seen or done, so far from home, Junior thought, was as bad as staying in the same place, day after day, or going home to the same house, night after night — a house that everyone else thought was empty, but which was really occupied by the wife he was supposed to have buried years ago. There were times when he wanted to say it aloud, to shout it in the streets: *my wife is alive, she isn't dead, sometimes I think she'll never die, sometimes I think she'll live forever.* But he never did.

He had married Estelle by chance. They had met at a party, when they were both drunk, and four weeks later, they had decided to get married. It seemed logical to Junior, the way things were supposed to be: you got married, found yourself a decent house, worked hard and went out drinking and dancing on Saturday nights. Later, maybe, you had children. Yet right from the start, as soon as they got back from the honeymoon, he could see that something was bothering Estelle. He tried really hard, he worked all hours to get her anything she might want but, in a matter of months, she just let herself go. She had always been a good dresser; now, all of a sudden, she started to just loll about the house in her nightie and slippers, or she'd get into an old sweatshirt and jeans and sit in the kitchen, drinking tea and gazing in bewilderment at the dishes stacked up around her. Every now and then, Junior would come home from work and set to, washing and scrubbing and drying, clearing it all away, putting things back in their rightful places, and she would just sit there, watching him, not lifting a finger to help. Sometimes she even let him know that she resented his interference, that he had no business doing the housework, since he was out at work all day, that he was only doing it to make her feel bad. He tried talking to her; he tried to get her to see a doctor, but she would have none of it. Sex stopped a fortnight after the honeymoon – not that it had ever been very important, but Junior missed that feeling of contact, of touching and being touched. He had always thought of sex as a secret between people, the one thing that happened that nobody else was allowed to know about, the one place where nobody else could go. Now, they had nothing. When he looked at Estelle, he realised that he had never known her, and never would. The woman he had married had disappeared into thin air, to be replaced by a phantom.

Some time after they introduced all-night television, she started staying up, no matter what was on, just to watch. From time to time, in the small hours, Junior would wake up and go downstairs, to where she sat with the big armchair pulled up close to the screen, watching some repeat of a police series from the Seventies, or a hazy documentary about Colombian drug barons. Sometimes she would have fallen asleep already; more often, though, she would look up at him, half-aware, pretending she'd been awake all the time, that she'd really been engrossed in the programme. It was something she did, not by any conscious effort, but automatically, as if it mattered, one way or the other: what she wanted Junior to understand was that, whatever she was watching, it was a programme she had intended to watch all along, the one she had waited up for. Junior knew it made her feel better if he seemed to believe that, though he had no idea why. He would wait a moment to see if she'd switch it off, and she would sit there, clutching the remote, waiting for him to go. Sometimes he could smell the sleep off her, the sickly-sweet warmth of her body, touched with the damp musk of dreaming.

34

'I'll be up soon,' she would say. 'I just want to see how it ends.'

Junior would hover, knowing she wouldn't come up, feeling whatever connection there had ever been between them dissolve, as he waited.

'It's three in the morning,' was what he would want to say, so she would know that he was tired of waking, for no good reason, because something – some instinct, some vestigial sixth sense – registered a gun shot or a scream through the fog of sleep and woke him up, so he would have to go downstairs and find out what was wrong. Sometimes he'd wake in the dark and think it was her, that she was the one who had been shot, or raped, or murdered on the stairs while he slept. Sometimes he had the clear and utterly absurd idea that she was being driven away, bound and gagged, in the middle of the night. It wouldn't be something he thought, in so many words, of course, it was just a vague and persistent fear, something that had been there all the time, implicit in the very fact of their existence.

This went on for about two years. He would come home from work and find her sitting in the front room, glued to the set; when he went out later, she would glance up, with a look of mild, slightly disconcerted wonderment, then she would turn back to the screen, as he stood watching her from the hallway. He'd started going out just to meet real people, to stand at a bar and talk to a woman – a barmaid, or one of the other customers – and see no ghost in her face, no phantom of terror or regret that he knew he would never understand, or even recognise. He'd started drinking too much; he'd had fantasies about dying, or running away, dreams about killing her, or himself, or both. He didn't know the boys, then; he'd always gone out drinking alone. Sometimes, looking back on that time, he would wonder what would have happened, if it had gone for another year, or even for another couple of months.

Then, all of a sudden, everything changed. It was around the time that he lost his job, when he'd had that bit of a problem, and he'd been out at the Liff for a couple of weeks. Estelle had never come to visit him, and he'd worried about her; it didn't bother him that she didn't care how he was – he preferred her not to see him out there amongst those others, anyway – but he was worried for her, in case she wasn't coping by herself. He wasn't away long; they gave him some special drugs and he felt well enough to go home, even though the doctors had said he should stay out there longer. He didn't like it. To be honest, he didn't like the people: they gave him the creeps. Some of them were so attached to their sickness, almost obsessed with it. He could see how that might happen, of course; he'd felt it himself, right at the beginning, before they took him away. There was something about the way it made you see, how you didn't care about anything, except maybe some detail, some pattern in a floorboard, or a cake of soap, some subtlety of light or texture that nobody else would notice. He'd seen how beautiful the world was, if you stopped being with other people and turned away: he had lain awake at night, listening to the noises in the dark, the traffic and people's voices off the street, and he'd sat in the kitchen in the afternoons, when he should have been at work, listening to the birds singing in the lilac bush outside, or the kids calling back and forth to one another on their way home from school. He'd seen how beautiful it was, and it scared him, because he knew what he really wanted was just to stay there, to stay and never have to come back, the way those people did at the hospital.

When he got home, Estelle had already taken to her bed. He didn't know how long she had been like that, and he reckoned she must have been getting up to get food, as well as washing and going to the toilet, but from that day on, over four years now, she had stayed in bed. He brought the television up so she could watch it – he'd gone out and bought a special aerial, because the picture hadn't been as good in the bedroom as it was downstairs – but she didn't seem interested. He brought her books and magazines; he even took her little baskets of fruit and vases of flowers from the garden, so he could go on pretending for a while that she was ill, like somebody in a hospital, but she didn't seem to notice. Over the space of a few weeks, she became more and more withdrawn, more and more silent. Sometimes he thought it was deliberate, a kind of act; he would tell himself that she was doing all this to stop him from dwelling on his own problems, and he'd imagine her as kind, as secretly, clumsily careful for his soul, or his hurt mind. Deep down, though, he knew that, whatever her problems were, whatever it was that had locked her up inside herself, it had nothing to do with him, and he realised there had never been anything between them, not love, or respect, or any sense of one another as separate individuals. They had come together by accident, and stayed from habit, or inertia. They had imagined life would be simple, that it would take care of itself. Only it wasn't, and it didn't. While he'd been in the hospital, he'd come off the drink, and the doctors had convinced him that that was the best thing; but, one night, when he couldn't bear it any more, he had left her there, lying in her bed – he had already moved into the spare room – and he had walked to the Mercy. He'd felt guilty and lonely to begin with, but he'd stuck it out and, after a couple of drinks, he'd started talking to another man who was standing at the bar, on his own, looking vaguely uneasy, as if he was waiting for someone. They had started off talking about the football, and ended up on country music. The man's name was Sconnie; Junior had vaguely arranged to have a drink with him the next night and, from that moment on, his life had changed. It wasn't just that he felt better for getting out of the house, and having someone to talk to; it wasn't even the power he felt now, all of a sudden, knowing he could go out drinking and control it; the real bit was, he could tell, whenever he started getting ready to go out, that Estelle looked forward to his absences. It was as much for her sake, he told himself, as his own, that he left her, first in the evenings, then later, in the afternoons as well, for the Mercy. Then, one day, when the boys had asked him if he had family, and he'd said he had been married, but his wife was dead, it felt almost true to him. As soon as he'd said it, he'd seen how logical it was, how appropriate, and he'd stuck to the lie with everyone he met, till he half-believed it himself.

Now, as always, Estelle lay quite still, her eyes fixed on the ceiling. For a while, she had pretended to be asleep when he came in, so he wouldn't disturb her, but that hadn't lasted more than a couple of months. Now, she made it obvious that it didn't matter to her whether he was there or not – if he spoke, she would blink a little, as if she were engaged in some difficult calculation and something, some minor disturbance, had interfered with her concentration, but she never replied, she didn't even move her head to look at him, or betray in any way that she knew he was there. He was as real to her, he knew, as the sounds that rose from the street below, the birds at the window in the early darkness, the buses and cars swishing by in the rain, the kids calling to one another on their way back from school. When he brought her food, she would wait till he was gone before she ate, even the tea he carried up to her was left on the bedside table till he went out. He imagined her when he was at the pub, sitting up in the bed, coming back to life, drinking the cooled tea, the cup flecked at the rim with old milk. He didn't care. Sometimes he remembered the dream he'd had, when they were first married, a dream he had assumed they agreed upon. Whatever happened, he would ask himself, to that simple life of work and beer and dancing? Whatever happened to people just living their lives, going out every day and doing a decent day's work for a decent day's pay, and knowing it would go on like that, for years, making or mending things, doing something worthwhile and then coming home on a Saturday night and getting dressed up to go out dancing or have a few drinks? It wasn't just that Estelle had changed: everybody had. Now, anyone who had a job felt privileged, and they were so scared of losing it, that they would do anything anybody asked just to stay out of trouble. Junior remembered a time when, if you got tired of a job, or some supervisor type started making trouble, you could just pack it in, and go somewhere else. Once, before he was married, he'd taken a charge-hand who was giving him a hard time and he'd dropped him off a gantry, breaking the man's arm. He'd walked away from that: the boy had told everybody it was an accident and, even though some of the others knew what had really happened, nobody had told the management. They all knew that boy had had it coming.

Now, as he stood at the bedroom door and watched Estelle playing possum in their double bed – the bed he hadn't slept in for years – he wondered how long it had been since she'd spoken out loud, to him or to anyone. Did she sometimes wait till he was gone then get up and walk about, talking to herself, just to hear the sound of her own voice? Had it changed, somehow, after such a long time? And if she had said something, if after all this time, she had finally spoken, would he understand what she said, or even care, one way or another? Junior didn't know. He had wanted so little, and he had hoped for a change for such a long time; now, years after it had happened, he saw that he had taught himself to hope for nothing, to expect nothing. There was a story he knew, that story you hear in bars all over Scotland, about the man who puts his son up on a table and tells him to jump, that he, the father, will catch him. He had always disliked that story; he had always been angry when people told it as if it was a good idea – how the father lets the boy fall and, as the child lies crying on the floor bends over and says, 'Let that be a lesson to you. Trust nobody.' He disliked it so much because it really had happened, to him and to others; his own father, out of bravado and sadism had put him up on a kitchen table and played this very trick, with a couple of his mates from the pub standing by – played it, so he said, for Junior's own good, so he would learn to be hard and make his own way in the world. From that moment on, he had wanted not to be like that, at any cost; from that moment on, he had wanted to take people on trust, and to trust himself. Even now, when everything had fallen apart, he wanted to believe, if not in love, or marriage, or justice, then at least in the possibility that such things might come about, if not for him, then for someone, somewhere. He remembered something he had read once, in a book he had borrowed from the library. It had said that when what we hope for comes to nothing, then we can make a new start, and maybe even find something better, something we hadn't expected. Or something like that. If there was one thing he wanted to believe in, it was that.

From time to time, Sconnie would have to remind himself that he didn't believe anything he said. Or rather, that he did believe some things – he did believe, for example, that television was a lie, not just on the surface, but on a much subtler, more pervasive level, and he really was angry when he saw how people generally behaved – but he knew in his heart that he wasn't altogether serious, that, when it came to the bit, he didn't really care much, one way or another. Having opinions, like telling stories, was a way of making space around himself, a way of keeping something intact, a sense of himself as separate. Years ago, just after his father had died, Sconnie had devised a scheme to make himself completely weightless, a near-phantom, almost entirely inaccessible to other people. It wasn't just a question of pretending, or of wearing a mask in company. His scheme had erased any sense he had of the potential for meaningful communication, or even contact, outside the sphere of casual conversation and bar-room banter. It had almost worked too: or perhaps it had worked, and he didn't really know it had. It was one of the beauties of the scheme, after all, that there was no way of checking its effect.

Sconnie didn't remember anything about his life, except for a few vague images of his father. He remembered, for example, how his dad's hair had turned grey, in a matter of weeks, and he knew it had been his fault. Sconnie's father had always been proud of his black hair: he was always the one neighbours wanted as a first foot at Hogmanay, and he liked to refer to himself as tall, dark and handsome, though he was only five foot nine and, while he had a certain basic charm, he wasn't what anybody would call good-looking. He would claim people had mistaken him in the street for Robert Mitchum, trying to make a virtue out of his heavy, hooded eyelids; everyone took that as a joke but Sconnie wasn't altogether sure that it was intended as such. When he had a few drinks on him, the old man would sing some old Scots or Irish song; he was proud of his voice, as well as his looks, though it wasn't very strong, and more often than not, he would be a little flat on the high notes. He always chose something slow and wistful to sing, a love song or a lament. Sconnie didn't think he could have sung anything else. Besides, just to look at him, you could see he was a man who believed in the sad songs. He always put on a show of being quietly contented, but Sconnie would look at him sometimes, when the old man was out in the garden, or washing up the dishes, and he couldn't help but notice the regret in his father's face, the definite air of disappointment. At the time, there was no reason to imagine he might be unhappy. He had a good enough job and a pretty young wife; there were never any arguments around the house – literally never – and because they were careful with money, there was usually enough for little extras, for those small luxuries that made life worthwhile. The old man didn't smoke, and he only drank on special occasions, at weddings and funerals and family dos; he was – or he seemed, before that last, sudden illness – healthy enough. Yet Sconnie could tell there was something troubling him, even though he would never have dared to ask about it. He had made a mistake, taken a wrong turn somewhere, and he had decided to live quietly with the consequences, whether from inertia, or some moral principle. He was the kind of man who assumed responsibility for the choices he made, even though he probably knew it made no difference whether he did or not. Maybe he couldn't see any way out; maybe it was a matter of honour. Maybe he wanted to avoid hurting someone. Of course, Sconnie had no way of checking on any of this: whenever he caught his father in these quiet moments, the old man would smile softly and begin talking right away, in that even, cheerful voice of his. He believed in self-improvement, especially for his son, and his conversation was always about something he had seen in a magazine, or heard on the radio. It was always along the lines of isn't science wonderful, or how do people think up such things. Even when Sconnie smacked him in the middle of the head with a golf club, he immediately began talking about something he had read somewhere. Anyone else would probably have passed out, or at least fallen over, but he managed to keep talking. The whole thing happened on a Sunday afternoon, in the park; thinking about it afterwards, Sconnie realised it was quite literally impossible for the old man to lose consciousness, or even show he was hurt, in such a public place.

It was an accident, of course. The old man had been trying to show Sconnie how to hold his club, and the boy had swung it back too far, the way he had seen people do on the links, striking his father square in the middle of his forehead. He heard the noise – a clean, hard crack – and for a moment he thought the worst, but the old man had just gone on talking, telling him everything was fine, and not to make a fuss, and maybe he should try to moderate his swing, because they were only putting, not driving off on the fairway. In one way he looked ridiculous; in another, though, Sconnie couldn't help but admire him. Once, when someone had asked him, at one of their family get-togethers, what he wanted to be when he grew up, he had pondered a moment then, unable to think of anything suitable, had said, simply, 'A man.' Everyone had laughed at that – they thought he was being funny – but, as he realised later, there had been something serious behind that answer. He had often wondered what it was, being a man. People would say to him, when he was hurt, or when things weren't going the way he wanted, that he had to *be a man.* He'd thought about it a long time, and he'd come to the conclusion that being a man, as far as the world was concerned, was being like his father. You had to conceal yourself, you had to pretend things weren't happening to you. Men who were men were supposed to be quiet and self-contained, to hold whatever anger or sadness they really felt in check. Control was of the essence, the one virtue a man could not do without, but Sconnie kept asking himself if that was all there was, if there might not be other, different qualities that he needed. Years later, this question still bothered him: late at night, when he had come home half-cut, but too restless to sleep, or when he was away on one of his long train journeys, he would try to describe his father for himself: gentle, humble, quiet, self-effacing, eager to learn. He wanted to find someone graceful and true, but the picture he kept coming up with was of that anxious, babbling idiot with a red weal in the middle of his forehead, trying to pretend nothing had happened.

Sconnie knew there were things you were supposed to put first in your life. Wife. Children. Home. Work. But his father had never given the impression of valuing anything especially: he took a mild interest in everything, from the migratory patterns of terns to his son's school report or his wife's gum problems. It was only after the old man died that Sconnie found what he really treasured, packed away in an old suitcase under the bed. A cheap leather bag, crammed with photographs and old letters; a couple of ribbons from his Air Force days; an old watch that didn't work any more; a signet ring that, as far as Sconnie could remember, he had never worn. The bag was decorated with ibises and jackal-headed figures, and Sconnie realised that it must have been made in Egypt for the tourist trade. His father had been in Egypt for a while: in the Forties, he thought. Sconnie didn't recognise the people in the photographs; the pictures were old and badly focused – men in service uniforms, a couple of the locals, dressed in overalls, some scenes inside what looked like a bazaar, a few pictures of camels. The letters were more interesting – and a little surprising. Sconnie had never imagined his father as a ladies' man, but he had obviously meant something to several of these correspondents. One, in particular, a woman who signed herself 'Liz', had written some pretty passionate stuff, and Sconnie had gone through the whole bundle, checking the dates, to make sure none of those letters came from the time after his father and mother had first met. Several of the envelopes contained snapshots: Liz was a slender, pretty girl, with curly blonde hair and very bright eyes. Sconnie wondered if his mother had ever seen those letters.

He read them all, but he felt guilty about it, even though his father wasn't around to worry about that any more. It was an odd sensation: he knew the letters had belonged to his father, but they seemed to be written to someone else, someone Sconnie had never known. It was as if he had broken into the life of a perfect stranger. He felt more comfortable with the other things he found in the suitcase, the ribbons and the watch, the ring – which fitted him perfectly – and a handful of official documents and pamphlets. The most interesting of these was, in some ways, the most revealing. It was a grimy, pink booklet, about four inches by six, entitled *Services Guide to Cairo*. It was obviously meant to fit into a pocket. The front cover showed a smiling Tommy, a windswept sailor and a handsome Air Force pilot, with his goggles perched on his brow, gazing off into the distance. On the back there were advertisements for Lebon & Cie, Le Caire – Alexandrie, Compagnie Centrale D'Eclairage Par Le Gaz et Par L'Electricité, and Manley House, facing Groppi's Rotunda, offering hot and cold running water, a spacious lounge, a reading and writing room, a gramophone and radio. Sconnie could imagine the pleasure his father would have derived from this booklet. It was packed full of useful information: where to shop, where to catch buses, what to see, services and amenities, clubs, cinemas, theatres. Of all the mementoes he found, this was the one he would bring out from time to time, just to glance through its pages. He would read sections aloud to himself and try to imagine his father yachting, or visiting the skating rink at Midan Malika Farida. He wondered what the old man – who would have been a young airman then – would have made of the passage that read: *For an Enjoyable Hour go to Femina, Imad-el-Din FREE to Troops in Uniform; from 10 a.m. to 2.30 p.m. – New Programme every Monday.* The last line was underlined in pencil, so Sconnie had to assume that his father had been there, at least once. Another favourite passage described the **INDIAN SOLDIERS CLUB CAIRO, 6, Sharia Galal (near Midan Twefik) – Telephone 50871**. *This club is for the use and benefit of all ranks of the Indian Army. A restaurant service is provided and supplies Indian food and cold drinks, at basic prices. Special rooms*

*exist for K.C.O's, V.C.O's and N.C.O's together with special
servants and a bar to meet their requirements. Two wireless sets and a
Ping-Pong table together with Indian Papers and Reviews are
available.* This announcement was circled lightly in pencil,
though Sconnie couldn't imagine his father ever being in such
a place. He would more likely have gone to the Homely
Club, on 42 Sharia Genina Ezbekieh, Cairo, which was 'set up
with providing a home wherein refreshments can be secured
and games played, and for men to share in spiritual activity'.
Or had he preferred the Ezbekieh Gardens Services Club,
with its open-air swimming pool and garden kiosk, run by
lady voluntary workers, where soft drinks, ice-cream, cold
lunches and sandwiches were sold at popular prices? Sconnie
could imagine his father, in an Egyptian garden, flirting with
one of the lady volunteers, and he began to love this little
booklet, for the pictures it gave him of a happier man, in a
simpler and more genteel world. He could see the old man, in
his mind's eye, on the way to the historic sites, sitting by the
window on Tram No 15, or waiting for the blue bus at Bab el
Hadid. Those were places he had marked with a pencilled X
in the margin: Pyramids and Sphinx, Mattaria and Heliopolis
Obelisk, the Barrages of the Nile. Sconnie assumed he had
gone to see them. He must also have made some effort to
understand the language: at the foot of page 16, in neat pencil,
he had written: Shari = Street; Midan = Square. Sconnie
couldn't remember his father ever talking about that era, or
making any informed reference to the pyramids, but he would
wonder, from time to time, if the old man had stood in the
shed at the end of his allotment, saying those words to himself,
under his breath, and remembering what he had seen and
become, on those long Egyptian nights.

Sconnie's father had died slowly, of cancer. He hadn't

complained; he was quite a young man still, but he'd taken it well. He had even tried, for his wife's sake, to keep up a semblance of normal life, to pretend nothing was happening. It was only during the last two or three weeks that the old man had stripped his existence down to the barest essentials. He would get up, but he hardly ever changed out of his pyjamas; he would go back and forth from the living room to the kitchen, making tea and toast, which was all he ever ate, or he would sit in his armchair, in front of the empty television, gazing at the screen as if totally entranced by what he was seeing. Or he would sit at the window, watching the kids come home from school. He looked like a ghost; his mouth was too red, his face like flour, his eyes almost black, the skin too loose around the bones. Sometimes he forgot to eat, or he pretended to forget. It must have hurt, just swallowing; by the time they took him to the hospital, he was so thin that, with his cropped hair and striped pyjamas, he could have been one of those prisoners from Belsen Sconnie had seen in television documentaries.

He would usually sleep through visits. Sconnie would sit by the bed and watch: he could see his father's eyes moving and he would be surprised at the idea of him dreaming – for some reason, he'd expected that to stop, now that the old man's life was coming to an end. Sometimes he wondered what those dreams contained – whether they resembled the dreams he knew that he himself had every night and immediately forgot, the way he forgot everything, with a moment's regret that was itself almost immediately forgotten, or whether they were deeper and clearer, filled with light and answers, with a dying man's ability to tune in to the background noise that the living are usually too busy to notice. Sconnie imagined him travelling back to the kitchens and shrubberies of long-demolished houses, or bridging the rifts in small talk from forty years before with the things he should have said; he imagined him searching through an empty house and finding the child he had never quite abandoned, finding him and returning some gift he had taken long before, and never used, squaring his life once and for all with something off-centre, some figure in the wings, who had watched and governed every moment of his visible existence. Sometimes he woke, quite suddenly, and it would be a second or two before Sconnie realised he was being watched: for those moments, the old man would seem immediately alert and aware of everything, as if his sleep had been pure make-believe, as if he'd been waiting all along to catch his son out. Yet when Sconnie asked how he was, or if he wanted anything, he seemed not to hear – or if he'd heard, he didn't understand. Sconnie would stay a while, sitting quietly by the bed, staring at his father's face, or the back of his hand, waiting for him to speak, yet knowing he was elsewhere already – even awake, he existed in his own world, somewhere between memory and the slow logic of decease.

At the funeral, he couldn't think of anything to say. People kept coming up to him and shaking his hand, and telling him they were sorry for his loss. Afterwards, at the pub, he had felt like a guest at someone else's do: he sat in a corner, letting people buy him drinks, and nodding whenever they spoke to him. He kept thinking his father had kept something from him, something important. Then, late in the evening, when the party was in full-swing and most of the guests were half-cut, he remembered a day trip they had made, on the train, to Edinburgh. As they were crossing the Forth Bridge, Sconnie had asked for a coin to throw out of the window, as tradition demanded. His father didn't like to waste money, but he had fished a penny from his wallet and handed it over. The two of them, father and son, were alone in the carriage – it must have been a special occasion of some kind, for them to have been travelling to Edinburgh without Sconnie's mother – and the old man watched in silence as Sconnie reached out through the narrow window and hurled the penny out to sea. When that small adventure was finished, they had sat back down in silence, as the train reached land and hurried on to Haymarket. For once, his father hadn't talked. He was wearing his good blazer, the one with the *Per ardua ad astra* badge, and a stripey tie: he always made an effort with his appearance, and Sconnie felt proud, for a moment, sitting there on a train beside his father, not talking, like real men, keeping their own counsel. Finally, as the train reached Haymarket, they were doused in the smell of warm malt, followed by a sharp, slightly bitter scent, and the old man had looked at Sconnie keenly, with an unexpected light in his eyes.

'Do you smell that?'

Sconnie nodded.

His father smiled softly and took a deep breath.

'I love that smell,' he said.

He looked at Sconnie for agreement, with that same brightness in his face.

'It's the best smell in the world,' he said. 'That, and the smell of the Forth, and that scent the desert has at night.'

It wasn't very much, and they soon lapsed back into the silence; then they were getting off the train, and moving off amongst all the people, making for the steps. But that evening, at his father's funeral, Sconnie remembered that look in his eyes again and he was glad.

A few days later, he began working on his scheme. He thought at first it was just a matter of self-containment, a

process whose logical end was weightlessness. It was a question
of discipline, of paring the body down to sinew and bone and
becoming one of those lean, wiry men you see out in fields
and pieces of wasteland, with their roll-ups and thin dogs,
standing in the wind, constantly on the alert, as if they knew
something was just about to happen, something dramatic, or
final. He didn't want to be like his father, weighed down with
his body and work and the family he probably loved, in his
way. Though he knew it wasn't a question of physical weight,
as such. There were men he could believe in, solid bodies
moving through well-defined spaces, making decisions, dealing with problems – men like Kennedy, or Perry Mason – and
they were hardly slender, or insubstantial, it was just that,
rather than being pinned down by the effort of being, the way
his father was, they seemed to possess the weight of their
bodies, to use it, the way a dancer, or a prize-fighter might,
and he wanted to be like that. It wasn't really a question of
weight, but it had something to do with gravity, and he knew,
deep down, that he had to adjust himself, beginning with his
body and moving on to his soul, to adjust his being in relation
to gravity. He had noticed, when he went out swimming,
how much stronger gravity seemed when he crossed a
riverbed, during those moments when he lost and regained his
balance, or a foothold slipped – how, for seconds at a time, his
contact with the earth would deepen and spread, till he felt he
was vanishing into its field. Maybe that was how the astronauts
felt, on splashdown, finding the weight in themselves that
echoed the earth's pull, possessing their flesh anew, the palms
of their feet, their fingers and ribs charged with gravity. As
time passed, they began to understand how bodies live for
weightedness: how bone starts to break down in space, losing
its form, the way it does in people who suffer from

osteoporosis. That was the special skill that some men possessed: nothing more than an intuitive understanding, an acceptance of gravity that allowed them to pass through the world with a certain grace. Sconnie was certain it was there in everyone: a hidden essence, a secret other. It had even been there in his father, who had seemed so ordinary, so heavy. He had caught glimpses of it, from time to time, in a moment's silence, or a gesture, in the way he looked, standing in the garden, with his back to the house, in an old white shirt and corduroy trousers, turning from his work to listen for something Sconnie could never hear, somewhere in the distance. It was there in his voice, sometimes, and sometimes in his smell, when he came in out of the rain, a mixed scent of dry-cleaning and hair cream, of warm skin and cologne and the faintest trace of smoke, not so much tobacco as leaf-smoke, as if he had stood in a clearing all day, tending a fire, alone, silent, bound to the stillness of the woods, when Sconnie knew all along that he'd been at work, taking orders from other men, and dreaming about his days in Cairo.

The reason for his scheme, the reason he had begun to wander aimlessly, taking the first train that pulled into the station, and travelling till he felt like getting off, was that Sconnie wanted to hear that distant noise, the one his father had been hearing. Because he knew it was there. When he was tired of being in the pub, tired of the pretence of being Sconnie, he would get up from the table and walk down to the station and stand in the queue, choosing a destination at random, from all the place names he kept in his head: York, Scarborough, Kirkcudbright, Inverness, Wick, Brighton, Halifax. Villages he had heard about on the radio, or seen on television, would come to mind, and he would have to ask if there was a station there and, if not, where the nearest station was. Then there would be the wait: he might change trains several times on his journey, or he might have to hang around a matter of hours for a connection, but that didn't matter. What mattered was the weightlessness he achieved, that sense of floating, like an astronaut, in infinite space. As soon as he got on to the first train, the one that took him away from there, he felt absolved: weightless and clean, like a new man, but until that moment, he was still Sconnie. If there was a delay, he would become more and more restless and unhappy. It was only when the train pulled out of the station, that he began to breathe, as if for the first time: he would find a seat next to the window, in an empty compartment if possible, and he would watch the world slipping by. It was the one time when he remembered himself; the one time when he was truly happy.

Now, at forty-four, he still felt like a boy inside, with a boy's love, a boy's wishes and foolishness. Some days it hurt, physically, just to hold it in, fluttering and banging in his throat, a searing hot pain that he pretended was indigestion. He would go to the chemist's and buy packets of Rennies by the dozen; he lived on them, cramming down handfuls between meals, like they were sweeties. There were times when he couldn't remember anything – what had happened the day before yesterday, his mother's face, the way home, where things were in the kitchen. There were days when he couldn't escape the bright, vivid memories of people and houses he couldn't quite place, and he would wonder if they were real, or if he had dreamed them, the previous night or twenty years ago. Maybe they were from a film he had seen, or a story he had read, back in the days when he still went to the pictures, or picked up a book. He knew the facts of his life as if he had learned them somewhere, reading them out of a book, the history of a man with whom he was, he knew, slightly acquainted: his son had died at the age of six, his wife had left him, he had worked down south then come back, he drank too much, he liked country music and stories about famous mysteries or serial killers. He liked to hang about at the station, watching the people as they met or told one another their goodbyes. He liked to watch strangers best, or those distant relatives who meet after years and are unsure about handshakes and kisses; he liked to see the people who step off a train and expect to be met, only to find they are alone on the platform, in a strange, cold, northern town, perhaps with nowhere to go, while the other passengers are taken away to cars and drinks and warm beds.

When he takes drink, his personality changes. Sometimes he ends up on a train, waiting for hours in some unknown station, or hurtling through the countryside, talking to some complete stranger as if he has known him since school days. Not that he knows anybody, other than the Mercy boys: the only folk he ever meets outside the pub are the people he catches in other pubs, or in station waiting rooms, where he sits by himself, with a can of beer in one hand and a fag in the other, minding his own business, till somebody chances along. As soon as he finds a listener, he's off. He talks about the same things to everyone he meets: the history of country music, or the famous clairvoyant, Ted Serios, who could make an image appear on a film just by staring at a camera. When Sconnie takes a drink, he can talk about Hank Williams, or Bob Woodruff, for two hours, more or less non-stop, allowing for interruptions. It's important to him that people remember that it was Juice Newton who sang *Angel of the Morning*; it's important to him that they know how Hank Williams died. At the same time, he knows that nothing is important to him.

Nothing he says is true, and he knows it: nothing can be true, not if it can be said. When he takes drink, Sconnie will tell people about his beliefs, which he also says he doesn't take seriously: he believes, he says, that there is a real world that we cannot see or directly experience unless we get outside ourselves, unless we forget who we are. You can't see it, but it's real, it's out there. What you see, most of the time, is what you expect to see and that's not it. It's real but, for most of the time, it's unattainable. You have to break through to it. When he takes drink, Sconnie says that the essence of wanting is not to have, that you cannot have what you desire, because as soon as you have something, you no longer desire it. So to want something is not to want to have it, he says. Nobody has any idea what he is talking about, least of all himself – and, if there is one thing in life that satisfies him, it is this fact.

Between the sessions, there were the nights and the early mornings; the private, invisible theatre, half-dreamed, half-real, of waking in the small hours at the foot of the stairs, or curled up on the kitchen floor, foetal position, shivering with the cold as the alcohol wore away; the blank theatre of unlit rooms and bathroom mirrors, of things shifting away and returning, transformed; the theatre of phantoms and shadows, of things disappearing, or looming up out of the darkness unexpectedly. Some mornings, Alan would be sick. It didn't bother him, it was just part of the routine by now, like eating, or sleeping. He would know when it was about to start minutes before it happened: he would feel the bile rising and he would walk into the toilet and stand waiting till it came: blue-black, sometimes, or dark-red, when he'd been drinking wine, but usually a slow, thin yellow, unpolluted with food, entirely liquid. It seemed almost magical, the way it came from nowhere, a transmutation his body had performed, something almost alchemical, an act of distillation, of transubstantiation. He knew, by now, how long it would take, how much of it would come at any one time, and he regarded the whole process with a mixture of patience and fascination. He never talked about those times – though the others did, cracking jokes and laughing it all off, exorcising the pain and

56

bewilderment of it all with half-told histories of shit and piss and bile. It was always a mystery to Alan, that they survived that theatre, day after day, week after week, month after month, when it seemed just one accident, one small miscalculation could finish any one of them at any time, forever.

Nevertheless, by half-eleven the next morning, the Mercy boys were back at the usual table, Sconnie in the same clothes he had worn the night before, Junior, as always, well turned out, in a clean blue shirt and black trousers, his shoes polished, his jacket pressed, even if it was showing signs of wear at the elbows and cuffs. It was important to him, in ways the other boys couldn't have understood, that he kept himself together, that he didn't let himself go. Most days, Rob would get there before the others, and they would find him sitting at the table, with his back to the bar, a three-quarters empty pint glass on the table in front of him, and no nip. It was sunny this morning, a bright day; as he'd walked down to the Mercy, Junior had noticed a mood in the air, an expectancy, a readiness for the pleasant surprise, that only ever happened on sunny days. As he walked into the bar, he could see that Sconnie and Rob were deep in conversation: Sconnie talking, Rob listening, a pleased look on his face.

Junior bought a round and sat down. From the highest window, sunlight was pouring in, flooding their corner of the room, glittering on the beer spills and the rims of the glasses. The bar was almost empty: it would fill slowly over the next hour, but it would never get packed – which was why each of the boys, for his own reasons, had chosen to belong there. Junior wondered idly where Alan was, then tuned in to the others' conversation.

'What's the worst thing, then?' Rob was asking.

Sconnie grinned. 'Pissing blood is bad,' he said.

'Pissing blood?' Junior came in, regarding Sconnie with mild, dismayed interest. 'When did you have that?'

'A couple of years back,' he said.

'What's it like?' Rob asked. He'd never pissed blood himself, but he'd had those couple of days of throwing up reddish bile, and he'd found blood in his shit once. At the time, he'd been surprised at how little it hurt. He'd thought about going to a doctor for a while, but he wasn't registered with anybody and it had cleared up soon enough; besides, he wasn't too sure he'd want some doctor checking him over in that general vicinity, when he came to think of it. Still, he could imagine pissing blood was worse. Anything that affected you there was bound to be bad. He remembered a bit in a book he'd read once – after he'd fucked some girl at a party, and then someone had told him afterwards that she had a disease, and was going round giving it to other people for revenge; he hadn't believed it for sure, but you never know, he'd thought, and he'd watched himself for any signs, for hot pissing and discharges, and he'd read this bit in a medical book, about people who had VD and urinary tract infections, so he would know what to look for. Pus. Irritation. Bleeding, even. The trouble was, he had too good an imagination: just reading the words was enough to start him off, so by the time he was finished, he was convinced his prick was rotting from the inside, the blood and tissue and muscle breaking down and trickling out, darkening his piss, giving off a faint, but unmistakable smell of disease. In the end, it turned out that he didn't have anything, but he'd got himself so worked up, he'd gone down to the clinic to get himself checked out, and some woman doctor in a clean white lab coat had given him a hard time about what she called his 'style of life'. Then, when he got the results, he was a bit embarrassed, as if he'd made the whole thing up, and he couldn't wait to get out of the place. That had been years ago, though, before he'd married Cathy. Nowadays, he didn't take those risks – or not most of the time, anyway.

Sconnie shook his head.

'It's not so much that it hurts,' he said, 'though it does. It's just the shock of seeing it, and how it feels, like your life-blood's running out of you.'

Rob snorted appreciatively and Junior turned to him with a questioning look.

'It's not funny,' he said, mock-seriously.

'Aye, it is, though,' Sconnie said.

'How's that?'

'Well.' Sconnie shook his head softly. 'You see things in a new light. Like those boys with the comet.'

They were all watching Sconnie now – he had their attention – but he didn't say any more, just picked up his pint glass and finished it. Then, with a neat, almost prim gesture, he finished off his whisky.

'Well, Sconnie, son,' Junior said, finally. 'It doesn't sound like a good idea to me.'

'Didn't say it was,' Sconnie answered. 'But it makes you think. Like what you see on television, all the hospital programmes, and things about your health. I mean – they talk about all kinds of stuff, but they never mention that, as far as I know. They never have a programme about what to do when you start pissing blood. And I wonder, why not?'

'Bounds of taste and decency,' Junior said, decisively.

'What?'

'You're not supposed to get stuff like that on TV,' Junior said. 'It might offend Mrs So-and-So in Broughty Ferry.'

'She's probably the one pissing blood,' Rob ventured.

'So what happened?' Junior asked Sconnie, 'ignoring that last remark.'

'Nothing,' Sconnie said. 'Went to the doctor. Got some big orange pills.'

'Oh.' The other two sounded disappointed.

'Talking about pills,' Sconnie said, 'there's a boy up my way, Tommy Lindsay, and he's talking to the boy downstairs from him, telling him how he'd got these headaches and dizzy spells, pains in his chest and neck, all kinds of symptoms. And the other boy says he's had that, and he got some pills from the doctor, and they worked wonders. So now Tommy is really impressed, and he wants to know which doctor the boy went to, but the boy says, never mind that, he's got plenty of the pills, he gets them whenever he wants on a repeat prescription, and he'll let Tommy have some from his own supply.'

Junior shook his head incredulously.

'He didn't take them, did he?'

Sconnie nodded.

'He did,' he said. 'And he felt fine the first few days, a lot better. It was about a week before he started seeing things, imagining there were people in the flat, walking about in the next room, that kind of thing. Paranoid. At night, he's scared to go to bed, because when he lies down in the dark, he sees this old woman bending over the bed, and her face is really ugly, but she's smiling at him, leaning over, further and further, till her face is just a couple of inches away from his, and he can hear her breathing and smell her halitosis.'

Sconnie paused, to let them consider the image, while he lit a cigarette.

'So Tommy goes to the boy and tells him what happened,' he continued. 'And the boy says to him, right enough, he'd been a bit confused for a while, too, but it soon wore off, and the doctor had warned him, anyway, that there could be some side-effects. Oh, and by the way, he wasn't taking any drink with them, was he?'

At that moment, Sconnie's head went up. 'Here's Alan,' he said.

By one o'clock, the room was full of light, and someone had put on some music behind the bar. Junior had nipped out and put a line on, and Alan had managed to slip Rob another tenner to buy his own round. He wondered, sometimes, if Rob was only tapping him, or whether he got the odd bit from the other boys. He didn't think so – he reckoned Rob would be too embarrassed to ask Sconnie or Junior for money. Still, not that it mattered. Every now and again, Rob would come in flush, and he'd buy rounds all night, ordering doubles of malt whisky, buying cigars and soaking them in brandy, the way he'd learned from some boy he'd worked with down south. Today, though, he didn't look that good. He seemed a bit pale and, even though he was acting his normal self, Alan could see that something was bothering him, and it wasn't just money problems.

For his part, Rob knew that Alan was watching him. He felt dizzy again, the way he'd felt a couple of times over the last week, when he'd had a few drinks and nothing much to eat. The boys never bothered much with food in the afternoon: Sconnie said the best way was to have a good breakfast – you should never miss breakfast, he said, because any doctor would tell you that breakfast was the most important meal of the day – then get home for an early tea about four or five o'clock, so that eating didn't interfere with your drinking later. He said it was a daft idea, to have three or four meals a day, all you really needed was breakfast and tea. If you were eating all the time, he said, your body was always working, digesting the food and getting rid of all the poisons and additives.

They were talking about dogs, now, usually one of Rob's favourite subjects; he was always complaining about the boy next door, Cathy's cousin, who had a couple of Rottweilers. According to Rob, they never stopped barking, and Sconnie liked to wind him up about it, suggesting ways of getting rid of the dogs: how he could put poison out for them, or grind up glass and mix it with their food, or maybe he could get some little pins, like women use for sewing, and hide them inside dog biscuits, or lumps of meat, and toss them over the fence. One night, they had cooked up an elaborate scheme involving a bowl of dog food, some super-glue, and a petrol can, and Rob had been so enthusiastic about the idea, Alan thought he was going to go back and try it out that very night.

Sconnie enjoyed these conversations. He didn't know why – he didn't like dogs much, but he'd never really bothered about them till he'd met Rob. Now he found himself thinking up all kinds of daft stuff. It wasn't that he cared about dogs, one way or the other, but there was something about the other man's anger that he respected – something he felt so deeply that he was compelled, by some inner force, to carry it through to its logical conclusion. He felt the same way when he met people who were in favour of hanging, or bringing back national service, or bombing Iraq; he would sit with strangers in bars and waiting rooms, moaning about the health service, or pollution, or all the foreigners coming into the country, and he didn't believe a word of it. It was just that he respected the other person's anger so much, he couldn't help being drawn in, to share it, to be a part of it.

'There's too many dogs about,' he said. 'You can't hear yourself think for the noise. And you can't walk along the street without stepping in shit. It's about time they were all put down and give us peace.'

'I thought they were supposed to be good for people,' Alan ventured, from his place at the edge of the circle.

Sconnie swung around. 'What is?'

'Having pets,' Alan answered, in a matter-of-fact voice. 'I read it in a magazine. It's supposed to be good for you, stroking them, having them around to talk to and all that. It's supposed to get rid of stress and stop heart disease—'

Sconnie held up his hand and shook his head. It was a gesture he performed from time to time, a sign that he was about to disabuse somebody of an erroneous belief. It was something they always respected: at some level, they knew that Sconnie wasn't talking for himself, that what he was saying wasn't in any way personal. It was like when you listened to the radio, and some boy was on, talking about some moral dilemma, or some necessary political measure: you knew he didn't really care what happened, he was just the expert they'd called in for the occasion.

'I'll have to stop you there, Alan son,' he said. 'I know what you're saying, and all that, because I've read the same stuff myself. But you have to ask yourself – who is it does all this research into such things, and why do you think they're doing it?'

Alan shook his head.

'I'm not following,' he said.

'The bit is,' Sconnie sat back and gave him a pleasant look, 'these doctors who say that pets are good for you. They must have a reason for doing that research in the first place. I mean – why aren't they out looking for the cure for cancer, or some new drug for multiple sclerosis, if they're so clever? Thing is, maybe that's the only work they can do, and maybe they've got reasons of their own for doing it. We all know the kind of things animal lovers get up to. They'll kill to protect a wee seal pup, but they don't give a shite about starving wee bairns in Sudan. They want you to believe cats are good for your heart, and the best thing for stress is a wee retriever puppy because *they* think animals are the bees' knees.'

He shook his head, and took a long draw on his pint.

'And another thing,' he said. 'Who is it pays for their work in the first place? Answer me that?'

He turned to Alan as if he really expected a response and, following his lead, the others turned too, like a gang of church elders rounding on a heathen.

'I don't know,' Alan said.

'The pet food companies,' Sconnie said, without missing a beat. 'The pet food companies is who. That way they sell more dog meat and cat biscuits and all that rubbish.'

'Aye,' Junior put in, 'it is rubbish at that. All horse meat and offal.'

'That's right,' said Sconnie. 'None of those dog lovers ever worry much about the New Forest ponies they're feeding to their wee pals. That's where they come from, you know.' He turned to Alan again. 'Did you know that?'

Alan nodded. He seemed to remember seeing a programme on television about some cull in the New Forest, or was it Dartmoor, lots of scraggy-looking ponies being brought down into yards and pens and knocked into pet food. The voice-over said it was a necessary cull, to get rid of the weak and the old that wouldn't survive the winter, but he didn't suppose the animals saw it that way.

'You see, Alan,' Sconnie continued in a softer vein, happy that his point was made, 'you can't believe any of this research. People don't do research to find things out, they do it to prove what they already believe. I mean – take a look at the statistics. Fact: According to statistics, being married is good for men, because married men live longer than single men do.'

Junior nodded. 'I heard that,' he said.

'So you did,' said Sconnie, absorbing the interruption like one of those preachers on American gospel shows, 'and the reason you did was, you were supposed to. And why was that?'

He looked around the table but the others had the good sense to know the question was a rhetorical one, so they didn't say anything.

'Society, as we know it, is based on the nuclear family,' Sconnie continued. 'Which would be ruined, when you think about it, if men didn't believe that marriage was good for them. Their own experience, of course, tells them otherwise – but then out come these statisticians to say, you think you're badly off, look at the boys who are single. They never point out that marriage is the norm in this society, and anybody who manages to stay single is probably some duffer anyway, somebody who's probably going to drink himself to death, or fall off a train, or something. They never point out that a good proportion of men are going to die young anyway, and they'll probably be the boys who are single who take the risks. They just say, married men live longer, and that's all there is to it. Forget about quality of life. Forget about control groups, or whatever. What they tell you is what they want you to know.

Get married. Get a cat and a dog and budgie and watch out for your cholesterol levels. That way you won't get heart disease or cancer. You'll be miserable as sin, but you'll probably live forever.'

He sat back and pulled out his cigarettes.

'Don't smoke, either,' he said.

Junior finished his whisky.

'And most of all, don't drink,' he said. 'So whose round is it?'

A few rounds further into the afternoon, while Sconnie was up at the bar, and Junior had nipped out to see how his horse was doing, Alan put Rob on the spot.

'Are you all right?' he asked.

Rob took a deep breath and nodded.

'You're white as a sheet,' Alan persisted.

Rob nodded again and stood up. The room shifted, then settled into place again. He waved his hand, then turned and walked, very deliberately, to the toilets at the back of the pub, hoping Alan wouldn't try to follow.

Inside the Gents was a wall of white tiles, with the old-fashioned Shanks Odourless urinals. He'd never really noticed this space before: how white it was, how cold. He steadied himself against the wall and tried to clear his head, but he could feel himself starting to go, the warmth draining from his face, his legs weakening, dark shapes forming in front of his eyes, like apparitions. Luckily, nobody else was there, but he was aware of the fact that anybody could come in, at any moment, and he stood still, his hands flat against the cold tiles, trying to breathe, to get some oxygen to his brain. This was worse than it had ever been before. He was about to black out: his head felt cold and empty and, for the first time, he was really afraid, not so much of whatever this was, as of losing control. He took another deep breath and tried to gather himself up; next thing he knew, he was down. He heard the slap as his body hit the floor, but he didn't lose consciousness – not for a single second – and he struggled back to his feet immediately. His only fear now was that somebody else might come in and find him there, lying on the floor like some old wino. Or Alan would come looking for him, and make some kind of fuss about it, call a doctor, or try to make him go home. He pushed open the door of the toilet cubicle and stepped inside. It was dark, and it smelled slightly of pine. He sat down on the toilet and put his head between his knees, the way they always told you to do in school, when somebody passed out at Mass. Breathing deeply, he could smell the fresh, slightly sickly pine disinfectant and, under it, something else. The thought ran through his mind that other people had probably sat here, sick and dizzy, in much the same situation. Maybe people had died in here. He lifted his head and took another deep breath.

On the wall opposite, in large black felt tip writing, a single piece of graffiti had survived the recent efforts of the cleaners. He studied it for a moment before he really read what it said.

MERCY BOYS
ARE ARSE
BANDITS

Christ, he thought. He tried to imagine somebody sitting there, on the lav, with his trousers round his ankles probably, reaching out across the width of the cubicle to write – no, print – these letters. What kind of person would do that? The image struck him as absurdly funny, all of a sudden, and he laughed out loud. His head was beginning to get warmer, the blackness had gone; carefully, he stood up and brushed himself down. The really stupid thing was, there was no such thing as Mercy Boys. It was just an ordinary pub where people came to drink. You got doctors here, students, builders, boys on the social; what you didn't get was Mercy Boys. Or maybe the closest you got to that sort of thing was him and Junior and Sconnie and maybe Alan, since they went there every day. None of them knew why. It was like everything else in life, just a question of habit, what you were used to. The only thing you didn't want, if you had any sense, was change. He slid the catch on the door and stepped out of the cubicle. He felt fine. Two minutes later, he was back at the bar, ordering another couple of pints with Alan's money. Everything was fine. He wouldn't have to go back home for hours yet.

For the first few months after they got married, Rob had expected to be happy enough. He knew he didn't love Cathy – if he had ever loved anybody, it had been Helen, all those years before – but he didn't think love mattered that much, as long as people got on all right, and had a good time together. To begin with, Cathy had been funny and easy-going, just what he thought he wanted in a wife. He'd always fancied her, even when he was still trying to get over Helen, and, when he'd first gone out with her, she'd been a good fuck; but then, after the wedding, everything had changed. It was the usual story, Rob had heard it a hundred times, but he hadn't expected it to happen to him. The worst thing was, when Cathy had started to get serious, talking about houses and babies and how he should get a better job, so they could think about taking out a mortgage and buying a place of their own, it was the sheer ordinariness of their rows that bothered him most. She wanted a house and a dog, and she wanted a car, so they could go out to the country on little runs; she wanted to save up for holidays abroad, like the other girls at work.

Rob had tried not to let it get to him; but he'd told her, even before they'd got married, that he wasn't interested in that kind of life, and it didn't seem fair to him, when she kept going on about it. Then, after a while, he'd noticed she was less interested in sex and, sometimes, when he came home from work, he'd find himself wanting her and not being able to do anything about it. If he started anything, she would slip away from him and start talking about getting a better house, about the things they could do if they had their own place. She would keep going on about wallpaper designs and paint and nice furniture, and he'd stand listening, trying to hide the fact that, right now, all he wanted was a fuck. It was ridiculous: he would feel sick with desire, and she would just sit there, showing him colour charts and samples of fabric. They still had sex, from time to time, but only at night and even then, when he reached out to touch her, he would sense her body stiffening a little, then gradually relaxing, almost by some deliberate effort, as if she were granting him a favour, against her own desire. Rob knew things changed when people got married: there were adjustments to make, there were things that had to be taken care of. He had read about that kind of stuff in magazines, and he didn't really mind if it came to that in the long run. He was quite prepared to accept that the initial excitement would fade, to be replaced by other, hard-won gifts: companionship, trust, understanding. Still, he'd expected, for a while at least, that the honeymoon would continue, if only for a year, or even a few months. Overnight, their affair had become an old, stale marriage, and he felt angry and cheated. It was like lifting a beautiful stone out of the river-bed and watching it dry in the air, seeing that the thing that had seemed vivid and bright, almost animate in the water, was really nothing more than a dull, bluish pebble. What had seemed almost magical in their lives, when they had first met, was now nothing more than a negotiated state, a bargain they made, day after day, to live at peace in the same narrow space. The worst thing was, he didn't know why she had changed;

he was pretty sure she didn't know how he felt about Helen, or the fact that, whenever he had a couple of drinks, he would still find himself thinking about her.

At first, they had lived in a bed-sit, and he'd been happy enough, going out to the pub, coming home for his tea, staying in for a night's telly or going out again, with or without her. He'd thought she was happy enough, too; she had her job, and he'd take her out from time to time, to the pub, or the pictures; the sex was still good, though maybe not as frequent as before – but soon she started going on about a new place, more room, better furniture, that kind of thing, and, finally, he'd given in and they had moved into this house, next to her cousin. Malcolm. From the first, it had been a disaster. Malcolm had invited them round to his house for a drink, to make them feel welcome, and they hadn't got on. Cathy had got all dolled up, and the boy who stayed with Malcolm, the lodger, had eyed her up all night, lighting her cigarette for her and paying her little compliments on the sly, when he thought Rob wasn't listening. Also, Malcolm was a complete wanker: he had long greasy hair, and he had these two big Rottweiler dogs in the garden, which he never exercised, so they kept barking and jumping around all the time. At one point, he let them in, so Cathy could see how big they were; Rob didn't like dogs, especially big dogs, and he sat frozen, trying to pretend he wasn't bothered, till Malcolm let them back out.

The other thing about Malcolm that Rob didn't like was his paintings: his front room was like an art gallery, with paintings all over the walls, except that these weren't paintings of landscapes or bowls of apples, they were just crap portraits of film stars, people like James Dean and Montgomery Clift and Marilyn Monroe; Malcolm painted them from photographs he'd cut out of magazines, then he hung them on the walls, so people could see his handiwork. Cathy seemed to think this was great.

'I really like that one,' she said, pointing to a huge portrait of a man in cowboy gear.

'That's Clark Gable,' Malcolm said. 'In *The Misfits*, the year he died.'

'It's great,' Cathy said. She turned to Rob. 'Isn't it great,' she said, prompting him.

'Yeah,' Rob said. 'Great.'

'*The Misfits* is my favourite film,' Malcolm said.

'Is that right?' Rob was looking at the picture, trying to remember what Clark Gable really looked like.

'The interesting thing about that film,' Malcolm continued, looking to the other boy, the lodger, for back-up, 'is the fact that three of the stars died not long after the film was finished. Montgomery Clift, Marilyn Monroe and Clark Gable. Some people think it was that film that killed them.'

'How do you mean?' Cathy asked.

'Well . . .'

Malcolm had gone on to spin some yarn about the film, but Rob had stopped listening; he was watching Cathy, the way she had started to come out of herself, giving Malcolm and the lodger little smiles and leaning in to get her cigarette lit, once or twice even touching the other boy's hand, gently, flirting with the two of them, letting them make a fuss of her. After a while, he got sick of the whole performance and stood up.

'Thanks for the drink,' he'd said. 'But we've got to go now.'

They had all looked confused then, as if they thought the evening was just beginning, and Cathy had been reluctant to go. It had even taken him another twenty minutes to get them out of there, and back to their own house. And he hadn't planned to do it – he'd never hit a woman before in his life – but when he got her inside, he'd turned and just given her a little slap, a light, quick slap on the cheek, so she would know she couldn't piss him about like that, in front of other people. He didn't say anything, he just did it, matter of fact like, and she hadn't cried, or said anything, she'd just looked at him, more surprised than anything else, but as soon as it happened, Rob knew there was no going back.

Later that night, after Cathy had gone to bed, he sat up with a bottle of whisky, and thought about Helen. He remembered the times he'd spent with her, out swimming in their special place on the river, or sitting in the woods, amongst the thick weeds, smoking draw, and listening to the birds, or the soft patter of rain on the leaves. There had been an abandoned hut on the old allotments that they used to go to when it rained: it was gone now, but it was still there on his inner map, a dingy wooden hut smelling of stale oil and chemicals, its roof broken in, the floor littered with newspapers and empty bottles. They had taken acid out there, for the first time, sitting in the lee of the hut, and waiting for the microdot to melt on their tongues; then, when the warmth flooded his body, he'd touched Helen's face, and she had kissed him, her mouth sweet and wet and a little feverish. When he remembered it, it was hard to believe that those days were a part of his own life, and not some film he'd seen, or something he'd read somewhere. That place – those places – had stayed with him, the way scenes from a movie stay, and somewhere, in some angle of his mind, he believed that he and Helen would go back some day to the stillness of the nettles around the hut, to the cleavers growing through heaps of broken stones and the dim indoors space where they had sat for hours, the roof patched with sky and whatever remained of birdsong and summer rain. It had something to do with fairness, with the idea that things should be right, that they would return to themselves, in this life, or another, their bodies misted with one unending summer's heat. They would replay that movie of ivy and scraps of cotton and the black inward of stopped bottles they had found in the shed, the crinkled tubers in long-abandoned boxes, with their black-green, sinister shoots, a nurtured life that had passed its prime and lay festering, rich with the last sugars of summers past. It had taken him a long time to abandon this notion; before he knew he had lost it, he was in the wrong movie, marrying Cathy like a man in a trance, or like someone out of his depth in deep, black water, who still believes, even as he is pulled under, that some kind of rescue is possible.

'You've never been happy.'

That was what Cathy said to him, whenever they started arguing. They'd come to a point, and she'd turn round and say it, half-pitying, half-angry, and he'd have to get away from her then, upstairs, or out the door, away from her flat, shiny face and that satisfied look of hers, the way she always knew she was right when she had no idea what she was talking about. Because he had been happy, once. He had known Helen long before he'd ever known her, and though it hadn't lasted long, he had been happy, for a while at least.

It had started when he was still at school. He hadn't liked school much: he'd hated the teachers, especially the men – the way they talked down to you, and swanned about the place as if they were God's gift, in their tweed jackets and knitted ties, flirting with the girls, or trying to pretend they weren't, not realising that they were being shown up, that the girls knew exactly what they were doing, and were laughing behind their backs. He hated the smell of the place, that mixture of boiled potatoes and damp, and how everything was old and second-hand: the desks were all scuffed up, covered with ink stains and graffiti, even the books had whole lists of other people's names inside the front, and stupid notes in the margins, to remind people of what the teacher said, so they could remember it for the exams. Most of all, Rob hated the other kids: the hard-working ones who tried to pretend they weren't; the keen, useless ones, who had a go at everything, no matter how stupid it was, eager to please, seeing themselves reflected in the teachers' calculated praise; the fat boys with their constant excuses to get them out of PE, or stupid explanations about how the dog ate their homework. When-ever a teacher got at him, Rob refused to make any excuses. He just sat and listened and waited till it was finished. They would shout at him; they would lean over his desk and ask him, in that soft threatening voice they kept for special moments, if he had anything to say for himself, and he wouldn't answer. He hated the teachers, he hated school, he hated the other kids. He even hated the girls. With one exception.

There were different rules for girls. Most kept their heads down, and tried not to be noticed, and that usually kept them out of trouble. Of course, there were different kinds of girls – some of them were little bitches, and some were a good laugh, there were girls who took the piss out of the teachers, or let you go round the back of the gym with them. Most girls just went through school, all the way through the third and fourth years, and into the fifth, and they weren't really there, they just stayed out of the way and handed in their homework and didn't answer questions unless they were asked, and nobody noticed them. It was as if they were invisible. That was how it was with Helen. She was in his class, but in all the years they'd been going to the same dingy little rooms together, for Science and English and RE, he'd hardly known she existed. Until, one day, the situation changed.

It was the summer holidays. In the afternoons, to get away from the others, Rob would get his stuff together and wander out along the river to a place he knew. It was a good place to swim, but nobody else seemed to know it. Rob thought of it as a long spit of land that reached into the water, but it was really nothing more than a couple of large stones and a sand drift, surrounded by bricks and weeds, screened off from the path further up by a stand of scrubby trees. He would go out there on his own and swim half the day, coming in from time to time and lying flat out amongst the weeds to get the sun, in the long heat of the summer afternoons. He liked the heat, and the smell of his skin as it dried. He liked the scent of the crushed grass and weeds, the warmth of his body and the odd shiver of wind that ran along his spine when a cloud covered the sun and it went suddenly dark, so sudden he could even tell through closed eyes, all that shifting and flickering on his eyelids melting away to nothing as he sat up and looked around, and it felt as if someone had just been there, watching him.

It was his own, private place and he was certain nobody else knew about it. Sometimes he even went there at night and swam in the dark. He wasn't afraid: there had always been something about the place that drew him in and made him feel at home, away from the houses. He'd often imagined himself coming out here and never going back or, if he did, going back to another place – another town, with different people – somewhere in America maybe, where they had guns and strange children, somewhere in the country, with swamps and long, empty roads going nowhere. He would spend hours imagining the house he would live in, if he could live in a place like that: a big, old wooden house, with a cellar and an attic, and upstairs rooms that nobody had been into for years, silent rooms full of old Indian masks and fish traps, and carbines hung on the walls. Or maybe one of those cabins where hired killers live, just a table and a couple of chairs, a plain wooden table and a couple of rickety chairs, and a little stove in the corner, a black pot-bellied stove with a kettle on it, and maybe a cup on the table, a white enamel cup with a blue rim, full of icy water.

Then, one afternoon, as soon as he arrived at the place, he knew someone had been there. It was like the time he had broken into that house in Blackness, when he'd found the dead man – he'd known right away that somebody was there, but he couldn't see who it was for ages. It was only the second house he'd done, but he wasn't scared. He didn't even care if he got caught, it would just give his mother and all the idiots at school something to think about. He'd been walking around, and he'd seen the window was open: it was about three o'clock in the morning, and the house was dark, so he'd just gone over and pulled himself up on to the window-sill, then dropped softly into the room – just like that – and hunkered down, listening, waiting to see if anybody had heard him. As soon as he did, though, he'd had that feeling – like he was being watched, or like somebody was there – and he'd stayed still, frozen, ready for whatever was coming.

That was when he'd seen what it was that was bothering him. He thought it was something else at first – a pile of clothes, maybe – but as his eyes became accustomed to the light, he saw that it was a man – and as soon as he did, he knew the man was dead. He could have been sleeping, sitting in the big old armchair, with his head to one side, one arm hanging down so it rested in his lap, but Rob knew he wasn't. The man was about fifty, Rob thought, and even in that light, it was obvious he was a foreigner; he had dark, pockmarked skin, and that dry, puffy look about the eyes that Rob had seen in some of the Indian or Pakistani shopkeepers, a dry, swollen, look that made him think of animals that aren't used to the daylight. In the half-light from the window, Rob could see that the man was wearing a V-necked sweater over a plain blue shirt, and he had tartan slippers on his bare feet. The thought went through his head that the man's feet must have been cold, then he laughed at himself and went through to the kitchen, walking in a crouch, so nobody passing by would see him through the window.

He wasn't really sure what he was looking for. He'd come expecting money, or maybe drink, or cigarettes, but all he found in the kitchen was a table and a fridge, a pile of dishes in the sink and, on the counter, some potatoes in a bowl that had already gone mouldy. Higher up, on one of the shelves above the sink, there was a leg of lamb, with big slices carved away; it had one of those wire covers over it, the kind you have to keep the mice away, but the meat was hard and plasticky-looking. Rob opened the fridge and stood in its cold blue light, looking for something – anything – he could take with him. He was annoyed all of a sudden that he had started this, and it looked like he wasn't going to get anything out of it. There was some cheese in the fridge, and a bowl of something that looked like lemon jelly, and that was that. Not even milk. He was thirsty now, and he'd wanted there to be something, milk, or beer, or something – just to see if he could drink it.

He checked upstairs; there was nothing. As he was searching the bedroom, he was taken with the notion that the old man wasn't sitting in the chair any more, that he had just stood up and walked out into the street, in his slippers, where anybody could find him. Rob felt a surge of panic, and he was tempted to switch on a light, but he got a grip on himself in time and made his way downstairs quietly, on the alert, listening for any sound, watching for any movement. The old man was still in his chair, of course – and, suddenly, Rob realised that, if he had any money, or anything of value, it would be there, concealed somewhere about his person. He walked over to the armchair and stood looking at the old man's face. He looked sad, as if he'd known, when he died, that somebody would find him like that. Maybe he'd even known who it would be. Maybe he had imagined a boy he'd never seen before, a foreigner, climbing in through the window to steal his money, or his watch, or whatever else he had in his pockets. The thought made Rob want to laugh. He'd always thought that dead people were just dead – like the animals you see by the side of the road, or the people in war pictures, who didn't really look much like people until you studied the picture closely – but this man wasn't like that at all. This man was as real as he would have been if he'd been alive, maybe more real. He had a presence, just like a living person; Rob had felt it as soon as he had clambered in over the window-sill and dropped to the floor. As soon as his feet had hit the ground, he'd felt that presence. And now the old man was putting thoughts into his head, trying to psyche him out, trying to protect the little he owned on this earth, even now, when it was useless to him.

Rob knelt down and looked at the man's hands. He wasn't wearing a watch, but there was a ring on one of the fingers. It looked like gold, plain and rounded, like a wedding ring, though it wasn't on the wedding finger. The man's hands were chubby, and slightly blue-looking in the half-light. Rob took hold of his fingers – gently, but firm enough to feel that he was quite cold – and began trying to prise the ring free. It wouldn't come. He wriggled it first one way, then the other, straining and pulling at the skin; he got it halfway, but he couldn't get it past the knuckle. The skin felt loose and puffy, and he thought, if he tried too hard, it would split or tear, and he experienced a wave of disgust at the thought of it. Finally he gave up. If the old bastard wanted to keep his ring, he could have it.

By now, he was beginning to feel uneasy. He prodded half-heartedly at the pockets, for any sign of money, or a wallet, but there was nothing and, with some relief, he realised there was no point in hanging around. He'd begun to notice a smell: it wasn't what he imagined as the smell of death, it wasn't like rot, or anything like that, but it was pretty foul, a bit like the bushes at the park, where people went in to piss, and it was getting stronger all the time. He was pretty sure it wasn't the old man: it seemed to be coming from the kitchen and, after a moment, he realised there was something in there, something he'd missed before; he was pretty sure, even, that it was something alive. He listened. There was a soft, scrabbling noise, as if whatever it was that was in there was trapped inside something – a cardboard box, maybe – and he walked through again to see what it was. Immediately, he noticed a large cardboard box, in one corner of the room – he couldn't understand why he had missed it before – and he realised that, not only the noise, but also the smell was coming from there.

He hadn't stayed to find out what it was, but later, when he got home and sneaked upstairs, he caught himself feeling oddly proud of the old man, even a little fond of him. He didn't tell anyone else about what had happened – it was a secret that belonged to him, and keeping it made him feel a sense of kinship, as if there was a secret, hidden thread that connected him to another world, the world of the dead who still had their own presence. That was what had mattered, of course: that presence. It was the same thing he felt, that afternoon, when he came to his private spot near the river and realised someone or something else was there, something invisible. It was several minutes before he saw Helen and even when he did, even though he knew who she was, it was like seeing a ghost, or like being in that room, with the subtle emanation of the old man's spirit hanging around him. It had been minutes before he'd seen her: she was quite still, standing amongst the bushes near the water's edge, and he'd had no idea who she was. She looked completely different from the girl in his class at school: thin, pale, with long dark hair, she looked like a mirage, something he could have imagined there, in the watery sunlight. It was a moment before she too realised that she was not alone, but she didn't seem surprised to see him. She had just smiled and come over to where he was standing, and he had noticed that her hair was wet, and there were damp patches on her blouse and jeans.

'Hello.' She looked at him as if she expected him to do something, perform some kind of magic trick, or tell her a story.

'Hello,' Rob answered. He felt stupid. He knew who she was now, but he couldn't believe it: it was as if she was a different person outside school, as if she had been veiled all the time she had been sitting there, in class, paying attention. There was a long silence, while they stood gazing at one another, each of them waiting for the other one to say something. Finally, Helen spoke.

'Have you got any cigarettes?' she said.

Rob had taken out the packet of Marlboros he had nicked from one of his mother's friends the day before and held out the pack to her and, somehow, as soon as she took it, the cigarette looked longer and cleaner and slimmer than ever, as if, just by touching it, she had made it more real, more perfect. It was like all those words they used for cigarettes, rolled into one – slim, clean, extra-long – and it had been enough, then, just to stand there, smoking in silence with this strange girl, and looking out across the water, as if each of them had been alone, and it was how he had learned to feel, as long as they had been together: a sense that, no matter what they did, or where they went, being with her was like being alone, only better.

After that day, they had met, often, but they had never told anyone else about it; and from that point of view, she was never really his girlfriend. It was a secret they had decided to keep, for no good reason: or at least, for no reason that Rob was aware of. The other thing was, even though he'd started to think that maybe he was in love with her, even when they'd kissed and smoked dope together, and sat out in the weeds dropping acid and watching whole days go by like some kind of mystery theatre, they'd never had sex – not the full thing, not intercourse. It amazed him, now, looking back, thinking about it, but at the time, he hadn't really been bothered – she didn't want it, and he'd not pushed it. Still, when Helen went off to college – she didn't really say goodbye to him, she just said she'd see him later, in a few weeks – and Cathy turned up, wet and giggly and a bit daft, it hadn't taken him long to change his mind. And Helen must have heard something about it, away at college, because she hadn't come back for ages, and when she had, she hadn't even come looking for him, or let him know she was there. She hadn't even written to him.

So it was much later, after he was with Cathy, but before they were married, that Rob met her again, up on the Perth Road. He'd seen her coming from maybe fifty yards away, and he'd been stopped in his tracks, dizzy with the sense of her, of how beautiful she was – how, as soon as he saw her again, he knew that she was the only woman who would ever exist – and he'd stood there, waiting for her to notice him. He'd been out buying drink for a party – his engagement party, in fact – and he was on the way home now, with a box of wine cradled in his arms. It wasn't till the last minute that she looked up and saw him there, looking foolish, holding the box to his chest and staring at her.

'Rob!' Helen seemed pleased enough to see him, but the look she gave him was the look she probably would have given on meeting any old friend from school. 'How are you doing?'

'Fine.' Rob smiled. He felt awkward, standing there, holding the box of bottles.

'I heard you got married.'

He shook his head.

'No,' he said. 'Who told you that?'

She craned her neck to see inside the box. She had changed since he'd last seen her, but when he tried to figure out what it was, he couldn't quite put his finger on it. Her hair was different – so were her clothes – but there wasn't just one thing he could point to, it was as if she had shifted slightly, and become an altogether new person.

'I don't remember,' she said. 'Are you having a party?'

'Sort of.' He smiled. 'Would you like to come?'

She shook her head.

'I can't,' she said. 'I'm only here for a couple of days.'

'Oh.' Rob tried to look casual, like someone taking no more than a polite interest. He felt awkward for having lied about Cathy – even though they weren't married yet, it had still been a kind of lie to say he wasn't married to her. He was as good as married, no matter what he said. The thought depressed him suddenly; he felt a spasm of despair, which he wanted her not to see.

'Are you still at college?' he asked her.

'Yes.' She laughed. 'For two more years.'

'Do you like it?'

'Yes.' She smiled. Then, as if there was some connection, she added, 'I'm going to France in the summer.'

'Oh.' Rob didn't know what else to say. She seemed distant to him now: she had moved on and left him behind and, all of a sudden, he felt as if he had been frozen, somehow – tucked away in a fold of time and frozen, like one of those bodies people found in ice-fields, in Siberia or somewhere.

Helen shook her head, then, and for a moment he thought she would say something that would make everything be the same as it was before.

'I'm glad I saw you,' she said. 'I wanted to wish you luck.'

'How do you mean?'

'You know,' she smiled – sadly, he thought, then decided he was only imagining it. 'With your marriage.'

Rob felt a wave of panic surge through his body. He knew she was about to go; in five minutes, two minutes, in a few seconds' time she would be gone and he would never see her again. He didn't know how he was so certain of that, but he was. In this life, he had read it somewhere and believed it, long before he knew why it mattered to him, there are people you meet again and there are people you lose forever. Helen was going to be one of those.

'Be seeing you.'

He nodded. It was the best time of day, that time of morning when the pubs are just opening all over town, and people are going in and standing at the bar, patient for the time being, anticipating that first drink. Somebody in the back would still be drying up the glasses, or getting stock out; a radio would be playing somewhere. He could smell the beer, that hops and malt smell, mixed with the scent of wax and smoke. All he wanted – it was true, it was all he wanted – was to take Helen's arm and bring her there, just once, to spend one perfect day together, sitting in a bar somewhere, with good music on the jukebox, in a big, empty, sunlit room. That was all he wanted: just one more day, just one more afternoon. He knew it was as much as he could have asked – she was different now, he could see that – and afterwards, thinking back, he wondered why he hadn't said anything, why he'd let her go so easily, when so much had depended on that day, on having it in his mind, the one thing nobody could deny him. But that was how it was: he let her go, and stood watching, as she walked away. He watched her till she disappeared into the crowd, hoping she would turn around, thinking, if only she turned around he would put the box down, then and there, and go after her. It would be a signal, he thought, a signal she maybe didn't even intend, but a signal nevertheless, if she just turned around.

The first time Alan had seen Jennifer was about six months earlier, on Halloween night, not long after he'd moved into the flat on Magdalen Green. He'd come in from the pub, and he was sitting in the chair by the window, with the CD player on, drifting back and forth between sleep and waking; random images were forming then disappearing in his mind, before he could altogether grasp them, images invented out of nothing, odd scenes and pictures from a childhood he didn't know he'd had. Sometimes, when he drifted like this, he remembered, quite clearly, in full detail, events that had never happened – or at least, not to him. Later, when he was fully awake, he would tell himself that these events were scenes remembered from books he'd read, or films he had seen long ago, but he couldn't quite put off the feeling that it wasn't so. The seemingly false memories were more real than that – more real, in fact, than much of what he did recall. It was as if he were catching a glimpse of another place, a place where he belonged – where, maybe, he had another life that was running all the time, even when he was absent from it. All he had to do was find that place – a space inside himself, inside his own mind – and he would be at home. As soon as he forgot himself, as soon as he drifted into that half-sleep, he was happy. At such moments, in that other place, he felt somehow

87

more real, more authentic, as if that was how he was meant to be, and everything else was forced upon him by some outside power and he wanted to stay there forever. He didn't know how long he had been in that place, when he started awake and realised there was someone at the door.

It was dark. He'd come in about the middle of the afternoon, when it was still half-light, and he was surprised at how quickly time had passed. He'd put the CD on repeat when he'd sat down and it was still playing; he remembered the record was Bob Woodruff, *Desire Road*, and the song that was playing when he woke up was 'River's Edge'. Something in his half-waking dream had been ravelled up with the song, so that, for a moment, he couldn't separate his own thoughts from what was happening in the music. There was something in Woodruff's voice, too, that suggested other possibilities, ways of being that were different from his own, and he'd wanted to go somewhere, to wherever that voice belonged, to find out what it meant, and how it came into being. Outside, close to the window, there was a whistling noise, followed by a burst of white light, a brief, vivid flicker over the green: it was like something alive, one of those fleeting creatures that flowered and melted away under a microscope, becoming something else – its own offspring, or some new, alien form – before it had ever begun to be itself. As the light faded, Alan switched on the table lamp and went to answer the door.

The visitor was a young girl, around eleven or twelve, Alan thought, though she might have been older. She was wearing a long white night-dress over her ordinary clothes, though it wasn't quite long enough to hide her trainers; her lips were a thick, greasy-looking stripe of dark-red, almost maroon lipstick and, except for the skin around her eyes, which was ink-black, her face was heavily powdered with what looked like fine white flour. When he opened the door, she didn't speak, but stood staring at him, waiting, as if she wanted him to just see her costume before she moved on.

'Hello,' Alan said. His voice sounded thick and distant, like someone talking in his sleep. 'What are you supposed to be?'

The girl made a face.

'I'm not *supposed* to be anything,' she said.

'Is that right?' Alan smiled. 'So is this how you usually look, then?'

The girl didn't return his smile, or make any attempt to respond to what she obviously thought was condescension on his part, and Alan felt vaguely shamed, aware, now, that there was something he was supposed to say or do, something more that he was supposed to have seen and remarked upon – some detail that made all the difference, and which should have been obvious to him. He remembered going out guising like this when he was a kid: all the children in the neighbourhood would get dressed up in different costumes – he always went in his mum's old summer dress, his face black with coal dust and grease – and they would go from door to door, telling jokes or singing songs to their neighbours. It was a way of getting money for the pictures, or for sweets, but it was also a big night, one of the special days in the calendar, like Christmas or the first day of the summer holidays. Nowadays, the kids just went around in ordinary clothes, their faces hidden under werewolf or witch masks, holding out their hands as soon you came to the door, and mumbling some rhyme about Halloween. He couldn't remember the last time he had seen anyone in a proper guiser's costume.

'I thought maybe you were a ghost,' he said. He felt vaguely embarrassed by the way she just stood there, staring at him; at the same time, he hadn't wanted to upset her. At least she'd taken the trouble to dress up.

'So,' he added. 'Are you going to sing me a song?'

The girl frowned.

'I can't sing,' she said.

'Oh.' Alan noticed that, set in the black make-up, the girl's eyes were a deep, bright blue, with a hint of darker blue around the edge of the iris, and her hair was a dense mass of black curls. The white face-paint wasn't very well applied: it was thick and patchy in places, thinner in others, and it was beginning to flake off where it met the dark rings around her eyes.

'How about a joke, then?'

She shook her head impatiently.

'I don't know any jokes,' she said.

'Oh.' Alan made himself look serious. 'Well.' He reached into his pocket and pulled out a handful of change. 'Anyway.' He separated out a single pound coin. 'There you go.'

'Thanks.' The girl took the coin, hitched up her night-dress and casually put it away in her pocket. Then she stayed right where she was, to show him that, while she would take it if it was offered to her, the money wasn't really what she had come for. She looked up at him curiously.

'Do you live here?' she asked.

Alan nodded.

'How long for?'

'A couple of weeks.'

'I've never seen you.' She said it as if it was a logical impossibility that he could have existed till that moment.

'I've never seen you either,' Alan replied. 'Where do you live?'

The girl waved her hand vaguely. 'Upstairs,' she said.

'Oh.'

There was a silence as they stood looking at one another. Alan thought the silence would embarrass her into going, but the girl stayed where she was, studying him curiously as if he were something inanimate, some object that had briefly caught her attention, while she figured out what it was. So he waited. It seemed rude, somehow, to disturb her.

'What's your name?' she asked, at last.

'Alan,' he said. 'What's yours?'

'Jennifer.'

'That's a nice name.'

The girl made another face.

'Not so,' she said. 'People always call me Jenny.'

'So what's wrong with that?'

She shook her head, but she didn't say anything.

'What would you rather be called?' Alan asked.

'I don't know,' she said. 'Something Spanish maybe.'

'Why Spanish?'

'I don't know,' she said. 'I just like Spanish.'

'Is that right?' Alan said. He felt like a kid, talking to her. He felt stupid, too, but there was something about her that held his attention, something that drew him in. 'Are you doing that in school?'

They'd talked like that for about half an hour, maybe longer, while he stood holding the door open, in his stockinged feet. At one point, some people came down the stairs and passed them, a man and a woman in the kind of clothes you only wear for a party, and the woman gave Alan a funny look. Later, when Jennifer had gone, and he was back inside, getting ready to go out, he realised he was still thinking about her, and all that night, as he sat listening to Sconnie and Junior arguing about the relative merits of Trisha Yearwood

91

and Alison Krauss, he kept seeing the girl again, in her ghost costume.

After that, he caught himself looking for her, at the end of the afternoon, when the kids came home from school. He would get back from the pub as the smaller ones came wandering past his window; then, later, the girls from the Academy started to arrive in twos and threes, in their red blazers and black ribbed tights. He got to know them all by sight: the fat asthmatic, her glasses perched on the tip of her nose, trudging by on her own, her head down, deep in thought; the tiny blonde girl who always tried to look older, with her hint of make-up and fussy shoes; the thin redhead from the end of the road who was obviously quiet and polite, and perhaps more intelligent than the others. Finally – always by herself, and always the last to get home – Jennifer came up the road and sat on the wall outside his window, as if waiting for someone. The first time he had seen her there, he had wondered why he'd never noticed her before: she was sitting just outside the window, her hair hanging down over her face; after a moment, he realised she was singing, or talking softly to herself.

Then, one afternoon, a fortnight or so after their doorstep encounter, she turned suddenly and looked straight at him, as if she had known all along that he was there. His first instinct was to duck away, to pretend he hadn't been watching her; a moment later, though, he was back at the window – he couldn't help himself – and she was still there, her face turned to the glass, a mock-puzzled look in her eyes that reminded him of something he'd seen in a film somewhere, or in a photograph of someone famous. Without the make-up, he could see more clearly how pretty she was, and how young. He'd half-expected her to turn away, but she didn't; she stood up, turned around fully, then, after a moment, her face expanded into a bright, unfeigned smile. It was too much. He tried to smile back – to make it neutral, to smile the way a grown man smiles at a kid he's met, somewhere in the neighbourhood – but all he could manage was a foolish grin, like someone who's had a clever joke played on him, and is trying to be gracious about it. For a joke had been played on him – he knew it – in that very moment. It had been hatching for a couple of weeks, ever since her visit, and it had come to fruition, in a matter of seconds, as he stood there, gazing out at her. He was pretty sure she knew it, too, because her smile softened, and she looked away, turning her head so her hair fell, obscuring her face, then she looked back, and she smiled again – a different smile, quieter, less bright, the smile you keep for surprises and small moments of beauty – before she was gone, walking away in the half-light, like any other girl on her way home from school.

On the way home, Cathy stopped at the shops to get something for their tea. The supermarket was crowded with people who seemed to wander aimlessly, not very sure why they were there, or what it was they wanted. The only ones who moved with any sense of purpose, making straight for the drinks section with fixed looks on their faces, as if they were afraid it might disappear if they didn't get there soon enough, were the boys from the pub, picking up a carry-out for the night's drinking. Everybody else seemed to be sleepwalking: women with children hanging on to them, ignoring their endless, elaborate pleas for sweets and comics; old men with baskets, standing in the biscuits aisle, staring at the shelves; people stopping to talk and getting in everybody else's way, with their trolleys at right angles to the frozen food cabinets, to cause maximum inconvenience. Cathy wasn't surprised they seemed so aimless: there wasn't much of a selection, really, only the basic goods, with the occasional special offer or Purchase Of The Week, which usually meant somebody had ordered too much of something useless, like frozen turkey breasts or hobnobs.

Cathy didn't take much pleasure in shopping any more. When they were first married, she had tried much harder to make things nice, to get the things she knew Rob liked, or the other, fancier things, she thought he might like. When they could afford it, she would take time to go to all the little shops, to buy nice pieces of fresh fish, haddock fillets or salmon steaks, say, and she would go to the greengrocer's for new potatoes and fresh vegetables, with the dirt still on them, baby leeks and carrots with their leaves, little cherry tomatoes, special salad leaves and mushrooms that looked so white and clean they reminded her of those old-fashioned light bulbs the shops used to put up at Christmas-time. She would cut the tomatoes in little wiggly patterns, with a sharp knife, so they came out looking like flowers, or she would frost the edges of the plates with spices, the way they did in magazines, so everything looked nice. She would buy wine, sometimes, on the weekend, and keep it chilled; she liked the better wines, not the usual cheap stuff, and she always looked out for anything special that might be on offer that week. Occasionally, she would try a different kind of sauce or gravy on the meat – oranges, say, or something spicy. To begin with, Rob had appreciated the little touches, especially the wine; he'd seemed to like it when she lit candles, or put flowers on the table; after a while, though, he'd stopped noticing, or if he did, he'd only tell her they didn't need to waste all their money on fancy things, he was happy with anything, he was happy with fish and chips, or beans on toast, stuff like that.

Of course, if she had a car, she wouldn't shop in the little supermarket. She would drive down to Tesco's, or over to the new Safeways in St Andrews, the one that had just opened last year. That was the thing about a car, it gave you the freedom to do whatever you wanted. If she had a car, she would go on long drives, up to the Highlands, or down to England; she would drive off early in the morning, when Rob was still asleep, and keep going till she got to Tobermory, or the Black

Isle, or maybe Newcastle, for the Metro Centre. She wanted to see that big angel they were building there; she liked the idea of it, standing guard over the people, its wings spread out to protect them. She'd seen the picture in the paper: a giant rust-coloured angel with outspread wings and a smiling, gentle face, and she didn't understand why everybody was getting so annoyed about it, about how much it had cost, or whatever. People needed something like that in their lives. Cathy had cut the picture out and put it in her box, along with the other stuff she kept there: photographs of her mum, a collection of corks she had kept, from special occasions, like her twenty-first, or her engagement party, when her mum had got them real champagne. She'd had the box for years – ever since she was small: it had all kinds of stuff in it, but mostly it was just postcards, pictures of places she had been, or places she would like to see; paintings from galleries she had gone to on school trips; photographs of harbour towns, or gardens, or little villages in the Cotswolds, where she'd never been but planned to see some day, as soon as she got the car. Rob didn't want to get one – he said it was too expensive – but she was saving little bits here and there, secretly, so she could get something; Malcolm had told her she didn't need to go to a car dealer, he had mates who could get her something at a good price, no questions asked.

What she really fancied was a Citroen, an Avantage, say, in red. Her dad had taught her to drive in his old Citroen – it was really old but he'd kept it in good condition; she couldn't remember what they were called then, but it was a long, purple-coloured car with funny headlamps that looked like the eyes on lizards, and she had learned fast. She'd passed her test first time, in fact, mainly because of that car, which made her feel comfortable and just right behind the wheel, and she was pretty proud of her driving ability, even though she never got any practice these days. She couldn't understand it, that Rob had never learned to drive. Of course, even if he had, she wouldn't let him drive her car when she got it – there was no guaranteeing, at any time, that he would be sober enough. Even if he was sober, she wouldn't be able to trust him to be careful. No. She would have the car to herself, and go on long drives every Sunday; she would keep the car spick and span and she would have one of those stickers in the back window, low down so she could still see. THIS CAR IS BEING EXPERTLY DRIVEN BY CATHY. That was what it would say.

The other thing she wanted was a pet, to keep her company. A dog would be ideal, but she knew Rob would never stand for that. Rob hated dogs. She'd tried to get him interested in a kitten, but all he'd said was, 'NO ANIMALS', in that voice he put on when he wanted her to know he was being final and there was no room for negotiation. He didn't understand how lonely she was – and, though it was a hard thing to say, Cathy had to admit that she was lonely. These days, Rob was hardly ever home, and when he was he was usually in a bad mood, or he would be asking her for money, so he could go out. She was lucky to have work to go to, to get her out of the house and amongst other people. Apart from the girls at work, and Malcolm, she didn't have anybody, now that her mum was gone. At least when she went to work, she could get a laugh.

Sometimes, on her days off, she would catch a bus up to Ninewells and wander about up there, in the grounds, or even in the main entrance area, where the shops were. Sometimes she went on to the wards, pretending she was looking for someone. She could wander about for hours, looking at the people in their beds, or the visitors walking about the corridors with bunches of flowers or boxes of chocolates, looking lost. It came as a surprise to her, that she liked hospitals: ever since her mum had gone, she had liked the thought that everyone was going to die, and it made her feel warm inside, knowing they were all going to see each other again. She believed in heaven, even though she didn't go to church any more. It had been difficult: she'd stopped going not long after she'd married Rob, and she'd kept it a secret from her mum until she died. It wasn't that she didn't believe in the church so much, it was just that Rob spoiled it for her. In the end it had been too much effort, dealing with the rows all the time. She'd felt bad, not telling her mum, but she didn't really feel guilty towards the Church itself, because God knew she was still a believer, in her heart.

Still, she was happy at Ninewells. She had thought of becoming a hospital visitor – she liked the idea of bringing comfort to people who had nobody else in their lives – but she wasn't sure what that involved, and she didn't want to take on too much responsibility. She could imagine she might get too involved – she had the kind of nature that naturally went out to other people, and it was probably too soon for that after her mum dying. Once, when she had been out there, walking along one of the corridors, she had come across this old couple, a man and a woman: they were both really old, and the man looked very ill – gravely ill, really – she could see it as she was walking towards him, that look of fear in his eyes, or not fear, really, more like embarrassment, like he knew he was going to get caught out, somehow – and then he was falling, the old woman was reaching out for him, her arms like a puppet's, stiff and useless, and Cathy was rushing forwards, staring at him, trying to hold him up with her eyes. She'd got to him in a matter of seconds, and she was on her knees, next to the old man, trying to think what to do, because she knew she could help him — she *knew* it; then there had been other people, and someone had shifted her aside, and they had taken the old man away, the woman following, leaving her there on her knees, alone and useless. It had really bothered her, that, because she'd known, at that very moment, that the old man was going to die — she had seen that look in his eyes — and all she'd wanted to do was help him, just to tell him that it would be all right, that they would all come back, and nothing would ever frighten him again.

Other times, she liked to go out in the mornings; especially on Sundays, when Rob was still sleeping. You could see what had happened the night before: you could read it right off the pavement, from the splatters of blood or sick, the clusters of cigarette ends, used condoms in shop doorways, chip papers, broken bottles, spillages of coins. She was disgusted, but there was someone inside her who wanted to handle these things, to bag them up, like the detectives on the television, and take them home, to show Rob. She wanted to gather up the coins, or the fragments of glass, and hold them between her fingers, like pieces of evidence — as proof of something. It was amazing that people didn't know about these things — or didn't care — they let it all pass as if it didn't matter. From the bandstand on Magdalen Green, she could see the airstrip, with its soft gold lights. They would be lit, even in the daytime, so the pilots could see them when they came in to land. Over the water, the low, friendly hills looked like a different country; though she knew it was only Fife, she still thought she could live there, especially on Sunday evenings, when the lights were up, and she imagined driving over the bridge, through the little Fifeshire towns and villages, under the orange lights, everyone sleeping in their beds, tiny dramas happening in every house she drove by. If you slept, you dreamed, but you always knew you were dreaming. If you stayed awake, though, you couldn't tell what was what. That was how she felt, sometimes, when it was soft and slow, on Sundays, or at night, when she woke up and had to go downstairs, to get away from Rob's snoring. Sometimes she went out in the dark, in the small hours, and walked up and down the lanes between Magdalen Green and the Perth Road. She liked it best when it was windy, when the alleyways were littered with blossom or dead leaves. Even in the middle of the city, you could hear owls and other animals, even foxes, sometimes. Nobody ever bothered her out there. It was as if she was invisible, or protected by some kind of special charm.

More than anything else, she wanted a child of her own, so she could bring it up to be clean and perfect. Not like its Dad. She still wanted it to be Rob's kid, because he was her husband, and that was how things were. But she didn't want him interfering. She had done everything she could with Rob: she had been good to him, but all he did was throw it all away. The trouble with Rob was, he didn't know how to be happy. He just couldn't help it. You could make him rich, you could give him everything he wanted, and he still wouldn't be happy. He wasn't capable. He thought he knew what he wanted, but he didn't. Like most men. They walked right past what they really wanted, to get to what they didn't really want at all, because that was what they thought they really wanted. They hadn't got a clue. She'd read a book once, that one of the girls at work had given her, about emotional intelligence, and how much more important it was, in your everyday life, than the kind of intelligence people usually took notice of, like being good at school and having a good memory and stuff like that. And it all made sense to her. She'd tried to get Rob to read it, but he wasn't interested. Which only proved her point. If he'd had any kind of emotional intelligence at all, he'd have had some idea of where he was going wrong, but he didn't, and he didn't want to know. That was the trouble with most men – they lacked emotional intelligence. Cathy reckoned, if she could only get Rob to read that book, and take it seriously, all his troubles would be over. He would be a new man. And maybe then he would be happy.

When the others drifted off for their tea – it was a ritual, a rule that must never be broken, that they went for their tea about half-four, or five at the latest – Rob headed off in the opposite direction, towards the centre of town. He was feeling strange – he wasn't sick, or dizzy, or anything like that, and he wasn't drunk, it was just that he felt strange, as if he'd come into a familiar room and someone had moved the furniture around. He walked down to the Nethergate, then he crossed the little square, next to Boots. He didn't have any money, but he had the card, and maybe there would be some money in the account, to get him through the night. He was sick of having to put the tap on Alan; he didn't like having to ask anybody for money, even if it was a pal.

By the time he'd been to the bank – there was only twenty quid in the account, but he took it out anyway – it was getting to be that time of night when the shops were closing up and people were coming out of offices and places and going to the pub for a couple of drinks before they went home. There were men in suits and ties, women in narrow trousers and fine white blouses under their raincoats, boys in their work-gear, coming off the sites, looking at the women going by, and giving them a bit of attention, all heading off for somewhere, without a care in the world, money in their pockets, nice houses to go back to, and maybe somebody nice waiting for them. He really missed that moment sometimes, the way it had been when he was younger: going out, at the start of the evening, with that excitement on the air, and the thought that anything could happen. He stuffed the bank-notes in his pocket, then separated them out with his fingers – a ten and two fives – then he went into the Rat and Parrot, which was where all the good-looking women seemed to be headed. It took him a while to get served at the bar – it was as if the boy there was deliberately ignoring him – and he'd been a bit annoyed. But he kept the heid, and he'd got a pint and a wee one, and he'd sat down, right in the middle of the room, where he could see everything that was going on.

At the next table, a tall, fat man was sweet-talking a tall, slender-looking blonde. From the way they were dressed, Rob guessed they had come straight from work: the woman was in her mid-twenties, with short-bobbed hair and very clear, almost transparent skin, and she was dressed in a close-fitting bright red suit. The man was older, close to forty, with large, horn-rimmed glasses; he was wearing what he must have thought was a bold dark-brown jacket and a blue herring-bone patterned shirt, with a bright maroon and gold tie. His mouth looked wet and fleshy as he leaned in close to the woman to whisper something in her ear; beside him, she looked like a doll, pallid and fragile as bone china.

Rob took a long swallow of his pint then knocked his whisky back in one. Immediately, he felt better. He sat back in his chair and took a look around: the people here were almost all shop and office workers, the men in suits and ties that he'd seen coming along the street, and women of all ages, dressed to look efficient and strong, in suits and shirts, with just a hint of softness here or there – a silk scarf, a hint of blusher – so people would know they were at ease with their femininity, like in the magazines. A couple of them weren't that bad-looking, if you could ignore the clothes and, like, the body language, but the woman opposite was the best of them, almost beautiful, really, in spite of the fact that she didn't seem to mind that fat boy leaning in and slobbering all over her. Rob took another swig of his beer and settled in to watch. She had red fingernails but she wasn't wearing make-up and he could see the faint freckles on her nose and a smudge of shiny sweat on her upper lip. He couldn't tell if she was wearing lipstick.

After a while, she became aware of him watching her and she shifted a little in her seat. The fat boy could tell she was being distracted by something, but he didn't know what. Immediately, she made a more determined effort to concentrate on what the boy was saying; but she could still feel herself being watched and, when Rob didn't look away, she turned and gave him a short, but longer-than-polite look, a mixture of defiance and apprehension. Rob smiled. The fat boy looked up and caught Rob's eye, but there was nothing in his face, no sense of himself, and Rob gave him a small, mock-friendly grin that brought him up sharp, his face glancing off to one side as if he'd been hit, or like a bird when it flies into a window and falls away. Now Rob watched them openly, listening in – they were talking about people at work, making little jokes, trying to pretend they weren't aware of him, but their hearts weren't in it, and Rob was enjoying himself, making them squirm. He hated people like this fat boy. This cunt. He was probably an accountant; he probably made a pile of money for doing fuck all, just sitting at his desk playing computer games, or strolling around the office, chatting up the women, or sitting around with his mates, in their flashy suits and ties, talking about cars.

He was trying to get in the girl's knickers, that was obvious. But tonight, it wasn't going to happen. It wasn't because of Rob – he knew that – the girl was just trying him on for size and she was deciding she didn't fancy it, or not tonight anyway. After a while, she gave him a little kiss on the cheek and stood up; then, when he made to get up, she shook her head.

'It's all right,' she said, quietly, as if she wanted Rob not to hear. 'You stay. I've got to get back.'

When she said that, he realised what the problem was and he shot a look at her hand. Ring finger. Two rings. Engagement ring. Wedding ring. He smiled and shook his head. The girl bowed her head and walked out quickly, away back to her husband, where she suddenly realised she belonged.

The fat boy looked confused. Rob could see that he'd thought he was on to something tonight, a sure thing maybe, and somehow he'd blown it. He was also looking worried. He could feel Rob there now, watching him, and he felt unhappy about that. He was sweating, and his hand was reaching up, loosening his tie, unbuttoning his shirt at the collar. Rob started to count. At seven the boy stood up and, trying to look casual, walked out the door and into the street. It was dark now, all of a sudden. Rob stood up, finished off his beer, and followed.

It was a stupid thing to do. He knew it as he followed the boy, along Reform Street and round into Bank Street, where the fat boy must have parked his car. There were people about, and it wasn't that late, but Rob knew it was going to be all right, he just knew in his bones that all he'd have to do was

look at the boy, and he'd hand over everything, right there
and then. He'd be scared shitless, in fact. It was stupid, but the
fact was, Rob didn't care and, besides, he was feeling dizzy
again, light and empty, and he needed to make something
happen. To take control of things.

He caught up with the boy halfway along Bank Street.
There was nobody else about.

'Hey.'

The fat boy turned. Rob stepped forward and pushed him
against a wall, his forearm up at the fat boy's neck.

'What are you? Eh?'

The fat boy didn't say anything. Rob tightened his hold.

'What are you?'

The fat boy let out a short gasp.

'Take the money,' he said. 'Take what you want.' He said it
mechanically, as if he'd maybe even practised the line. Like
he'd been watching too much television.

'I won't say anything,' he said.

Rob laughed.

'I will,' he said. 'But first I want you to tell me what you
are.'

A flicker of understanding lit the man's eyes and he shook
his head.

'I'm nothing special,' he said. 'I'm just—'

'What do you do? For a living?'

'I'm a financial manager.'

Rob grinned.

'That's what I thought,' he said.

He tightened his hold on the boy's neck a bit more, then he
reached into his inside pocket – the breast pocket, on the left-
hand side, and lifted the boy's wallet. It was as easy as taking
toffee off a bairn. At this, the fat boy started to cry; he was

trying to say something, but Rob couldn't make out what it was. Quietly, with almost no force behind it, he brought his knee up and into the boy's groin area, just to shut him up and keep him distracted for a while. Then he let go his hold of the boy's neck, stepped back and took a look round. There was a girl standing at the far end of the street, next to a red car. She must have been watching, but when Rob turned, she got into the car quickly, and started up the engine. The fat boy was on the floor now, and he'd stopped crying. Rob opened the wallet, emptied out the cash, and put it in his back pocket.

'Tell anybody about this,' he said, 'and I'll fucking find you and kill you.'

He paused to let that sink in. Then he dropped the wallet on top of the fat boy's curled up body, and walked away, quickly, but not quick enough to draw too much attention to himself.

When he got to the Mercy, the boys were there. They were arguing about films.

'Dan Duryea,' Sconnie was saying.

'Who?'

'Dan Duryea.'

'Never heard of him,' Junior said, shaking his head. 'Anyway, it was Robert Ryan.'

Rob bought a round and sat down. He didn't want to talk, he just wanted to listen, to sit back and let their stupid argument wash right over him. He didn't know what they saw in those old pictures anyway. They were a lie, just like the television. They had nothing to do with life. Rob recalled how his mother had known everything about those old films. She could remember the words to every song Judy Garland or Fred Astaire had ever sung, words she barely understood half the time, lyrics about Topeka and Santa Fe, or the lights on

Broadway. Like Junior and Sconnie, she was dreaming of places she would never see, clothes she would never wear, journeys she would never make. As a boy, he had been mystified by the allure of Astaire, or Frank Sinatra: to him, they looked like middle-aged American men with half-decent voices, singing corny songs to women who became stars if they were pretty enough and managed not to look too bored by the whole thing. This was a private world that only she inhabited, the Sunday matinees with Bing Crosby and Vera-Ellen, the musicals and romantic comedies, where the clothes were all that mattered and the people seemed strangely bloodless. There were hints, from time to time, of something real: Cyd Charisse, in *The Bandwagon*, had caught his attention once and, later, when he'd first met Cathy, he'd convinced himself there was a vague resemblance, a fleshier echo of Charisse's body. Most of the time, though, he felt uneasy, as if he had been cheated in some way. There was something about its seeming innocence, about the asexual beauty of Katherine Grayson or Deanna Durbin, something about the knowing looks on the men's faces, the facile sturdiness of Van Heflin, the calculated unease in Alan Ladd's eyes that made Rob look for the flaws, the creaking machinery behind the stage sets.

He didn't understand why they had to dream about all that stuff – books, pictures, country songs. All that crap. His mother had lived on it all her life and then she'd died, still putting her make-up on, day after day, week after week, while the cancer ate her up inside. Even then, when the life was running out of her, draining away visibly, she had watched those old films, whenever she got the chance, though the drugs she was taking confused her, so she didn't know the difference, half the time, between what was happening on the screen and what was happening in real life. Even in death, she was just another fan, watching herself fade into black and white, with Nelson Eddy singing in the background, and some lanky boy riding away into the sunset.

He reached into his back pocket. The money was still there. He'd stopped on the way to count it, when he'd come to a quiet place, and he couldn't believe his luck. The fat boy had been carrying more than two hundred in cash, in tens and twenties. He must have just been to the bank. He was probably planning to use it to impress the girl in the red suit, maybe take her out for a night on the town, to see where that got him. He'd had another think coming, though. Now Rob was planning his night: stay in the Mercy till closing, then get a carry-out and either see if he could go back to Alan's, or take it home and hope Cathy was in her bed before he got there. Because he didn't want to see her. Not right now. If he saw her, the way he was feeling, he didn't know what he would do.

At three the next morning, Alan woke from his usual nightmare. It had been happening for weeks now – not every night, but often enough, and it was always the same: the same sensation, the same time of the night, when it was still and quiet, the same voice receding into the distance of his mind, followed by the sound of his own heart, like something that was loud somewhere else, a muffled noise of machines, or maybe someone chapping at a door, at the far end of a very long corridor. The voice he could hear was his own: he would hear himself cry out and then he would be awake, sitting up, half-out of the bed, as if he was about to go somewhere. He would never know if he really had cried out aloud, or if it had only been in his dream, but he could still hear it, no matter, even when he was awake, a cry that was almost a scream, half-fear, half-anger, fading away to the edge of his awareness. Then, as the shock wore off, he would settle back, nestling into the warmth and the darkness. He was awake now, but he was still half-dreaming, caught between two states of being, and he could see Jennifer's face in the dark above his bed, as clearly as he would have done had she been standing in front of him, in the cold light of day.

In his dream, she was teaching him Spanish. She was telling him the names of things, the word for house, the word for tree; the ways people talked about the weather and how you asked somebody their name. She was wearing her school clothes, with the white Halloween nightie over the top. In one hand, her left, she was holding a tiny animal, something small and warm and furry – a mouse, perhaps, only more tropical, with reddish fur and bigger, rounder eyes. It was cradled gently in her fist and he knew, if she closed her fingers, the animal would be crushed to death. This was what distracted his attention away from her face – this animal in her hand. It was only for a moment, but it was enough time, in the dream, for her to change and, when he looked back, her face was gone, just an emptiness framed by her hair that made him feel sick and dizzy, a little bit scared, but also angry, so that he cried out, and woke, and sat up, so he could come back and find her face in the dark, as she really was. Jennifer. Jennifer. Jennifer. He said her name over and over again, whispering it softly to himself, like a spell. Sometimes he thought he was the only one who was keeping her whole, half-dreaming, half-awake, keeping her alive while she slept upstairs, dreaming of God knows what, totally oblivious.

As soon as he woke, Rob remembered the money. His jeans were on the chair where he'd left them, and Cathy was up already. What time was it? What day? It must be Saturday, he thought; he could hear noises downstairs – she was clearing up and he wondered how he'd got to bed, and if he'd disturbed her, or left any mess. He'd thought of asking if he could go back to Alan's, but he'd changed his mind and come home, with a good bit of the money still left in his pocket. He'd paid Alan back; he'd bought a few extra rounds; he was going to give the twenty from the bank to Cathy, and say he'd got it out by accident or something. Even then, he'd still have enough left for himself. He seemed to remember counting it, some time late in the evening, and there had been plenty, almost a hundred. He reached out, pulled his jeans off the chair, and felt in the back pocket. The money was still there. He pulled it out and counted: a ten, a twenty, a twenty, a twenty. A five. Seventy-five and change. He lay back. It was Saturday. He had enough money for the whole weekend. Everything was going to be fine.

In the quiet times, in the early morning, before he went to the pub and Estelle was still asleep upstairs, Junior would fetch the camera out of its box and sit it on the edge of the coffee-table in the front room. It was something he and Sconnie had agreed: they would both try that trick Ted Serios used to do, where you stared into a camera and made a picture happen on the film, just by the power of your thoughts. Sconnie had been trying it for years, but Junior had waited a bit, practising, trying to get the picture clear in his mind first, so he didn't waste film or energy. Serios had made his pictures look like everyday things – buildings, pieces of furniture, ordinary familiar objects – but Junior thought the only way he could do it was to think of a scene, something that had happened to him, some event with its own innate power. He'd tried several things, and the one he'd come up with, finally, was a memory he wasn't sure he really had, something that had happened when he was about fourteen or so, going out with his first girlfriend.

It wasn't the best choice, but it was the best he could do. His trouble was, he remembered all the wrong things. He remembered what he hadn't understood at the time, things that went wrong, insignificant failures, the moments and chances that slipped by without his knowing. Most of all, he remembered Hannah. When he closed his eyes, and tried to picture something he could put on film, it was her he saw, clear as day, in his mind's eye, cycling home from school. It was an indelible image: the light on her hair and skin, her slender legs perfected by the dark stockings that fifth form girls were allowed to wear, that smile of hers, including everyone she met in some private happiness – or maybe some private joke. Maybe, for someone else, the picture would be too ordinary, but not for Junior. Even though it had been thirty years, he couldn't help remembering how Hannah had looked that winter, when he had abandoned her.

She was the one who started it. He'd always thought she was so beautiful, so self-assured, too good for the likes of someone like him. He used to see her on the way to school, or at the baths on a Thursday night; he'd watch her swimming, admiring her slow, graceful stroke, the way her legs kept up the even, fluttering kick, the way she never seemed to come up for air. After the baths, he'd hang around till she came out, then watch her walking away under the pale orange lights. He lived two streets away from her at the time, but it never once occurred to him to ask if he could walk her home. That had been her idea.

It was autumn-time. The air was damp and still; the trees in the park had just begun to turn butter-yellow and crimson, leaves were falling here and there, drifting slowly down and settling on the wet grass. Everything was touched with silver: not quite a frost, but more than a dew. Junior had been standing at the corner, between the baths and the park gates, waiting for her to appear. She was taking longer than usual, and he'd begun to think he'd missed her, when he was startled by a voice at his back.

'Are you waiting for someone?'

He turned around quickly and she was there, all smiles, the keeper of secrets.

'No,' he'd answered. 'I'm just—'

'Want to walk me home, then?' she interrupted.

Junior had tried to look nonchalant.

'Okay,' he'd said, and they had walked home together through the wet streets, like people in a film. She did all the talking, and he could still remember every word she said. She talked about her mother and the people they knew from school; she asked what music he liked, if he listened to jazz, and when he said he didn't, she told him about the records her uncle had given her. It made her sound really sophisticated, when she talked about John Coltrane and Miles Davis, people Junior had never even heard of. It made her sound older and smarter and she knew it, but the funny thing was, he knew that she knew, he even knew she was trying to impress him, and it didn't make any difference. Here she was, asking him to walk her home, talking like crazy, trying to sound clever, asking him questions and taking an interest in everything he said – and Junior was still scared stiff. It was too difficult to imagine that she would be interested in him. He just walked along with her, in the quiet after the rain.

And that was how it had started. When they'd stopped at her front gate, Hannah had turned to him expectantly and, when he didn't say anything, she asked if Junior would like to see her again. He remembered the scene as if it were something he'd read in a book: a dark hedge, a pretty girl, a boy who couldn't think what to say, the cars driving by, swishing softly on the wet tarmac. He could still remember the smell of her skin, that cool, damp smell of autumn faces touched with dew. Maybe it was that smell – the memory of it, so real, so vivid – that carried the real power, the power to fix an image on the film, an image that would, just for a moment, carry the cool fresh scent of a girl he hadn't seen for almost thirty years.

That autumn was the happiest time of his life. It was a big romance with Hannah: it wasn't really sexual, but he didn't care; they would kiss and touch each other shyly, but they didn't take it very far. Some of the other boys in his class told amazing stories of things they'd done, usually with girls from other schools, and, some of the time at least, Junior only half-suspected they were lying. It would worry him sometimes, that Hannah didn't want things to go further. He thought maybe he was doing something wrong. Maybe he was supposed to push harder; maybe she was expecting that. Maybe she was disappointed when he didn't force the issue. Some of the boys in school said a girl says No all the time, she has to say it, to show she's not a slag, and it was up to you to know when she really means Yes. You couldn't take her word for it. But Junior didn't really believe that. Or maybe he just didn't care. Most of the time they were happy together, just as they were, going to the baths, or the pictures, then coming home and sitting in her kitchen, while her mum watched telly in the front room.

Junior loved going to her house. It was warm and musty and lived in. Hannah's mother took in lodgers, men who were in town for weeks or months at a time, and she would cook for them, from a late dinner on Sunday night to an early breakfast on Friday, when they would leave for a weekend at home. The men came from all over. Most were Scots, but a few came up from England. There was one man, a civil engineer from Derby, who stayed for several months. Hannah practised every day till she could mimic his accent; sometimes, when she met him on the stairs, she'd say 'good morning' in broad Derbyshire and he'd grin, pleased to be the object of her attention. All the men liked to flirt with her; some of them – the shy ones – gave her presents, or sent postcards after they'd gone, thanking her mother for all she'd done, but addressed to them both, so Hannah would know they'd remembered her. Others made suggestive jokes, but Hannah just laughed them off. That was how she was. She only had to flash that smile of hers, and she got what she wanted from just about anyone. It even annoyed Junior, sometimes, how much she got away with. For a while, there, he'd thought she knew exactly what she was doing; he'd thought she was completely in charge of her life. He didn't know about Francis, then.

Francis was Hannah's uncle, the one who had given her the records. He was a big man, with thick, dark hair and wide, strong-looking hands. He worked on the building in the day-time, but his real job, his reason for being, was playing tenor saxophone in a local jazz quintet that went around doing parties and socials and such like. The women all thought he was the cat's pyjamas. They would come up to the stage between numbers and ask if they could blow his horn, and he'd lean over, with the saxophone still strapped around his neck, lowering the mouthpiece just enough for the woman to reach, if she stood on tiptoe. The resulting squawk made everybody laugh, and Francis would grin and start playing with the others. The rest of the band went along with it all, because Francis was a natural front man, and he got them a lot of work they wouldn't have got otherwise. They probably didn't like him being the centre of attention, but they didn't have much of a choice. Francis could really play and, as Hannah's mother used to say, he could charm the hind legs off a donkey.

Junior sometimes wondered how things would have turned

out if it hadn't been for Francis – if he'd never existed, or if he hadn't come to the party that Christmas, or if Junior hadn't gone upstairs that night. It was a great evening. Hannah's mother had made biscuits and mince pies, old-fashioned sausages rolls, pasties and apple turnovers, a real Christmas cake. Francis was supposed to be playing with the band, but he came round instead, and stood in the middle of the room, laughing and talking loudly, the life and soul of the party. Junior sat with Hannah in the corner: it was his job to fetch the drinks from the kitchen, and she was in charge of doling out the plates and napkins. She looked so beautiful, in her dark-blue dress, with her hair up and a string of her mother's beads around her neck. When Francis came to get his food, he took her in his arms and kissed her on the cheek.

'How's my best girl?' he asked.

Hannah smiled and tipped her head, but she didn't answer. Junior had seen Francis kiss her before: it made him cringe, the way Francis took hold of her, and pulled her against him, but she didn't seem to mind. Afterwards she would be flushed and a little breathless. Francis would move on and she would follow him with her eyes.

It had snowed that night. Junior wanted to give Hannah the present he had bought her. He'd been saving up for months and he'd planned the whole thing: he would give her the little box and tell her to open it; at first, she'd refuse, she'd try to keep it for Christmas Day, but he'd insist, and she would tear away the plain gold wrapping and find the ring, nestled amidst black satin. He would know what to say to her then, when she put it on her finger – it wasn't an engagement ring or anything like that, it wasn't even very expensive, and they were far too young for all that, but she would know he meant it as a promise, a pact between the two of them, their own secret.

Everything would have been fine, everything would have gone according to plan, if it hadn't been for Francis. Junior waited till Hannah went upstairs, to fetch something for her mother, then he slipped out into the hall. There were small puddles of meltwater on the floor near the door, where people had hung their coats to dry, and the stairwell was filled with the water-and-evergreen scent of winter. Junior took the box from his coat pocket and started up. He could hear someone moving, but he didn't see Francis till he reached the bathroom door.

Francis was holding Hannah from behind, pulling her to him, sliding one hand over her body, his face pressed to her neck. They were standing with their backs to him, but Junior could see Francis' arm moving in the bathroom mirror: it slid downwards, then up, lifting the hem of the dress, gathering it up in his fist so her legs were naked; then his other hand moved down and Junior heard her gasp. She didn't move: it was as if she had sunk into him helplessly, surrendered to his will. That was what bothered him most, later – that she was so willing, so utterly lost in it all. She wasn't struggling, she wasn't crying. A moment later, Francis looked up and saw Junior in the glass. He didn't say anything. He didn't even stop what he was doing: his hands kept moving as he tilted Hannah's body forward, manipulating her like a doll, tipping her head forward so she was leaning over the sink. All the time, his eyes held Junior's, through the glass. There was no shame, no fear of being found out, only a slight, almost good-humoured mockery. That look said he could do what he liked, he didn't care what Junior thought. He was proud of himself.

There were times when Junior still wondered about that moment. He would go over the scene in his head, looking for the clue he had missed, refilming it in his mind's eye. In the remake, he would take two steps forward into the room and punch Francis in the face, then he would pull Hannah away and she would fall into his arms, grateful to be rescued. Francis would slink away, cowed and shamed, vanishing into the night, never to be seen again. Sometimes they would call the police, sometimes they would see what a sad creature he was, and they would let him go. But the truth was simpler. Too simple. He should have known more, there should have been more time to think things through. But there wasn't and, in a moment of fear and confusion, Junior had run away. Quite simply. He had run downstairs, pulled on his coat, and walked out into the cold night air.

He hadn't expected Francis to follow him. He was out of the gate and fifty yards along the street before Hannah's uncle caught him up.

'Where are you going?' he called.

'What's it to you?' Junior could hear the tremor in his voice and, it was hard to have to admit it, but he was afraid of Francis then. He was a big man, after all, and no telling what he might do.

'Listen son,' he said, 'why don't you just get back in there and pretend nothing ever happened. What you saw was just a bit of fun. You don't want to spoil Hannah's night.'

'I'm going home,' Junior had answered.

He'd started away, too, but Francis had taken hold of his arm. Junior had tried looking straight into his face – he wanted Francis to see that he didn't care about him, or Hannah, or anybody else – but he couldn't help himself. His fear got the better of him and he looked down, shamefaced, as if he was the one at fault.

'Have some consideration,' Francis said, with measured contempt.

'What? Like you?'

Francis was silent for a moment, staring, then he'd let go.

'Christ,' he'd said then. His voice was still soft, still quiet. 'You really think you know the score, don't you?'

'I know what I know,' Junior answered. He could hear himself sounding like a child, petulant and silly, trying to be clever.

'You think so?' Francis asked softly.

Junior nodded, and Francis sighed quietly, as if he really was dealing with a naughty child, being reasonable, trying to stay patient.

'You don't know anything, son,' he said. 'Maybe you saw something. But you can't always believe what you see. Maybe you're telling yourself she doesn't want it. That would make it okay. But do you think I'd do anything she didn't like? I can have any woman I want. I don't have to force myself on anybody.'

'I don't care,' Junior almost shouted at him, close to tears. 'I don't give a fuck about any of you. Do what you like.'

Francis smiled then, and shook his head.

'Go home, son,' he said, turning away. 'I'll tell them you're not well. And don't worry about Hannah. I'll give her a dance.'

Now, as he tried to fix the image of Hannah on the film – an image of her as she had been, in the days before he had betrayed her – he was ashamed, to think that he had half-believed Francis that night. For years afterwards – long after it was too late – he would stop in the middle of the day, in the middle of some ordinary chore, wishing the earth would open up under him. He would try to rationalise it. He would tell himself that things were different back then; and it was true, for a long time he had thought that other men were better than he was. They were always more certain of themselves, less likely to be wrong, and he imagined they were keeping a secret of some kind, some recipe for self-regard or common sense that he, Junior, ought to have worked out for himself, and hadn't: a skilfulness with rope or machinery handed down from father to son; an ability to stay hidden when they chose, to remain inaccessible to shame or judgement, to brush off failure and turn things around; an instinct for the right moves, for knowing when to talk and when to keep your mouth shut. As far as he was concerned, he hadn't been man enough to face up to Francis, and he never would be. It was perfectly natural that someone like Francis should lie to him and get away with it, just as it was perfectly natural for Junior to accept what he said. The following week, when he broke up with Hannah, he could barely talk. He didn't even want to hear her side of the story. The fact was, he had hated her. He'd thought she could have stopped it if she wanted: she only had to call out and someone would have heard. It must have been that she was willing: what she had always kept from Junior, she had yielded to Francis with a shiver of pleasure, a ripple of pure joy that ran through her whole being. From the very first, she'd wanted it to happen. She'd strayed into the dark, where he could find her, and she'd given herself, when her mother wasn't there, in the front room, in the kitchen – wherever Francis had found her, he did what he wanted, and she let it happen. That was what Junior had decided he believed. When he'd told her he didn't want to see her any more, she didn't even argue, she just shrugged and walked away.

That was the problem with him. He remembered all the wrong things. He remembered Hannah's face, when she opened the door that night; he remembered the sound of her voice, how she smiled as she let him in, how she tasted when he kissed her. He remembered how she would laugh when one of the men left her a present and slipped away without a word. He remembered how small her hands were. When he went into town he would imagine he saw her everywhere, though she had left home years ago. First, she went to college; then she got married. Junior used to see her in the Christmas holidays, and once he had walked over and stood outside her mother's house on Christmas Eve, just listening to the music and the voices, half-afraid, half-hoping she would come to the window and see him there. Of course, she didn't appear. After a while, a tall man came to the door and looked out, then he stepped outside, lit a cigarette and stood there, gazing up into the starry sky. Junior couldn't see his face, but he knew it was Francis. He looked so big, so sure of himself. It was hard not to imagine that he was happy.

Now, with Estelle asleep upstairs, he sat in the front room, staring into the lens of the camera and trying to make the picture of a girl appear on the film. It was a mental exercise – or that was what Sconnie called it – but it was also something else. For Junior, it was an almost religious act, a kind of penance. He didn't doubt that Hannah had forgotten him long ago, but he hadn't forgotten her. Maybe if things had been different with Estelle, he would have done, but his bedridden wife had created a space in his life, a space that he couldn't honourably fill. When he had been out at the hospital, he had understood this: it didn't matter what the story of your life was, all that mattered were the spaces you had to fill, and how you filled them. That first night he'd met Sconnie in the Mercy, they had talked about Ted Serios, and he'd realised what this mental exercise was all about. If you were lucky, you got to live a normal life, with somebody you loved, and work to do, and children to bring up. If you weren't, you were on your own. It was up to you. You had to fill the spaces in your story, any way you knew how.

Rob watched as Cathy made herself busy at the sink. This was her usual way of letting him know that she didn't give a fuck about what he was saying and, at the same time, that there was work to do and as usual she was the one doing it. She looked like a normal woman, in her black skirt and the blue shirt knotted around her waist, her thick black hair tied back in a pony-tail, with just a few stray wisps catching the light from the kitchen window. The skirt was too tight across her hips, accentuating her figure, and she wasn't wearing tights, just the gold sandals Malcolm had given her for Christmas. What with the gypsy earrings and the smoothness of the material across her arse, what with the fine red of her mouth and the way the shirt slipped up, revealing the white skin around her waist whenever she leaned forward, he couldn't help wanting to start something, even just to touch her, or better to reach around her and cup her heavy, round breasts in his hands – but he knew it was useless because, even though she looked like a normal woman, she wasn't, she was a cold bitch, and he knew she would pull away at the slightest contact, with that air of amused contempt she reserved for him these days, whenever he let her see that he wanted her.

'Well?' she asked.

'Well what?'

She stopped washing the dishes and looked at him.

'Well did you have a good night out with the boys?' she said.

Rob didn't answer. He could feel the slow ache rising in his groin – in his loins, the Bible would have said – and he wanted to just have her, then and there, on the kitchen floor, with all the dishes and shit all around them. It wasn't fair to have to live like this; it wasn't natural. Couldn't she see what she was doing to him? Couldn't she see that he was going to end up hating her?

'What time did you get in?' she wanted to know.

'About midnight,' he said. It was a guess. He remembered being in the Mercy at midnight, when they called last orders, but he wasn't sure what had happened after that.

Cathy snorted.

'And the rest,' she said.

She turned away in disgust, and went back to the dishes. He thought of stepping forward and having her there, right up against the sink, lifting her skirt up and getting into her from behind, holding her down over the sink and having her, then going out to the Mercy with the rest of the money. He'd be fucked if he'd give her back that twenty now.

'How much did you spend?' she said, her back still to him, scrubbing at a saucepan.

Rob shook his head. 'That's none of your business,' he said. 'It was my own money.'

'Oh yeah?'

'Yeah.'

She turned around.

'So where's the money you owe me, then?' she said.

'What money?'

'The money you borrowed from me last week.' She put an

126

extra little stress on the word borrowed. The truth was, he'd taken it out of her bag when she wasn't looking, and then forgotten all about it. He'd meant to give it back to her, of course. It was just that it had slipped his mind.

'I've got it,' he said. He slipped his hand into his back pocket and pulled out a tenner. 'See?'

'Where's the rest?' she asked.

'What rest?'

'You're not telling me that's all you've got. You wouldn't have handed it over so easily if you didn't have more.'

Rob picked up his jacket, which was draped over the back of one of the chairs, and shook it. The loose change in the pockets jingled, and he looked at her.

'That's me,' he said.

'Fucking isn't.' She sounded like she was about near the end of her tether now. Any minute she was going to cry, or throw a wobbly. He thought of giving her the rest of the money, and see if it got him anywhere, but he soon put that idea out of his head. He didn't want some fumbling, begrudged fuck in the old marriage bed anyway, when it came down to it. The best thing to do now, he thought, was to get the hell out of there. While the going was still more or less good. He put on his jacket and started for the door.

'Where are you going?' she said.

'Out.'

'Out where?'

'Where do you think?'

She stepped forward quickly and grabbed hold of his arm.

'You're not going to the pub,' she said. 'You haven't got any money.'

She stood there, breathing hard, challenging him, hanging on to the sleeve of his jacket, gripping it tight. Rob shook his head. Even now, if there had been even the off-chance of something real happening, he would have stayed home. But there wasn't. She didn't want him, he thought, she wanted the money, and then she wanted him to be the way she wanted, to buy her a puppy-dog and give her kids, and get a proper job, as if there were any proper jobs to get. Quietly, with almost no effort, he pulled his arm free.

'I'll go where I fucking like,' he said softly, leaning into her face, showing her his contempt. He pulled on the jacket and walked over to the door, picking up his fags and lighter from the table as he went. 'At least down there, I've got friends.'

'You've got no friends,' she called out after him.

'Think what you like,' he said, quietly.

'You go out that door, Rob Watson,' she said, 'and you'll not be coming back.'

There was desperation in her voice, something forced and quavering. If anybody had been listening, Rob thought, they would have seen through her bluff right away, and he almost felt sorry for her. She had some idea, at the back of her mind, that he didn't really belong to the house, that he was a guest there – a lodger, like the boy who lived next door with Malcolm; when she talked to people about the work they had done about the place, she would always say how *she* had done this, *she* had done that, with no mention of him. As far as she was concerned, the house really was hers and she had the right to put him out of it, if he didn't play the game – she had even tried it once, locking the doors on him, and he'd had to come in through the back window and smash the kitchen up, to show her she couldn't mess him about. Even then, she'd stood there, shouting and screaming at him, trying to provoke him to some further action. There were times when he even thought she wanted him to hit her – but, in all the time they had been together, he'd never raised his hand to her, except for that once – and that was just a wee slap, anyway. He grinned.

'I'll come and go as I please,' he said, slipping his fags into his jacket pocket. 'And don't you try and stop me.'

Alan slid open the back door to the close and stood gazing at the rain. It was small and fine, a real wetting rain, a few degrees this side of mist. When he held out his hand, it was colder than he had expected, colder and more penetrating, numbing his fingers to the bone in a matter of seconds.

Someone had left their washing out, two white shirts and a pair of blue underpants, dripping over the empty patch of grass like failed pennants. He turned his arm around and around in the cool air and let the rain fuzz his hand, then he rubbed his wet palm across his face. The cold water tasted sweet and sooty. He took out his pack of cigarettes: there was one left, and he lit it carefully, with the last match in the box. In a matter of moments he felt light-headed, the way he always did when he smoked his first cigarette on an empty stomach. He held the smoke in his lungs as long as he could, then breathed it out slowly through his nose, watching it vanish into the air as he exhaled. He wondered, sometimes, where it went: smoke and dust and the skin that flaked off your body day after day, worn clothes and dead birds and the bodies of rats and hedgehogs on the roads. He'd heard, once, that the human body sheds all of its skin every seven years, as it grows a new body, tiny particles falling away all the time, vanishing into the air and becoming something else. Everything becoming something else, all the time.

Over on the other side of the close, he could see a woman moving about in her kitchen, preparing a meal. He'd watched this woman sometimes: she was clean-looking and pretty, with long dark hair; she always dressed nicely, with thick patterned jumpers, or brightly-coloured shirts; her boyfriend came round some nights and she made them both a meal, standing in the kitchen with a glass of wine and a recipe book open on the table. Sometimes he could even smell the food: garlic, tomatoes, chicken smells would waft across to him, and he would wish he could walk into that room, and be welcomed by a woman like that: a glass of wine, a smile, a little kiss. Later, after the meal, he would imagine them going to bed and making love, warm from the wine and the heat of the kitchen. It hurt physically, when he thought about it, and he turned away, leaning with his back to the door, while he finished his cigarette. Though he hadn't been aware of the fact when he'd come out, he'd been hoping he would find Jennifer in the close and he was disappointed when he saw that she wasn't there.

A couple of minutes later, he was heading for the Mercy. He stopped in at the newsagent's for some more cigarettes, and there was a bunch of girls there, about five of them, all silly and giggly. Jennifer wasn't with them, of course. Back outside, he tried to get into the mood – to get lost in that feeling he would have sometimes, seeing himself from the outside, alone, with nowhere to go, just the evening opening up in front of him. Gangs of people were wandering up and down the Perth Road, shouting and laughing and calling back and forth; boys with beer cans and cigarettes, girls walking by, damp-looking and sweetly-scented with cheap perfume, too fresh, too moist, heavy and misted with dew, like exotic fruits. Alan felt different from these people, the way some character in a film, walking in a crowd scene, looks apart from the others, picked out by the camera and by the lights, even by the soundtrack – at the same time, he could feel something in the air, he didn't know what, a sense of expectation, maybe. There had been times when he loved that sensation: to go out, in the cool of the evening, to mingle with the crowd and yet still feel that inward camera picking you out, to mix in with the others and go, just to see where it took you. There had been times when he felt happy with just that, but all he could think of now was how absurd it was, and how little it had to offer. He crossed the road and started doubling back on himself. As soon as he reached Thompson's Lane, he was out of the light and the noise and he kept walking, breathing the cool air, till he reached Magdalen Green. At the foot of the lane, he smelled the water, a cold, sharp smell, like ice, or new frost. At the same time, a man came out of the darkening air, with two bottles of whisky in his hand.

'Hey!' The man looked startled, as if he had seen a ghost. Alan turned away quickly and started walking, not too fast, towards Roseangle. Without looking back, he could tell the man was following him.

'Hey!' The voice came again, louder and more insistent. 'I know you.' There was a pause, for thought. 'Alan!'

Alan turned and looked back. All of a sudden, he knew that the man's voice was familiar, though he couldn't tell where he'd heard it before.

'Alan.' The man looked pleased and held out his hand.

Alan nodded. The other man was lean and hollow-eyed, with odd, yellowish lines etched into his face; he had thinning, sand-coloured hair and a sparse greyish moustache.

'Don't you remember me?' the man asked.

Alan nodded again, though he had no idea who the stranger was. He was wearing a thin white nylon shirt and track suit bottoms, with slippers on his feet. Obviously he had just come out quickly to get a carry-out; he hadn't even bothered to put his coat on.

'It's George,' the man said, with a short, hard laugh. 'Remember?'

Alan nodded, feeling stupid.

'Yes,' he said. 'George. I remember.'

George guffawed with laughter now and lunged forward, taking Alan by the arm.

'Good to see you, son,' he said, breathing smoke and whisky fumes into Alan's face. 'Good to see you.'

'It's good to see you, too, George,' Alan answered quietly, trying to slip out of the man's grasp. Now he was desperately racking his brain for some memory but, try as he might, he couldn't place him.

George laughed.

'It's a good thing I met you,' he said. 'I've got a couple of bottles of Dewar's here, just now. Come on back and we'll have a drink.'

Alan didn't want to go, but there was something odd about George – some inner blackness that was only visible in his eyes and his voice – that made him reluctant to refuse. Ten minutes later, he was sitting in a strange front room, a room he was sure he had never seen before in his life, with a half-pint glass of whisky in one hand and a fag in the other, and George was sitting opposite him, waving his fag hand around as he talked, a serious look on his face. There was a six-pack of beer and a bottle of whisky on the coffee-table and next to them lay what looked like a gun, though Alan couldn't tell if it was real, or a replica. It could even have been one of those fancy cigarette lighters. He didn't know; but the idea of it, lying there, maybe real, maybe loaded, bothered him.

George was talking about women. Alan had no idea how they'd come on to the subject, but somehow, almost as soon as they'd walked through George's front door, they were on to the evils of the female sex, and the Bible, and some other book George had read, called, as far as Alan could tell, *The Gospel of Thomas*.

'Everything else is in code,' George said. 'The Gospel of Thomas is the only one that says what it really means.'

Alan nodded. He had no idea what to say; he was still wondering how he'd even come to be there, in this strange house, listening to George's ravings. He looked around. The walls were bare, there was no television set, no CD, nothing like that, just a settee and a couple of chairs, and the coffee-table with the beer and the gun on it. It looked like a room that burglars had just exited, taking everything that was valuable with them.

'What do you think?'

The question came out of nowhere and took him by surprise. He looked up. George was leaning forward in his seat, waiting for him to answer the question, which was fine, except that Alan had no idea what the question was about.

'I'm not sure,' Alan said. 'George. Can I use the bathroom?'

He looked confused for a moment. Obviously he hadn't expected the conversation to take this particular turn. Seconds later, though, he was up and headed for the door. Alan thought he was going to come to the toilet with him. They stopped at the foot of the stairs.

'Quiet now,' George whispered. 'The wee boy's asleep up there.'

134

'Oh.' Alan nodded. A moment before George had been shouting his head off, about God and the Bible and how women were sent out by Satan, and now he was saying to be quiet.

'It's at the top, on the right,' George said.

Alan nodded and started up the stairs, slowly, taking care not to make a noise. George waited a moment and then went back into the front room.

At the top of the stairs, Alan could see there were four doors, all leading off the little landing, two to the left, and two just to the right. He found the toilet, and had a piss, then he stood, debating whether to flush it or not – maybe George wouldn't like it, if he made a noise, but then, he might not like it if Alan left his toilet dirty – when he heard a sound, a kind of low whining, from somewhere behind him. He opened the door. The noise was coming from one of the rooms opposite, the one on his left, he reckoned, the one directly above the front room, where he and George had been sitting. This must be the wee boy, he thought – but then, something was wrong because, even in his sleep, he shouldn't be making noises like this. He crossed the hall and stood at the door, listening. The noise came again – only this time, it was a low, strained whimpering sound, coming from directly behind the door, and he didn't know why, but he was certain it was a woman in there, not a wee boy. It was a woman, and she was hurt, or scared, pressed against the door, listening, just as he was. He tapped softly with his fingers – he didn't want George to hear – and listened. The noise stopped.

'Hello?' he said, in a whisper, but there was no reply. He didn't want to rouse George's suspicions, and the thought came to him that there was a way of making even a whisper heard – the way actors did it – only he didn't know how.

'Is anybody there?'

The whimpering sound resumed and he felt something move, rubbing softly against the other side of the door, somewhere near the floor.

'She can't hear you.'

Alan spun around. The wee boy was standing in the doorway of the other room. He was wearing a pair of grimy, damp-looking pyjamas with cutaway sleeves and some cartoon character printed on the front – Alan couldn't make out what it was. The boy was about six or seven, Alan thought, a clever-looking wee boy with close-cropped hair and brown freckles all over his face. Alan wondered where he had come from so quietly.

'She's deaf,' the boy continued, his eyes fixed on Alan's face, casual-seeming yet accusatory, as if he suspected Alan of some intended betrayal – or rather, as if he wanted to ask Alan's help, and was afraid of being betrayed.

'Is she all right?'

The boy shook his head.

'She's been bad,' he said. 'Dad grounded her. He says she can't help it, but that doesn't excuse what she did.'

The boy looked down at Alan's feet.

'I like your trainers,' he said.

Alan couldn't tell if he was being serious. They were nothing special, not some kind of name brand, just trainers.

'What did she do?' he asked.

The boy looked up sharply.

'What?' he asked, as if he'd just been wakened up.

'What did she do that was bad?'

'Oh.' The boy fixed his eyes on the door and, as if by some prearranged signal, the whimpering stopped and something shifted away, a weight, a mass, shifting away into what Alan pictured as a pitch-black, silent space.

'She drank the milk,' the boy said.

Alan stared at him. For the first time, he noticed the shadows under his eyes, and the redness in his eyes. At the same time, a noise rose from below and the boy retreated back into his empty room.

'What's going on up there?'

George was standing at the foot of the stairs with a can of beer in his hand. Alan turned and started down the stairs.

'Sorry,' he said, as he reached the foot of the stairs and waited, with George blocking his way. 'There was something wrong with the handle.'

'Oh.' George nodded and handed him the can. He looked suspicious, but he was obviously deciding to let it go. 'Well, never mind about that. This fucking house is falling apart round my ears, anyway.'

He shifted back into the front room, with Alan reluctantly following, and poured out some more whisky. As soon as they sat down, he started again on his tirade against women and devils.

'There are devils everywhere,' he said. 'There's not just one. They live in the house, and the women keep them hidden. They're what people used to think were fairies – tiny little beings with fish-hook claws to help them fasten on to you. They're drawn to the smell of women – and children sometimes. They feed on left-overs, carrion, women's blood –' a little bow of the head here, to show his distaste – 'you know, whatever they can get.'

Alan didn't say anything. There was nothing to say, anyway.

'Jesus came to redeem the man from the woman. That's the

truth. That's what it says in the Gospel of Thomas, but it's been kept secret. Suppressed.' He gave a short laugh. 'If the eye offend thee, pluck it out. If the hand offend thee . . .'

Alan shook his head.

'How do you mean?'

George shook his head in turn. 'I'm telling you,' he said, 'you have to be ruthless. If any thing offend thee, cut it off. We must put away the works of the woman. That's what the Gospel says. It's logical.'

He went on like that for another hour. After a while, Alan stopped listening. He was still thinking about the woman upstairs, and the wee boy, and what might be going on in this place. George was telling him what the most important thing in life was, the one thing you had to remember, which was this – he got to that point about five or six times, then interrupted himself with some quote from the Bible, or this Gospel of Thomas, so when he did get to the bit, Alan wasn't really listening.

'What I'm saying is,' George was saying, 'what I'm saying is that what you think is good is what kills you. You have to suspect everything. Anything that looks good is secretly evil. That's how the devil works.'

Alan nodded. He helped himself to another can of beer without waiting to be asked, lit up a fag and waited. George was on to the second bottle of Dewar's. Finally, his speech started to thicken and, finally, at last, in a moment of blessed release, George's head lolled sideways, and he fell asleep in mid-sentence. Alan leaned forward. He finished his beer – no point in wasting it – then he put his fags in his jacket pocket and slipped the jacket on. He looked at George's face. The man looked dead to the world. Alan stood up, as quietly as he could, and started towards the door.

'See me?' George said, sitting up, with one hand in the air, as if he'd never left off talking. 'See me, son?'

Alan looked at him, trying to feign casual interest. There was something different in George's face now, a new look of impatience, or irritation.

'My old man treated me like I was his dog,' George said. 'He made me sleep in a box under the stairs. I had to beg when I wanted food. He would be sitting there at the table, holding out scraps of food, and I'd have to sit up on my hind legs and beg. Can you imagine that? When it was dark, he would take me out to the park and tell me to go do my business in the bushes, like the other animals. Other times I'd wet myself, but after a while I got used to it, so I could hold it in. Sometimes he brought me treats home, after the pub, little chocolate chips and stuff like you give to a dog. He'd throw them and I had to catch them. This went on till I was seven. I didn't know I was seven, of course. I didn't know what age I was. I'd never been to school, or seen inside a book. All I knew was what I saw on television, sitting on the floor by his chair, with my knees tucked up under me, and my hands out in front, the way he made me. If he hadn't of died, maybe I would have been a dog forever.'

He looked at the half-empty whisky bottle as if he'd forgotten how it came to be that way, then lit a cigarette.

'I'm making up for it now, though,' he said.

Alan stood up. He didn't believe a word of George's story. 'Yes,' he said. 'You are that.'

George started and Alan realised he had just given himself away, that George hadn't known he was still there. He'd been talking to himself.

George wheeled around.

'Where are you going?' he asked, surprised, his voice thick with the drink again.

'I've got to go home now,' Alan said.

'Oh.'

'All right?'

'Yeah. Okay. See you.' George didn't seem to care any more. He sat staring at the whisky bottle, while Alan headed for the door.

'You don't believe me,' George called after him all of a sudden, as if he had read Alan's mind. He reached out, picked up the gun and lurched to his feet. 'You don't believe me, do you?'

''Course I do,' Alan said quickly. 'I'm just a bit tired, to tell you the truth.' He was trying not to look at the gun, and then he was aware of himself as he must have looked to George, trying not to look at it. George was staring at him – and for a moment, Alan thought, he really did look like a dog, a big, ugly Rottweiler, waiting to strike. George gave a short, bitter laugh.

'I've got a dog of my own, now,' he said. 'You want to see my dog?'

Alan shook his head.

'I'm not that good with dogs,' he said.

George smiled.

'All right,' he said. He grinned. 'If the eye offend thee,' he said, almost in a whisper.

Alan stepped out into the hall, and George followed, carrying the gun. His shirt had come unbuttoned at the waist and Alan could see the dark line of a scar on his belly.

'I'd better get home,' Alan said quietly. He wondered if the woman and the boy were listening. 'You get some sleep.'

'All righty,' George said, in a bad American accent. 'But you all come back now, d'ye hear?'

Alan opened the door. He could smell the air, feel the cold of it, and he realised they weren't really that far from the water here: he could taste it, a thin sweetness in the night, tainted with weed and diesel.

'See you,' Alan said.

George gave him a long, blank look, as if he wasn't quite sure how Alan had got there. Finally he nodded.

'Remember what I told you,' he said. 'You know. About the woman.'

'I will.'

'Best way.'

'Aye.'

'It's the only way.'

'I know.'

'Cheerio, then.'

'Cheerio, George.'

Alan turned and stepped out into the cold night air. He could feel George moving up to the door behind him.

'Mind now.'

'Uh-huh.'

He walked to the gate, opened it as gently and casually as he could, and stepped through. Then he closed it as gently as he could behind him. He didn't want to seem too much in a hurry, so he looked back, for one last goodnight. The door was still open but George was gone: the door stood empty, a sudden and appalling vacancy, and Alan wondered where he had gone. He looked up at the upstairs rooms. They were dark, the curtains drawn, no sign of life. He wondered if the woman was in there still, and if she was, what she was doing.

Then George appeared again, with the gun in his hand. He walked quickly to the gate and held it out, stock first.

'Take it,' he said.

Alan shook his head.

'No, man,' he said. 'I don't want it.'

'Please.'

His eyes were pleading and Alan realised, all of a sudden, why George wanted him to take the gun. He reached out, gripped it and felt the weight of it shift to him; it felt cold and heavy and hard in his hand. A good feeling. Balance and rightness. He nodded, as George let it go.

'See you, then,' he said.

'Aye.' There was a hint of tears in George's voice, and Alan wondered again if he'd maybe been making the whole thing up. Or some of it anyway. Maybe he was crazy, and he had begun to know it. Maybe that was why he wanted Alan to take the gun, in case he did something stupid. Which was all for the best, he supposed. He turned and walked away quickly, then; though he didn't look back, he knew George was there, watching him go, standing at the gate of his house in his stockinged feet.

After he left the Mercy, Rob went for a walk into town. It was late in the afternoon, and he didn't want to go back to Cathy, to her rounded warm body, so close and so far away from him. He didn't want to have to listen to her going on, either, or crying, or trying to be sarcastic. He just wanted to be on his own. He was fed up with everybody and fed up with having no money; he was even a bit fed up with Sconnie and Junior. What he really needed was female company, like that woman he'd seen in the Rat and Parrot the other night, or one of those students from the Uni, the girls he'd see all the time, walking up and down the Nethergate or the Perth Road: English girls with long brown or golden hair; little Oriental girls who always shied away when you looked at them; girls in sweatshirts and jeans, or girls dressed up to go out for the night, in skimpy T-shirts and gypsy ear-rings; girls with really short skirts to show their legs, long and naked, with no tights on – he really liked that look – or done up to the eyes in make-up, with little black dresses and strings of pearls. He didn't care; he wanted them all: tall, short, thin, fat, pretty, plain, whatever. He just liked women. When he was a kid he used to stand by the side of the road and watch them go by: women in the family car, bringing home the shopping; business women in crisp suits and white blouses; big women in delivery vans, cigarettes dangling from their mouths, in blue shirts and tight uniform trousers; and once, a woman in an open-top sports-car, with a Great Dane beside her, stock-still, like it was made of wax. He loved watching them, and thinking how, one day, he would meet women just like them.

He had been watching them for as long as he could remember. It was like when you went on school visits to the zoo; he would recognise all the animals from the picture books in the library, or nature programmes, but in the flesh there was something strange about them, they were larger and more immediate, a hundred times more vivid and dangerous. He wanted to know what they were thinking, as they paced the cages; he wanted to know what they felt, but they were a complete mystery to him – and women were like that, too: a complete mystery, because you could never tell what they were thinking, you could never know what they were feeling and, as far as his experience went, which wasn't that great, nowadays, they had no idea what *you* were feeling or thinking. Things you imagined were insignificant, stupid little trivial things, would come out really important to them, whereas they would take something you really cared about, like the football, or your pals at the pub, and make it all out to be nothing. It was a permanent mystery – but Rob didn't think it had to be a problem. It didn't have to be all doom and gloom all the time, all that men are from Mars, women are from Venus rubbish. It could be interesting, too. That was how it was supposed to be anyway, wasn't it? It made things more interesting, the games you had to play, the little stunts you pulled, the things you had to do, sometimes, to get what you wanted.

He couldn't understand how he'd come to be living like this, though. The thing was, he really did love women. Not just the ones he fancied, but all women. They fascinated him. Once, when he was just a boy, he'd been out wandering, looking for some trouble to get into. He'd been out in the country somewhere, in this stretch of woods, and he was just sitting by the side of the road. There hadn't been any traffic for a while, then a car had driven up and stopped, just opposite where he was sitting. It was autumn. Two women got out and walked purposefully into the woods – and Rob had followed. Whether it was his stealth – he liked to think of himself as stealthy, like Hawkeye, moving silently through the woods, invisible to the observer – or maybe because they were in too much of a hurry, the women hadn't noticed him. One was tall and dark and pretty; she was called Sally. The other one was shorter and plumper, with ash-blonde hair and a double chin; because she had done most of the talking, Rob hadn't heard her name, but he didn't care. Sally was beautiful. He kept hoping the women would wander apart, though he had no idea what he would do if they did. If either one of the women had seen him, he'd probably have run a mile. Not that it mattered, anyway. They had stuck together, searching for something amongst the fallen leaves, moving only a few feet apart, before coming together again, their heads bent, eyes fixed on the ground. He'd followed them around the woods for an hour, and they hadn't found what they were looking for; eventually, when it got dark, they walked back to the car and he'd followed, entranced, almost sick with desire for the dark one. Sally. Even now, he still remembered her: if he closed his eyes, he would see her, a detailed picture in his mind, like a photograph.

It was getting on for evening. Rob stopped at the bottom of the Nethergate and thought about Sconnie and Junior, away back to their empty houses for their tea, and he wondered about the night ahead. He had some money left, so he wouldn't be short, but he didn't think he could face another Saturday night just sitting there in the Mercy, listening to Sconnie's stories, before he went home to Cathy and her cold bed. It was a funny thing, but hardly any women ever came in to the Mercy. The odd one or two, usually student girls with their boyfriends, or middle-aged women with their men, but that was it. There had been a nice-looking barmaid a while back, but now it was just the two boys, and big Jo, who must have weighed about twenty stone. Rob wondered why that was. There were some pubs women just didn't go into, and there were others that were always full of them – he'd go down to the student places sometimes and sit there, just watching, lapping it up, especially at the end of the year, when exams were finished, and they were all getting pissed, in little skimpy tops and jeans, laughing and mucking about and inviting you to join in, if you wanted. They didn't bother. Not that it went anywhere, mind. He thought, sometimes, he would do anything to get off with one of those beautiful, crazy girls – just for a day, just for one night. You could go a long way on one good night, one good afternoon, getting pissed with a nice-looking young girl and going back to hers. He'd done it a few times, when he'd had a bit more money and confidence, like, before Cathy had sapped him of all his sense of himself. Still. That seemed a long time ago, now.

He stopped walking when he got to the Nethergate and stood there, like somebody who suddenly realises he's lost. A woman came out of one of the university buildings. There was something odd about her – she looked as if she belonged to another time, in her long brown coat, her curly light brown hair hanging over her shoulders – another time, another season, another way of life. There was something odd about the place, too. The sky was starting to turn grey, and there was a heaviness in the air, a sudden change in the pressure that made him feel dizzy and slow. There were people on the street – students and people coming away from work, but there was something wrong. He couldn't account for it at first, it was only after some time that he noticed the child soldiers: a group of boys on a corner to begin with, then a couple of girls at a bus stop, in green and brown camouflage suits, then a mixed gang of them, maybe a dozen, walking towards him from the town end, laughing and mucking about – and he saw that they were everywhere, all over the place, boys and girls standing in pairs, smoking, talking, kissing goodbye, walking away. They were all wearing the camouflage jackets, or green jumpers with brown boots and those padded trousers with all the pockets; a few wore flat black caps, with a red pom-pom on the top. It all looked wrong – artificial – the way it would look on a film set, if they were making a picture about the Fifties, or a ghost story, maybe. The woman in the brown coat came down the steps and she looked at him as she passed, as if she was wondering what he was doing there – and the idea came to him that he was the ghost, he was the one who was out of place. He turned to the woman and looked at her – which must have scared her a bit, because she turned quickly and started walking away, up towards the Perth Road. He carried on.

There were three boys sitting on the steps outside the next lot of buildings. Two of them were huddled together, half-cut, sharing a cigarette, the other – older, dirtier, with a thick grey beard and rheumy blue-grey eyes – lurched into Rob's path and held up an arm to stop him passing.

'Excuse me, son.' He tilted his face upward and Rob caught

a whiff of bad breath and drink and stale tobacco. He stepped
to one side, but the man followed.

'Get out of the road,' he said, quietly.

The other two boys looked up to see what would happen.

'Excuse *me*, son,' the older man persisted, barring the way
with his body now, both arms outstretched. It was too much
for Rob. He was pissed off, and he was beginning to feel a bit
depressed, and now he was looking for any chance to lose his
rag. In a split second, before the old boy knew what was
happening, and before the other two could intervene, he put
the head on the boy, butting him square and hard in the
middle of the face, knocking him to the ground. The old
bastard let out a roar of anger and pain, and Rob immediately
turned and squared up to the other two, just in case. They
looked at each other, and one of them said, 'Fuck', quietly,
almost under his breath, but they didn't move, not even to
help their mate, they just stayed where they were, at the foot
of the steps.

'It was his own fault,' Rob said. 'Right?'

One of the boys nodded.

Rob moved on, then, alert to any movement behind him, if
it should come – past the Queen's Hotel, past the bank,
past the pub and the take-away place. At the bottom of the
hill, next to the underpass, he stopped and looked back.
Nobody had followed. He took a deep breath. He didn't
know what had come over him, putting the heid on that old
boy like that. He met those boys every day: they were just
harmless old farts, hanging around the Uni trying to get
money out of the students, either by begging or, later, when it
got a bit dark, by putting it on a bit, pretending they were
hard men, to scare up a bit of loose change. The students
would fall for it, too. Boys up from England, wee thin boys

with round glasses and floppy hair would stand there, on the street, handing out their last few coins to those fuckers, who they probably thought were so hard. It was a shame they didn't know any better but that was life. If you were prepared to give it away, that was your own look out.

Alan woke suddenly. He had slipped off the sofa and on to the floor and he was cold and uncomfortable now. His left arm had got bent under him and he was aware of a dull ache between the elbow and the wrist. It was still daytime, but the light was a soft gold in the corner of the room. He pulled himself up and sat propped against the sofa. He had been dreaming of the old days, that time on Blackburn Drive, when they had lived in the prefabs, and he would play with Marie and Stewart, on the bit waste ground out beyond the woods. It was strange how dreams would be like that sometimes, mixing in real memories to seem more true: he'd watched it all like he was at the pictures, and he'd seen Stewart's leg, the time he'd jumped into that pit and landed on a big piece of wood, all covered with nails, hidden in amongst the weeds. He'd seen Marie, the time she had taken off her knickers and showed herself, and he'd remembered how naked she looked when they examined her, the little slit there naked with that same tender, unfledged nakedness of baby mice, when you found them in their nests. He saw the coalman's horse, standing at the end of the road, its head lost in the harness and the blinkers. It had all been so vivid, like being at the pictures. Then, somewhere at the back of the dream, he'd remembered the woman in the town who was supposed to have given birth

150

to a baby with two heads – and he'd seen it too, just the way it had been described to him. One of the heads was perfectly formed, quite beautiful, in fact, but the other was hideously ugly, all nose and ears, with tiny pin pricks for the mouth and eyes. The child was supposed to have died quite soon after it was born, and the woman was supposed to have gone mad from seeing it. People would talk about how she'd be seen in the town, pushing an empty pram along the High Street, with a thick scarf over her head, covering most of her face, as if she was the one who had been born deformed. It was only a story, of course. But in the dream, Alan had seen the baby and then someone, some voice behind him, from somewhere he couldn't see, had told him that he was the baby, and he'd looked into the pram, and seen it, with its two faces, and he'd known both faces were his.

He shook his head and pushed himself up. Six feet away, perched on a kitchen chair, Jennifer was sitting bolt upright, watching him.

'You're awake,' she said simply, with a hint of sarcasm.

'Yeah.' Alan looked at his hands. They felt grimy, as if he'd spent last night playing in the dirt.

'How did you get in here?' he asked her. His voice sounded like it was being poured through a funnel.

Jennifer laughed.

'You left the door open,' she said. 'You shouldn't drink so much. It makes you forgetful.'

Alan struggled to his feet.

'I know,' he said. 'How long have you been sitting there?'

'Oh, a long time,' she said. 'A couple of hours. Did you have a nice dream?'

'What?'

'Did you have a nice dream?'

'I don't know. How do you mean?'

She stood up.

'You were talking to yourself,' she said. 'Talking in your sleep.'

'What did I say?'

'I don't know. I couldn't make it out.'

'Oh.' For a minute, he'd thought she was going to tell him he'd been talking about her, but she didn't say any more about it, she just stood up and gave him a twirl, to show off the dress she was wearing. It was a thin yellow and blue frock, quite old-fashioned, like the ones the girls used to wear to school when there was a dance, or a Christmas party.

'So?'

'So what?'

'So, how do you like my dress,' she said. 'God, you really are stupid today.'

'It's very nice,' Alan said. 'What's it for?'

'Nothing. I just came to show you.'

'Oh.' Alan looked at her. She was smiling at him, holding the dress by its hems and spreading it so it caught the light – and she looked so beautiful at that moment, so happy and pleased with herself, that he suddenly felt sorry for her with a kind of grief and loneliness that surprised him. If he could have had anything in the world, he thought, he would want this girl to go through the rest of her life being happy, just as she was right now, for no good reason, because that was the only way to be happy – if you relied on something else, something from outside yourself, you wouldn't be happy long.

'You look beautiful,' he said. She was standing close to him now and, without even thinking, he reached out and touched her, gently, on the shoulder. The material felt soft and cheap under his fingers and he could feel the warmth of her through

152

it; then, realising what he was doing, what he had just done, his fingers closing, almost caressing her shoulder, he pulled his hand away like he'd just been burned. Jennifer looked up at him. She was startled. Then, in a single, unstoppable movement, she fell against him, pressing her head to his chest, and wrapping her arms around his waist.

Alan froze. He could feel her against him, warm, thin, pressing against his body, close, then closer still, her grip tightening around his waist, and he felt a quickening, somewhere in his stomach and thighs, a thick, dark heat rising from his groin and filling him, from his scalp to the soles of his feet, not just desire, but longing, an immaculate and imposs-ible love. Before he could pull away, he was hard; pressed against her belly's warmth, his erection felt like a violation in itself, a tiny rape, and she must have felt it, she must have known what he was feeling. He knew she must, and in his shame, he tore himself away from her, disgusted, sickened, dizzy with fear and desire. Jennifer remained where she was, her arms hanging by her sides, her head down.

'Sorry,' Alan said, after a moment.

She didn't move. She didn't look up, and she didn't say anything.

'I shouldn't have done that,' he said.

She lifted her head then and he saw her face. She knew, of course, but she was pretending not to know.

'What?' she said.

'I shouldn't have touched you.'

'Aren't you my friend?' she said.

Alan nodded his head. 'Yes,' he said, 'of course I am.'

She had tears in her eyes now. Maybe she didn't believe him – or maybe she really didn't know what he'd done, what he'd wanted in that instant. But if she didn't, how could he explain it? And how could he let her stay there a moment longer?

'You'd better get home,' Alan said. 'I've got to get cleaned up and stuff. I'll see you later, all right?'

Jennifer nodded.

'I really like your dress,' Alan said.

She nodded again, then she turned and ran out through the open door, her footsteps echoing in the close, flat splashes of noise, receding into the masonry. He waited a moment, then he went to the door and closed it. Now that he was alone, he couldn't believe what had happened. He could still feel the warmth of her, not just in his fingers, but everywhere, and he recalled again what had gone through his mind; or not his mind, for his mind wasn't even there – it was just him, somewhere deep down in his sick flesh. It was unbearable. He tried to put it out of his thoughts, but he couldn't. It would always be there – there was no going back.

Quickly, then, he walked through to the kitchen. He filled the kettle with water from the hot tap, then stood waiting, while it came to the boil. Soon the steam began to rise, clouding the wall, so the paint looked almost green, instead of the usual powdery blue. He thought deliberately, now, about Jennifer. He didn't see her, he put away the warmth of her body, and thought about her, the way you might think about a picture you had seen, or a puzzle you were trying to solve. He wanted to tell her he hadn't meant anything when he touched her, or, if he had, it hadn't been what she had thought. She had just looked so beautiful, in her thin frock. He had wanted her to know that he loved her – really, loved her, in a way he hadn't imagined possible – but it wasn't sexual, it was just that he loved her because she was beautiful, and because he felt sorry for her too. He wanted her to know that he would have done anything rather than hurt her. But it wasn't true. None of that was true. The truth was that he wanted her. The only real fact in his life that he could be sure of was that she was the one he wanted to come home to and lie down with, she was the one he wanted to touch and kiss and make love to, not the woman across the close, not her or any other. In other words, he was a pervert, a sicko, a child molester – and it didn't even come as a surprise. At some level, he realised now, he'd known that all along.

The kettle clicked off, and the steam cleared. Alan unplugged it and carried it to the sink; then, holding his left arm out, palm upward over the basin, he poured the boiling water over his hand, keeping the fingers apart so the water would flow between them, scalding the insides of the fingers, where it was the most tender. The pain was searing, but even as he did it, he knew it wouldn't cause permanent injury. It was just enough to make him remember what he had done. For now he realised that it would never be the same with Jennifer; he would never be able to explain to her, she would never trust him again. She would think he was just like all the others, all those dirty old men. There could be no penance, and no redemption. The situation was irreversible.

At the foot of the Nethergate, by the underpass, a small, thin, freckle-faced girl was sitting on the wall, watching the passers by. She'd once had long red curls, but they had been cut off so the hair came to an abrupt end just below her ears. It gave her a crazed, slightly shocked look.

As soon as he saw her, Rob knew she was on something. She must have noticed him looking at her, and she fixed him with her eyes and started towards him, flaring out into his path and looking up at him, with a fixed, too deliberate smile on her face. She wasn't nice-looking, or anything like that. If anything, she looked a bit odd, and if it hadn't been for the slides in her hair, and the slight softness around her hips and breasts, he wouldn't have known for sure that she *was* a girl. She had big doll's eyes, though, and bright-reddish freckles; her hair was held back off her face with two thin, bright-blue slides; there was something about her, a softness, a vulnerability, that attracted him.

'Hiya,' she said, taking hold of his arm, as if she had known him all her life. 'How's it going?'

Rob stopped dead and looked at her. Her pupils were huge, black and empty, like the inkwells on the old desks they used to have in school.

'Hi,' he said.

'I know you,' the girl said. 'Right?'

She gave him a bright, ingratiating smile that revealed a row of tiny, sharp-looking teeth.

Rob nodded. Why not? He'd never seen her before in his life.

'Right,' he said.

'You got any fags?'

'Yeah.'

'You got any money?'

'Yeah.'

'You want to get a carry-out and come back to mine?'

Rob looked at her. Over the last couple of years, he'd had other women when the opportunity arose — if it came on a plate, he wasn't going to say no — but if there was ever any need for some effort on his part, some obvious move, he would let it pass. Which usually meant he missed out on the best chances, and ended up with whatever was left, like this girl here, some half-cut or stoned woman he'd meet in a bar or off the street, whose name he wouldn't remember afterwards, if he ever knew it. It wasn't exactly what he had in mind, but there was a balance he wanted to preserve, a balance in himself: he didn't want his hunger, his wide-eyed married-man's desperation to show.

Not that the women he met didn't guess right away that he was married. He didn't wear a ring, but that wouldn't have made a blind bit of difference to most women, if they were up for it. Some of them were married too, no doubt, and they had their own reasons for playing away — reasons which didn't interest him. But there was something deep-rooted — something old-fashioned, even — that shamed him when he'd been with another woman and was stealing away from her bed, or her front room — because he shouldn't have had to be doing that. It should have been Cathy. If she had only allowed it, they could have had something between them, a secrecy, a private game that only they could play, a conspiracy of desire that would have held them together. It was her fault, mostly, that he was here, in places like this. Sometimes, when he was sober, he would look back on those other women with disbelief and horror; but after a few drinks, he'd do it all again, as low as it got, any chance he got, and he'd justify it all without a second thought. If you were starving at home, he'd say, you had to go out and find a take-away.

The girl was still hanging on to him, looking up into his face and grinning.

'How about it?' she said, slurring the words slightly, and Rob realised she had no idea who he was. She probably thought he was somebody else, somebody she knew.

'Yeah,' he said. 'Let's go.'

The girl gave a little squeal of laughter.

'Bacardi,' she said. 'I want some Bacardi. You like Bacardi?'

'Yeah.' Rob gave her as much of a smile as he could manage. 'I love Bacardi.'

Somewhere towards the end of the afternoon, Alan came to his senses. He was sitting in the graveyard on the Perth Road, on a strip of grass, at the foot of a huge white angel. His hand hurt like hell, where he had poured the water over it. Two girls were walking by on the next path, and they were looking at him − and that was when he realised he'd been praying, talking to the angel out loud, asking for mercy, with tears in his eyes, completely gone, wanting to be forgiven. The girls were staring; when he looked up, they burst out laughing and walked away quickly, covering their faces and emitting little gasps of laughter, like somebody had just told them a dirty joke. Alan stood up and walked to the gate.

Outside, it was starting to get dark. The lights were on all along the Perth Road. There was a cool breeze from somewhere, cool and wistful, a breeze from the west, from the Carse of Gowrie, or further away, and he had a sudden image of the distance, of roads and towns in the dark, motorways and woods and hills, the utter beauty of elsewhere. Suddenly, he knew what he had to do. He was sick of everything, that was the problem. He'd been drinking too much for far too long − ever since he'd won the money − and he had made himself a bit crazy. All he needed to do was get into his car − he'd had the car for months, now, and he'd somehow forgotten all about it – and drive away. There was nothing wrong with him that couldn't be fixed by getting out of Dundee and starting again somewhere. It didn't matter where. All that mattered was being alone, out on the road, driving all day and late into the night, watching the miles slide by, and letting the road take you away.

He didn't know how much of the money was left. Letters would arrive, some days, and he would sit at the table in the kitchen, staring at the clean, crisp envelopes, trying to decide which one to open. He didn't like opening letters. When he was a kid, and they were moving about so much, they could go for weeks without getting a letter – and he'd liked that, it was as if they had moved away to another world, where nobody could find them, and the new people they lived amongst would be like the people in films, quite normal-looking, quite ordinary, but no more substantial than ghosts.

His bills were paid through the bank. He got his money from the cash machine and he never requested a statement. Every month, a letter from the bank arrived, and he would set it aside, with the other letters he didn't want to open; he didn't destroy them, he just chose not to open them. That was an odd thing about letters: they would be so clean, so perfect, when they lay there, untouched, on the doormat, but as soon as you opened one, it became almost painfully banal, ugly and creased and grey-looking, a small betrayal. It was the same thing with food: when you bought the tins, or the packets, or the cling-wrapped boxes of runner beans or tomatoes from the supermarket, they looked clean and fresh and appetising, like the food in magazines, but when you prepared it all, the results would always be ugly and disappointing. That was why he had started with the pet food. He didn't see that there was anything wrong with eating the stuff – and he was right, it was okay as far as food went. It was nourishing and it didn't make him sick, the way some take-away food did. He also liked the cheap tins of own-brand economy stuff with no pictures on the label. At least those products didn't raise any unrealistic expectations; you just ate them quickly, straight out of the tin if you liked. And letters were the same. He didn't want to know what was in them, because, usually, it was nothing.

Still, he knew that, eventually, the money would run out. Though he didn't want to know about it till the time came. It had been an accident anyway, that he'd got the money in the first place. It had happened while he was still working: he'd not been drinking much, and he'd had some money left over – a couple of hundred quid – money that had just accumulated one way or another. He'd had a kind of a girlfriend then, Maria, and he'd bought her presents from time to time, when he had money to spare, but she didn't really like him doing that, so he'd stopped. She didn't want him making any assumptions, she said. As far as she was concerned, they were just good friends, and she didn't want to spoil that. He didn't see why giving her presents would spoil it, but he didn't argue with her. So one day he was walking home, and he'd just been to the bank, and he had this money that he didn't know what to do with. He'd thought he would build up a big collection of CDs, but after he'd got about a dozen or so, he couldn't think of any more that he actually wanted all that much. He'd thought of buying a video machine, but that would mean getting a television, and he didn't like televisions. And he'd stopped reading books, pretty much.

So he was just walking along – past the chemist's, past the shops, past the bookies – and he'd thought about how he'd never gone in there, the way his dad had always done. He just wanted to know what it was like, really, to see what his dad had got out of it all those years, and then he was going in, before he could think twice about it. Inside, it was smoky and dim; there were boards on the walls with newspapers pinned up, and there were men standing around, smoking and thinking and scribbling things on little scraps of paper, almost nobody talking, a place of study and speculation. Alan realised he didn't know exactly what to do, but he'd met this boy who was there, quite a friendly boy, who explained how it all worked, and showed him how to write out a line. All Alan had done was choose some horses off one of the boards on the wall, picking them for the sound of their names, without paying any attention to the form or the odds, the way the boy had said you should do, then the boy had helped him place the bet. It felt quite interesting, like conducting a tiny experiment in chance, so Alan put on all the money he had in his pocket. The other boy had looked a bit surprised, then, and he'd asked Alan if he was sure, and Alan had said, yeah, why not? He wasn't expecting anything to happen, he just wanted to know what it was like – though he didn't tell the boy that. The girl at the counter gave him a slip of paper, and the boy had told him he should go and get a drink or something, and come back later, to see if he'd won. It was funny, though, because the boy was different now: after he'd seen all that money, his attitude had changed – it was as if he wanted to get away from Alan as quickly as he could, as if he thought Alan was some kind of jinx, maybe.

But he'd won. It was a shock, because it was so much money, and he didn't really feel right about it. He could see his dad's face – all the hope that was there, when he thought he was on to something – and he felt bad, as if he'd cheated at something. Because he hadn't felt that hope; he hadn't felt anything at all. He had just done it, to see what it was like, and he had won more than his father had ever won or lost, or even dreamed of winning, probably, in his whole life. It was like cheating a dead man. A couple of days later, when it had sunk in how much money he had won, with his beginner's-luck bet, he'd stopped seeing Maria, and after a while he hadn't bothered going to work any more. There didn't seem to be any point, when you could win more than two years' money in one afternoon. To get rid of some of his winnings, he had bought a second-hand car, and parked it on the road, outside the flat, but he'd only used it a couple of times, in the early days. He'd had fantasies of taking Jennifer out for drives, but he'd never even dared to suggest it. Which was just as well, now. He thought of Jennifer again, and he wondered where she was, and what she was doing and whether, maybe, she was thinking about him.

The girl was stoned out of her head. They'd drunk the Bacardi, and now they were lying on the floor, and she was kissing him, her mouth wet and sticky on his face and neck.

'Tell me what you like,' she said, as she slid her hand down over his stomach and started fumbling with his belt. Rob remembered the sensation he'd had before, that she didn't know who he was – or rather, that she thought she did know him, only she was mistaking him for somebody else. Now she was talking to somebody else, asking somebody else what he wanted her to do, only she would be doing it to him. Not that it mattered. The image of Cathy flashed through his mind as the girl opened his trousers and slid them off his hips: he had wanted to be with her, as a man would be with a wife, secretly, in the light and the dark. He had tried to forget Helen, and he would have done, if she had just accepted him – if she had only reached out and touched him, and let herself be touched. Now, she had driven him to this, and he hated her for it.

'You like this?'

The girl shifted and lowered her mouth over his groin. Her fingers were working on him and then she began to suck, tentatively at first, then hungrily, like some animal, fastening around him, flesh on flesh, or like something from the sea, wet and sticky and hungry, feeding on him. He felt a last wave of resistance pass through his body, then he slid into it and let go. It was almost unbearable.

The next day, when Rob got home, Malcolm was there, sitting at the table in the kitchen, where the Sunday dinner should have been, his dirty wax jacket draped over the chair next to him. Cathy had made him some coffee, and they had obviously been sitting there for some time, over a plate of Digestives, having one of their heart to hearts. Rob could just imagine what they had been talking about.

'Hello, Rob.' Malcolm was putting on his only-trying-to-be-friendly voice. Cathy looked up at him but she didn't say anything. The television was playing in the other room; it was *EastEnders*. He hadn't realised it was so late. Through the wall, inside Malcolm's house, the dogs were barking, the same hard, urgent sound he'd heard all the way up the road, just as he almost always heard it, on his way home.

'Malcolm,' he said. 'Do you think your dogs are all right?' Malcolm smiled.

'Oh yeah,' he said innocently. 'They're fine.'

'They're making a bit of a racket,' Rob persisted.

'Are they?' Malcolm craned his head to listen, then gave Rob another tight little smile. 'I can't hear anything,' he said, reaching into his jacket and taking out his tin of rolling tobacco.

'I suppose,' Rob said, 'you're so used to the noise you can't even hear it anymore.'

Malcolm finished rolling his cigarette and licked the paper. His mouth was wet and red, and fine wisps of tobacco were stuck to his lips and tongue.

'I suppose,' he said, after a measured pause.

At this point Cathy, sensing danger, interrupted them. She had been keeping her head down – she had probably forgotten the time, too, or she would have got Malcolm out before Rob came home, so she could give him something to eat and get him off to the pub early as possible. She liked her Sunday nights in. All her favourite programmes would be on, and she'd get herself a bottle of wine, or some cider or something, and have what she called a quiet night in.

Now, all of a sudden, Rob wondered what she did when he was out. She said she watched television, but how was he to know whether that was the truth? Even if Malcolm really was her cousin, it didn't mean there was nothing going on. Besides, it had always been something of a mystery, this family connection with Malcolm. Rob recalled how, at the funeral, there was nobody else there who seemed to be connected to Malcolm, no mother, or sister, or whatever, and none of the other mourners seemed to pay much attention to him. Now Cathy looked up and gave him a nervous smile.

'I bought a picture,' she said. 'It's in the other room.'

'What?' Rob looked at her.

'I bought a picture. Yesterday. It was in the sale.'

'I heard you,' he said. 'What kind of picture?'

'A nice one,' she said. 'It's in the other room.'

'You said.' Rob looked at Malcolm, who sat back, his legs extended in front of him, under the kitchen table, flicking ash into the ashtray with tiny, annoying little flicks.

'I can take it back,' Cathy said. 'If you don't like it.'

Rob shook his head. Malcolm was making no move to go, there was no sign of anything to eat, and now she was telling him she'd bought some picture. Without another word, he turned on his heel and walked through to the other room. Malcolm's dogs had stopped barking next door, for the time being at least, but on the TV, Cathy Beale was having an argument with somebody; the picture was lying on the table and, beside it, there was a large claw hammer and a double size picture hook, still in its wrapper. Now Rob understood why Malcolm was there: Cathy must have asked him to come round with the hammer, since they didn't have one of their own, and he'd taken advantage of the opportunity to stop in for a coffee and a chat about cars. Rob looked at the picture. It was a colour photograph, in a black wood-effect frame, of two cuddly little black and white kittens, sitting nestled together and looking out at the camera, as if they were posing.

Rob couldn't imagine Malcolm with a ready supply of picture hooks, so it must have been Cathy who had bought the triangular, two-nail picture hook, for extra strength, even though the picture was too small to need it. It was just like her; for anything she wanted, she had to get the best. The more he looked at the picture, the more Rob wanted to laugh – the faces of the kittens were too intelligent, too alert, like the faces of human children, only cuter. It was ridiculous. He'd seen things like this in shops, usually in those discount places that opened for a couple of months, then closed down again: tightly packed, temporary-looking places with all the kinds of stuff nobody could ever want – out-of-date diaries, cheap toys, badly-made kitchen gadgets, those stripey black and orange fur cats for the inside of the car, with suction caps on their feet and Garfield faces – mixed up with bulk lots of washing soda and unbranded fabric conditioners, disposable razors and jumbo packs of dishcloths or scouring pads. He'd seen people in shops like these, wandering the aisles, picking over the goods, peering into nooks and crannies amongst the stacked picnic stuff and badly-stuffed panda bears, as if they thought they could find something worthwhile, something real amongst all the rubbish.

Rob walked back into the kitchen. Cathy was up and about now, standing at the sink, making some tea at last.

'Well,' she said, as he came back in. 'What do you think?'

'Fine.' Rob glanced at Malcolm. The thought crossed his mind that Cathy's so-called cousin had stayed around on purpose, just to see the look on Rob's face when he saw the picture. Though maybe there was another reason. There was always that. Come to think of it, Malcolm seemed to be around a lot, these days.

Cathy swung round, holding a potato in one hand and a scrubbing brush in the other. She always scrubbed the potatoes, never peeled them; she had read somewhere that the skins were the best things for you, that if you scraped them off, you were losing most of the goodness. The other thing she'd read was that you shouldn't cook them too soft, or all the vitamins would be lost. So there she would be, serving up lumpy potatoes with their skins still on, which Rob couldn't stand. He liked his potatoes white, the way potatoes should be, soft and white and smooth, with loads of butter mashed in.

'You like it?' Cathy looked pleased. 'It was in the sale. I thought it would go nice above the telly.'

'Fine,' Rob repeated. He turned to Malcolm. 'What do you think?'

Malcolm looked up and gave him a mock-quizzical look. 'How do you mean?'

'What do you think,' Rob repeated, quietly, in an even voice. 'Do you like the picture?'

'Oh yeah.' Malcolm turned and gave Cathy a little smile. 'It's very nice.'

'All right, then.' Rob looked at Cathy and then back at Malcolm. 'I'll put it up then.'

Nobody said anything. Cathy's smile had faded – she had only just realised how much he hated the picture, in spite of the fact that she should have known better than to even bring it in the house – but Malcolm just sat, head down, a slight smirk playing about his lips.

Rob went back to the other room. *EastEnders* was just finishing. He unwrapped the picture hook and set it down on the table, with the little round-headed nails set out so he could get to them easily. Somebody on the television started talking about a collie that had been rescued from neglect, and the steps that were being taken to lead it to a full recovery, and next door, as if on cue, Malcolm's dogs started barking. They were close to him, right on the other side of the wall, and they seemed to be barking directly at him, as if they could sense or smell him through the partition. Rob couldn't believe it. It was the middle of a Sunday afternoon, he was hungry, still dirty from having stayed up drinking and fucking half the night, and here he was, standing above the telly, hanging up a picture of some kittens. The other boys were probably down at the Mercy, on their third or fourth drink, wondering where he was. He couldn't believe it. He just could not believe it.

He turned off the television. Then, with his thumb and two fingers pressed against the picture hook, he took the hammer and tapped in the first nail, very gently – but the more careful he was, the more the wall seemed to give way, the nail slipping sideways, little crumbs of dampish plaster breaking loose and dropping on to the floor. The more he worked, the more he could feel the anger building inside him, not boiling, the way it usually did, but simmering, slowly, almost deliberately, coming to a head. He knew the wall was no good; he knew he shouldn't be trying to hammer in nails; he knew he should just take the picture out of its cheap frame and stick it to the wall with Blu-Tack. Finally, he gave up and put the hammer down on the table. For a moment, everything went quiet. He could almost feel Cathy and Malcolm in the next room, waiting, listening. The dogs were barking next door; the kittens were gazing out at him, from the safe confines of their fluffy, soft-focused world, the absurd, ridiculous emblems of something he couldn't have named, but loathed, all of a sudden, with a precise, logical, all-consuming hatred. He could feel Cathy and Malcolm, like spies, or lovers maybe, sitting in the kitchen, laughing at him, and something was breaking up inside his head, splintering into tiny pieces. Suddenly everything went silent and he knew – *he knew* – that Cathy and Malcolm had been there all day, probably having it off in his bed, while he'd been out, and now they were sitting in the kitchen, playing the innocent.

He walked back into the kitchen. The hammer was in his hand. He hadn't planned to do anything with it, he hadn't planned anything at all, he'd just wanted to tell them that he knew what they were up to, but when he saw Malcolm, sitting there, smirking, he just swung the hammer up and hit him, hard, right in the middle of his face. He felt something break there, and then he heard the chair fall, as Cathy stood up; he heard her screaming, just once, before he swung the hammer again, hitting Malcolm's forehead, and knocking him back, still in the chair, so that he went flying, spilling coffee and sugar and tobacco over the floor. It was amazing, the ease

171

of it. It wasn't really him doing it, or not exactly, it was just something that was happening. It was something that was happening, like a scene in a film, a film which he was watching, and he couldn't believe how beautiful, how very simple and easy it was. Malcolm didn't make a sound as he went down, but the cup clattered and slid along the floor with a clean, rattling noise. Rob turned to where Cathy was, as she was backing away, towards the door, then he stepped forward, swinging the hammer up as he went, and hit her on the side of the head with the first blow. He hit her again, twice, before she fell, the blood and stuff splashing on to his arm. She didn't cry out, the way people do in the films, she just gave a weird, disappointed-sounding groan, as she slumped to the floor. The dogs were going berserk next door, as if they knew something was happening, and then Rob was on the floor, half-kneeling between the two of them, bringing the hammer down on first one, then the other, smashing into the skulls and soft neck meat and shoulders over and over, till his arm was aching.

He didn't stop till he was too tired to go on. He hit one, then he hit the other; they kept moving around, trying to get up, but still neither made a sound, and he just sat there, hitting them every time they moved. He wasn't really thinking about it, he just felt pleasantly tired. Something came into his head: that advert on the television, the road safety one, where the boy comes flying across the back seat and hits his mother, and she is killed, her head crushed in by the force of the blow. It was as if he knew that woman, and he felt sorry for her, not just because of how she died, but because of the way she had lived, the decisions she had made, her sad, cheap wedding, all the ugly furniture and wallpaper and the curtains she had made from last season's fabric, the cheap, blotchy fabric she had bought reduced. He was covered in blood now. Malcolm had stopped moving, but Cathy's hand was still stretched out, and he could see the tension in it, the last thread of her life, running along the arm to the clasping fingertips. That was how the whole thing worked: he remembered it from school. The brain sends out a message, and the signal gets turned into tiny electrical impulses and rushes out along the nerves, like telegraph wires. That was Cathy's last message, that tension in her arm. It lasted a long time after he stopped hitting her, maybe a minute, maybe longer, then it faded away. It was just like they said: the two bodies, which had been Malcolm and Cathy just ten minutes before, were lying beside him now, completely still, like switched-off machines. The life was gone. Already, it was as if they had never existed.

When he woke, that Monday morning, Junior knew something had changed. He looked out of the window: it was a bright, clear day, and the thought passed through his mind – a fleeting image, no more – that he could leave, now, just like that. He could walk down on to the bypass and stick his thumb out and go, in just the clothes he was standing in, wherever the first car took him. He remembered the time when he was still young, in his teens maybe, hitching around the south of England, looking for work. He'd got a lift from a lorry on the road to Brighton, but the driver had turned off about halfway, and left him standing on a grass verge, just outside a village whose name he couldn't remember. He'd stuck out his thumb and waited; there had been quite a few cars, but they were mostly reps and types like that, and by the time it started raining, twenty minutes later, he was ready to give up. He could see straight down the main street of the village and there was no place to take cover, not even a shop doorway or a bus shelter. There was just a row of houses on both sides of the road and a church, set back a bit in its own gardens, at the far end. He reckoned it would probably be locked, but the church was his best chance, so he pulled his jacket up over his head and ran the full length of the street, up into the porch.

The church was called St Michael and all the Saints. He'd
stood in the porch a while, just waiting, watching the rain as it
got heavier and everything went dark. There was nobody
around – he'd noticed that, round about here, how it always
looked empty, whenever you were passing through, just
gardens and houses and the odd cat. By rights, he should have
been pissed off, standing there with no money, in wet clothes,
with no job and nowhere to go, but he wasn't, he just felt as if
nothing really mattered any more; and suddenly he realised he
was happy, even: happy like when you were a little kid, and
you were out for the day, away from everyone, with nobody
bothering you. After a while, the rain stopped, and the sun
came out. He could have gone back to the verge and started
hitching again, but there wasn't much traffic and what there
was, he knew, was no use to him. It was warm now, and the
surface of the road had begun to steam, wisps of vapour rising
in the hazy air all through the empty village. Birds were
singing in the hedges, the air smelled of new grass, and Junior
felt unaccountably happy, as if he had just come home, to the
place where he belonged.

When he went upstairs, he noticed that Estelle's door was
open – which was odd, since he usually closed it when he
came back from the pub. Though he couldn't remember if
he'd done it or not the previous night. He went in, still in his
pyjamas. Usually, when he stopped by her room, before he
went out, or when he came in, he would be fully-dressed,
clean-shaven, neat and tidy. It was a matter of principle,
somehow, so she would see that her behaviour wasn't
affecting him. But this time, he knew it would be different.
Estelle was lying in the usual place, in the middle of the bed,
but as soon as he saw her, he knew she was dead. He walked
around to the foot of the bed, so he could see her face. For

whatever reason, he didn't want to get too close. He wasn't sure what he was looking for – she could look like death-warmed-up at the best of times – but he knew, as soon as he saw her face, that she was gone. And he realised that the difference between death-warmed-up and really dead was huge. There was nothing that resembled death, not even remotely. When you see death, when you look at a dead person, whether that person is someone you care about or not, you know that death is final, no question. It was always a surprise to him, how priests and people could go on believing in an afterlife, when they dealt with dead people all the time.

He didn't feel anything. It was a matter of recognition, and that was all. He had been married to this woman for twenty-odd years and, for most of that time, she had given him no sign of real affection, never mind love. She had been cold, empty, almost absent, for years before she died. He wasn't thinking about sex – God knows he had never expected much from her on that score – it was just the small details of married life, or maybe of what he had imagined of married life, that were lacking. He had read in magazines, out at the hospital, or when he was waiting at the doctor's, how men were lacking, how they couldn't express their feelings, and all that, but Estelle had never given him a chance to express anything.

There were things he would have to arrange – he knew that. But, now, for this one morning, that would have to wait. Right now, he needed a drink, and, contrary to his usual habit, he went back to his own room, got dressed in the same clothes he had worn the day before, and headed down to the Perth Road, without even stopping for a bite of breakfast. It was ten fifteen. At the newsagent's he bought himself a packet of Marlboros and a couple of papers, then he crossed the road to the Mercy. The sky was brighter now, and the light was already streaming in through the high windows, making long, watery patterns on the floor and walls. He stood at the bar, the first customer, ordering a pint and a wee one. There was that smell he liked, the malt-smell of beer from somewhere in the cellar, the stored richness of it, a golden-brown scent touched with the darkness of wood. He ordered a pint of eighty and a Grouse, then sat at the table by the window, to be in the light and the warmth. It felt good, being there. Something had been removed, some vague pain in the middle of his chest, cut out, surgically removed and discarded, so he felt wide and light and empty, all of a sudden, and he remembered, again, that he could sit there for as long as he wanted, or he could go home, and it wouldn't matter, because Estelle wouldn't be there. He could sit all day, drinking and smoking, then he could go back to the still, silent house, and put Reba McIntyre or Trisha Yearwood on the CD, and play it as loud as he liked. For the first time in years, he was alone, and he was surprised at how glad he was.

Alone. He almost said it out loud. *Alone. Alone. Alone.* He bought himself another pint and a double Grouse and he sat there for another half-hour, in his usual chair, with the empty seats around him. It felt good. He was glad the other boys weren't there. It was his moment, a moment he'd been waiting for – he realised now – for as long as he could remember.

By the time Sconnie got there, the Mercy was full, but there was no sign of the other boys. Jo told him Junior had been in earlier, but he'd gone off after a couple of drinks, so Sconnie bought a pint and a nip and sat down at the usual table, next to a couple of women, who shot him a quick, hostile look, before resuming their conversation. Sconnie couldn't help noticing that they were both very ugly: the older one was thin and pinched-looking, with a faint greyish moustache on her upper lip, stained purple from her rum and black; the other woman had bluish, short-cropped hair, slicked back and shiny, as if she was wearing Brylcreem, or brilliantine, and she kept clearing her throat, holding her fist to her mouth and making soft coughing sounds. They had a large bag of crisps open on the table in front of them and every now and then they would dip in, picking up little handfuls of crumbs with their stubby, gloved fingers. They reminded him of crows at a road-kill, the way they worked at it, taking turns to alight upon the bag, or sip at their drinks.

'I can't remember when the funeral is,' the Brylcreem woman said, leaning in slightly, as if she wanted to prevent Sconnie from hearing her.

'Aye, well, look in the paper,' the other woman replied, handing over a copy of the *Advertiser*.

The Brylcreem woman looked dubious, but she opened the paper at the announcements page and studied it closely. It was obvious to Sconnie that she had difficulty reading. It was some time before she raised her head.

'It's tomorrow,' she said.

'Is it?' The woman with the moustache sounded surprised.

'Yes.' The Brylcreem woman shook her head. 'Which is a shame.'

'How do you mean?'

'Well. I was supposed to be going to go to Betty's.'

'You'll have to send a card, then,' the woman with the moustache replied, a little too sharply.

'Well. I'd like to go.'

The two women gazed at each other as if pondering some unfathomable mystery.

'Maybe I could slip out early,' the Brylcreem woman ventured.

'Aye. You could.'

'I could get a bus from the crematorium.'

The other woman nodded encouragingly. She seemed glad to have been of some assistance. There was a long pause as they sipped at their drinks, then the Brylcreem woman looked at her friend with some alarm. 'Is there a bus?' she asked.

Sconnie finished his drink and left. Even though he hadn't waited long, he was pretty sure the other boys weren't going to show. Besides, something about the women's conversation bothered him. It was a feeling he had, from time to time: a notion that, no matter who he was, no matter who he might have been, there would always be times when he would detest his own, whether they were women like that – women he had seen in pubs and cafes and queues all his life – or the boys he had met over the years, boys at work, boys from the pub,

179

talking about football or music or life as if what they were
saying actually mattered. That was the real reason, he knew,
for going off on the train, or catching buses out to nowhere,
to sit with the dead in the cemetery, listening to their
reassuring silence. Now, once again, he didn't want company.
Or if he did, it was the company of strangers; most of all, he
wanted to wake up in another town, to the noise and feel of a
strange city, early in the morning, when he was hung over and
nobody else was about. What he wanted – what was, for some
unknown reason, more important to him than anything else –
was the fleeting scent of a new place, a scent that had
something to do with bakeries and the fumes from passing
trucks, a sweetness touched with newsprint or cut grass, always
slightly different, and always the same. When you stopped to
think about it, when you forgot what you were supposed to
like and just paid attention to the things that really mattered, it
was always a surprise. That was what pleased him most about
going away – the fact that it was his choice; that nobody else
would have known what he was talking about if he had tried
to describe it to them. It was the same with women. What he
liked about women was their paraphernalia, their curlers and
brushes and little packs of things, their handbags full of lipstick
and paper hankies and odd ear-rings, the materials they used,
the colours and scents and textures of their lives. He liked the
way they talked about different shades, how they would say
things like cerise, or turquoise, or amber, when all he saw was
red, or green, or a kind of orangey-brown.

It was even the same with the drink. In practical terms, he
could see that his life had been a pure waste, what with
drinking and not looking after himself and spending all his
money at the pub. There had been a time, years ago – it was
painful to think how long it was – when he had been two

people: the sober one, and the one he would become when he'd taken a drink. For a while, he'd liked the sober one better; he was an easier man to get on with in the long run, no trouble, just a bit vague and ill-defined, like someone standing behind net curtains – a shape, a man with no distinguishing features. He was fascinated by that idea, always had been, and he would wonder, if he was ever found dead somewhere, lying in a ditch, or under a hedge, or huddled up on a piece of waste ground with an empty bottle by his side, what distinguishing features would they find, what tiny scars, what irregularities on the skin? Sober, he was nondescript, and he knew it; drunk, he became someone else: his mind shifted into a different gear and he felt a loose, dark, yet at the same time joyful energy, half-rage, half-exhilaration, rising in his throat from the pit of his stomach, and the pain in his chest would suddenly disappear. Other people didn't like this man – he wasn't as predictable, or as negligible, maybe – but Sconnie grew into him and thrived. After three or four pints he was already halfway there, sliding into an alchemical state, into a process of transmutation that allowed him to imagine anything was possible. He would have his doubts, sometimes, but it always worked; it had never gone away. He had never become a hardened drinker, like some of the other men, who drank all night then walked home, straight and steady, as if they hadn't touched a drop. He didn't see the point in that. Surely you drank to be drunk, to become something new. At one time, he had woken up in the morning wondering what he had done the night before, in an agony of shame and terror. Now, whenever he was sober, he was a man in waiting: the first drink was like a sacrament, a healing draught that released him from himself. The thought had passed through his mind, not once, but often, that it would kill him some day. Along the way, he'd been sick, he'd vomited and pissed blood, he'd woken up in places he didn't know. He could feel the decay in his body, the homoeopathic chemical signals of disease and death. But he didn't care. Something had ended in his mind: a line that had been playing out had stopped, all of a sudden, and he didn't know what to do next. It was like that feeling you got, when you woke up in the early morning, with the light just coming up at the window, and you thought nothing would ever happen again, just that moment of grey light and silence. At times like that, he thought, he could do anything that boy Serios had ever done. More, even. Once he had even got up and fetched the old Instamatic out of the drawer; then he'd put it out on the kitchen table, and he'd sat there, gazing into the lens, trying to think what image he would make on the film. He knew he could do it: it was just a case of choosing one thing, and focusing on it totally, with his entire mind. He knew how Serios did it: he knew that most of the time, people used about one tenth, one hundredth, of their mental faculties; it was just a question of getting in touch with the deep brain, and focusing it on the task at hand. You couldn't do that deliberately, the way you did a crossword or fixed a plug; you had to sweep away all the shit of everyday life and other people and things, before you could get in contact with your true powers. It had to be at moments like that, when you woke up and you didn't really know who you were, when you weren't encumbered with the limits and expectations of others.

At first he was going to make a box of matches appear, because that was something he'd read that Serios had done – but the image that came into his mind was a memory, a whole picture of a house and a garden, something much more complicated than anything Serios had ever achieved. Still, he didn't want to risk changing his mind, now that he had started, so he stayed with what he could see. And even though he'd known it was too rich, too elaborate a picture, he was almost convinced that it would appear on the film, or if not on this film, in front of him, then somewhere, clouding someone's holiday snaps. The scene that had come into his mind was partly invented, but it was also part of a memory, from a time years before, not long after he met Mary. He hadn't realised till then how important that moment had been, even though nothing had really happened, or at least, nothing he could have told to anyone else.

He'd been at a party, somewhere in Blackness. It was pretty boring, and he didn't know anybody, so he'd picked up a couple of cans and gone out in the garden. Soon as he'd lit a cigarette it had started to rain; just small, fine drops fuzzing his glasses and damping his skin, so he felt cool and fresh. He hadn't wanted to go back in – he hadn't even bothered to take shelter at first, but when it got heavier, he went and stood under a tree by the garden wall. He'd been standing there, with a can in one hand and the fag in the other, when a woman came out of nowhere, stepping into the square of light from the kitchen window. The moment he saw her, he'd been struck with the feeling that he knew her from somewhere, though he couldn't have said where. She was medium height, with long, blonde-brown hair; without really thinking much about it, he noticed she was pretty, beautiful even, maybe a couple years younger than him, in a loose blue top and jeans. She lifted her hand and pulled back her hair; by the light from the window, he could see the rain on her face. He knew then that he had never seen her before – or not in the real world anyhow. Maybe he had dreamed her. It was just like a dream, even then: him standing there, watching, and her just a couple of yards away, not knowing he was there. Maybe he moved then, or maybe she just became aware of his presence, the way you do sometimes, without knowing why, just feeling the tension of a live body, somewhere close, before you've even seen it. Or maybe she still hadn't realised he was there when she turned and saw him: it didn't really matter now, because the image was fixed in his head, forever, every detail inscribed on his memory like the details of a map: the back door, the light, the way she held her head, tilting it back slightly, the darkness in her eyes, the first flicker across her face of suspicion, then judgement, ending in a half-smile, as she decided he was all right. She walked across to where he was standing, and asked him for a cigarette. Her voice was soft and even, and he thought, from the look of her, and the sound of her voice, that she might be a student.

'Terrible party,' she said.

'Terrible.' He struck a match and cradled it in his hands; when he held it up so she could get a light, he felt her breath, warm and light, on the back of his hand. Then she took a drag and the cigarette end glowed red in the half-dark. She swayed away, flicking back her hair. He noticed her face was quite well-tanned, as if she had just been on holiday.

'Are you a friend of Bill's?' she asked him.

Sconnie shook his head.

The woman smiled.

'Thought not,' she said. 'I didn't think I'd seen you before.'

'No.' Sconnie looked at her. He didn't want her to think he'd gatecrashed the party, but he didn't want to lie to her either, for some reason.

'Is he a friend of yours?' he asked her, quietly.

The woman laughed.

'Yes,' she said. 'I suppose you could say that.'

She looked at him and waited, then she laughed again.
'You don't know whose party this is,' she said. 'Do you?'
'No.'
'In fact, you crashed it, right?'
'Yes.'
She laughed. 'Must be a disappointment,' she said.
'Not really.'
'Then you're easily pleased.'
'Not really.' Sconnie didn't take his eyes off her. He was thinking how it couldn't be disappointing, to have met her, to be standing there, in a dark garden, talking to her, as if someone had sealed them in a bubble of darkness and slowed time – and though he didn't say so, she must have known what was going through his mind, for she laughed again; then, giving an odd little shake of her head, she turned and walked away, back towards the house.

He hadn't ever seen her again. About two months later, he'd got married and then he got a better job, driving delivery vans. Mary got pregnant and they'd had Jamie and then Jamie had died. All that time – even when the boy was in the hospital, and he knew they couldn't do anything much for him – he had remembered the woman, whose name he didn't even know, and he felt vaguely guilty, as if he had committed some deliberate sin. Sometimes he would even dream about her. He knew, if he met her again, he wouldn't do anything. Probably she wouldn't even remember him. She was a different kind of person from him; somewhere, at the back of his mind, he knew he could never really get close to someone like her, no matter what happened.

That was the image he had wanted to materialise on the film and, for a while at least, he thought he had done it. He had concentrated really hard; he had seen every detail, every freckle on her face, the way her hair looked, damp with the rain. He had even been surprised when he got the film developed and nothing was there – or, rather, there was something, just a blur of yellow and reddish light, at the edge of the frame, but that could have just come from the light getting in, or a mistake when they were printing. Now, as he walked to the station, that image materialised again, and he caught himself thinking that this time, somewhere – in Sheffield, or Derby, or Leicester – he would meet her again, and she would know who he was, because she had been looking for him, in those intervening years.

The first train was crowded. Sconnie found himself sitting opposite an elderly couple, the woman neat and prim and watchful, knitting a sweater that nobody would want or ever wear, just for something to do; the man buried in his paper, with that cowed look on his face that Sconnie had seen in so many men, when they had been married a long time to women who watched them like hawks, waiting to pounce on any mistake or slovenly act, intent on coping, on keeping their houses and lives in order, at any cost. When he thought about it, now, he realised Mary would have been like that: what she wanted, more than anything, was order, an illusion of control that she no doubt saw as an illusion, even as she worked to maintain it. When Jamie had got sick, she had felt betrayed by something, some force in the world that also included her own husband, a force with which Sconnie had obviously collaborated because, if it hadn't been for him, there would have been no room for chance in her life, no space for the random. He'd realised that much later, after she had left; from the first moment, when the doctor told them that Jamie had cancer, she had blamed him. Everything he had ever done, every word he spoke, every move he made, was riddled with alien possibilities – and, strangely enough, it hadn't surprised him to know that she believed such things. He even half-believed it himself.

The couple opposite sat almost frozen, the woman with her knitting, the man with his paper, till they reached Kirkcaldy. They hadn't spoken a word till then, and Sconnie had been glad of the quiet. He sat by the window and watched as the countryside flashed by: fields, then rainy towns and ceme-teries, then the jagged, blue-brown coastline, with its rock falls and dry docks and wide, grey-to-silver sands. Then, at Kirkcaldy, a fat woman with a cat in a basket had fought her way down the aisle and plumped herself down in the seat next to the couple opposite. Almost immediately, the women were talking. It was obvious that they had never met before but, after some preliminary remarks about the weather, and the obligatory exchange of destinations, they moved on to their favourite subjects.

Illness.

Operations.

Disease.

Death.

Sconnie had seen it coming: the only surprise was how quickly they got started. Within five minutes, maybe even sooner, these two women, with no regard for the other people in the carriage, were discussing, with obvious relish, their friends' and families' kidney infections, bladder failures, lung shadows, heart bypasses. Almost as soon as they began, the old man closed his eyes and turned away, pretending to be asleep. Sconnie wondered how often he had sat through conversa-tions like this one, willing it to stop, bored out of his skull, and he felt a surge of pity, for this man and every other man like him, forced to dwell with, not mortality so much as squalor, every day of his life.

The two wifies were talking about the Kirkcaldy woman's son.

'He's in medical science—'

'Oh well,' the other one said, 'sometimes – well, if you're in that line, you'll, well, know what the result is going to be.'

'That's right.' The Kirkcaldy woman gave the other an almost satisfied look, a look of righteous justification. 'He knows just what to look out for.'

Sconnie turned back to the window. The rain was blowing hard, streaking the windows in long sideways lines, so hard he could barely see the waste ground beyond. He was waiting for when the train reached the bridge, skirting along the edge of the bay, past the docks and the headland of windblown gorse. He loved crossing the bridge. It reminded him of years ago, when he'd been working in England, only coming home every few months, when he could afford to.

'If you go to Harley Street they only treat you for one thing,' the Kirkcaldy woman said.

'Yes.'

'Whereas, if you go to the hospital, they treat you for everything.'

The train entered the rust-red cage of the bridge. Sconnie could see the muddy harbour of North Queensferry, the fish-coloured roofs, the off-white of the hotel. The rain was gentler now.

'Once or twice she phoned me herself.'

There were boats in the middle of the firth, moving slowly inland. Sconnie remembered the story of the whale that had somehow got lost up here, drifting off its normal route into the shallow water and becoming stranded on one of the bankies.

'She never took a right epileptic fit. But she was an epileptic.'

The people had called it Moby; they had tried to get it going again, encouraging it, crying over its dried-up body when it didn't make it away. Sconnie tried to imagine the confusion the animal must have felt, with all that alien noise around it, the boats and people and land sounds reverberating in its backbone and lungs. It must have hurt; it must have felt as if the world was ending. There had been an artist he'd read about once, who had walked for days to see a whale stranded on the beach, just so he could draw it. Sconnie remembered the book saying that this artist – he couldn't remember the man's name, but it was a long time ago, in the Middle Ages maybe, or just after, somewhere on the continent, in Germany, or Austria – this man had wanted to show things as they really were, that he couldn't trust somebody else's description of the whale, he had to see it with his own eyes. Sconnie had been impressed by that.

'Well, I mean,' the Kirkcaldy woman was saying, 'I had to go in for a cataract operation.'

'Oh, that's not so bad now.'

'No. I was only in for the day.' The woman checked to see that her cat was all right, then she took a flask from her bag and poured herself a cup of thick, milky tea. 'They told me to come in for ten o'clock. Which I was. Then the nurse came and said the doctor wouldn't be able to see me till after lunch.'

'Is that right?'

'So they did all the checks. They took my blood pressure four times. And four times it was always the same. And I think it was about half past twelve when they took me through.'

Sconnie wondered if the whale was dead when the man drew it. Or whether he watched it die, just to see what that was like. Maybe he made sketches of it, as it lay there in the sun, its life bleeding away. Sconnie thought of Johnny Cash. *I shot a man in Reno, Just to watch him die.* Those words had always bothered him.

'So it was a local anaesthetic you had.'

'Yes.' The Kirkcaldy woman nodded happily.

'I'm not sure I could have that.'

'Oh, it's not so bad. They put a cover right over your face. And he said you'll maybe see colours. Bright red, blue, that sort of thing. And he said if you want to move tell me and I'll stop what I'm doing. Or if you want to cough, just tell me.'

She paused for effect, and took a sip of tea.

'So I never moved.'

He had always felt uncomfortable about all that Johnny Cash stuff. As far as he could see, that wasn't what real country music was about. It was about roads and going away and not making any connection with anybody, not even to shoot them. Like Hank Williams. Or Dwight Yoakum.

'She says to me, do you want some lunch? And I said just some tea and a bit toast. So I sat a wee while then, and they brought the toast. And it was so dainty.'

Sconnie glanced across at the husband. He had woken up again, if he had ever been asleep, and sat listening politely. He looked old and frail and sapped. Sconnie could see that he was waiting for them to finish; there was a kind of mute appeal in his eyes, which his wife must have seen and ignored a thousand times.

'Put your head back, Jimmy,' she said, fussing. 'Have a rest.'

The other woman was still talking.

'So they just put in a needle . . .'

A tall man in a check shirt and baggy corduroy trousers walked by with a brown paper bag in his hand, and Sconnie caught a whiff of bacon and that sweet white bread they use for the baps, the way it smells when it comes out of a microwave.

'I had cystic – what's it called—'

Sconnie got up quickly and walked back towards the buffet car.

He had a couple of cans of eighty and swigged some of the Teachers from his jacket pocket, and felt much better. He didn't like it when the trains were crowded: it was better when the carriages were empty and you could sit there, staring out at the world going by, the trees and horses and graveyards sliding by in the rain or the wet sunshine, like an illusion, like some conjuring trick that he could almost see through, but not quite. Once, he'd been somewhere in Yorkshire – he never really did find out where it was – and he had travelled across a long stretch of spare, rain-darkened land. Sitting in the empty carriage, he had caught a glimpse through some trees of a huge fire, burning, it seemed, in the middle of nowhere, attended by no one. It was one of those moments he remembered – a moment that felt like a gift, or a signal, maybe, and he'd had a sudden premonition, simple and unemotional and in no way sentimental, of his own death, of the very moment at which he would die. For some reason, he'd been convinced that it would happen on a day just like this one: on some dull, rainy afternoon, a sudden quiet, then the rainfall noticeably ceasing at the window; a thick, nut-coloured skin forming over his coffee, then silence, absence, a last glimmer of blue before the dark. He would stop being: it was a thought that had occurred to him hundreds of times, probably, but it had never meant so much to him as then, and he had never found it so appealing, so very comforting. There was something he had read somewhere, about a man dying, in his garden, and the birds singing through and beyond his death, the shadows moving across the lawn – something like that. The fact of that death was all of a sudden real for him: something real, the one thing he couldn't ignore. Now, remembering that sensation, he felt uneasy, as if he had spilt salt, or stepped on a crack in the pavement. It was bad luck – not to have the thought in the first place, but to remember it.

The next train was almost empty. Sconnie got himself a couple of cans of export and found a seat in the one smoking carriage, beside a small, dark, squint-eyed woman with her cigarettes and lighter laid out neatly on the table in front of her. Sconnie asked for a light, and she handed the lighter to him with a soft, shy smile. She looked at his beer cans.

'I didn't know there was a buffet,' she said.

Sconnie nodded.

'It's just back there,' he said, pointing towards the front of the train.

'Oh.'

She smiled again then she turned and looked out the window.

'Do you want a beer?' Sconnie asked, pushing one of the cans towards her.

The woman looked at him. She had the kind of eyes that seem to be looking in two different directions at once, and he wasn't sure which eye was looking at him, or which one he should focus on.

'Thanks.'

They sat in silence for a moment, then the woman asked him where he had come from. Sconnie told her Dundee; then he asked where she was going. She was obviously waiting for this, because she immediately began talking in minute detail about the journey she was making, and all the other journeys she had made, over the past year and a half, saving up her money and her days off work, so she could travel all over the country, bit by bit, to Blackpool and Alton Towers and other places he'd never heard of. It was her hobby, she said, going to theme parks and funfairs. She would go for the whole day, sometimes two days in a row, so she could try all the rides, then she would write about them in a little book she kept, her own unique record of all the theme parks in Britain. At the moment, she could only afford to go to the British ones, she said, but what she really wanted was to get to EuroDisney in Paris, and some place in Belgium where they had amazing water rides. Eventually, when she had enough money and time, she would go to America – to Disneyland and Disney World – and that would be the best of all. She wouldn't be able to afford it for a while, she said, not on her wages, but eventually, with a little bit of effort and faith, it was bound to come. When Sconnie asked what her job was, she told him she worked in a Spar shop; then, before he could even think to ask, she told him she lived with her mother, to save money, because two could live cheaper than one, and her mum liked having her around the house. Sconnie listened as she talked and he felt a sudden rush of pity, for no good reason – pity and shame, because this woman, who must have been thirty or older, this woman who lived with her mother in some little flat, was making something, some fantasy, maybe, but something special, from the little she had. When the beer ran out, he asked her if she wanted another, but she insisted on buying him one and she went off down the carriage, swinging to and fro with the motion of the train, a woman on an adventure, a mission, full of secrets and somehow beautiful in ways he could never have explained to anyone else.

By the time he got off the train he was a little drunk. He'd left his travelling companion, who said her name was Judy, a little reluctantly; at one point he had even thought of asking if he could go with her, to wherever she was going, to eat ice-cream and walk around some theme park in the rain, but he'd realised that would have scared her, that she'd only been able to talk to him so easily because he was a passing stranger, someone she would never meet again. Now, all of a sudden, standing in the station forecourt at Sheffield, he felt lonely. He hadn't been there for a long time, and everything had changed – the station, the town, the walk to the centre – it was all different, even the old landmarks looked alien, surrounded by so much that was new. Finally, he found a pub that seemed familiar, and he walked in. It was early evening; he asked for a pint of Ward's and sat by the bar, listening to the radio that was playing through the back somewhere, and thinking about where he would go next.

These journeys had taken him to some strange places. Once he'd woken up, sobered by a sleep of minutes or hours – he couldn't tell – and he'd found himself sitting in a cinema. He had no knowledge of how he had come to be there: it was one of those places that used to show matinees when he was a boy – long Saturday afternoons of *Scaramouche* or *The Scarlet*

Pimpernel, films with Stewart Grainger and Peter Cushing – only now he realised it wasn't showing that kind of film any more. As things came into focus, he saw two slow bodies, scuffed-looking and really quite ugly, engaged in what must have passed for sex somewhere, their bodies constantly shifting, the man guiding the dark, oriental-looking woman into new positions every few minutes, her legs wrapped around him, or her face pressed down into the pillows so he could take her from behind, ambiguously, the camera moving in to show the details of hair and moisture, then cutting to the woman's face, as she twisted her mouth and screwed her eyes shut in a series of ecstatic and very obviously false climaxes. A moment later, they would be moving again, businesslike and matter of fact, the screaming orgasm of a moment before forgotten, as they searched for some new position, some further suggestion of impossible pleasure. Sconnie hadn't realised how explicit it would all be, how utterly lacking in mystery or beauty, and he sat watching, a little shocked – he'd never seen one of these films before – and dismayed, too, by the realisation that he had no memory of getting there, of buying a ticket and finding his way in the dark to his seat, while those massive grubby bodies tumbled and heaved on the screen above, their movements too practised, their absurd moans and cries building, again and again, towards the necessarily unachievable fulfilment. He'd heard films like this were boring – and it was true, they were boring, but there was also something ugly, almost vile, about the performance. At the same time – and he wasn't altogether sure that very ugliness didn't have something to do with it – he found, to his dismay, that he was unable to get up and leave, and he stayed where he was, his eyes fixed upon the screen, feverish and ashamed, but hopelessly aroused.

That had been one of the first times. Mary had gone; he had lost that sense of direction that had come from having her with him, watching and blaming but somehow guiding him, too, providing a map of how things ought to be. After she left, he didn't mourn – he knew that he had never really loved her – but he did feel lost and, at some point, he couldn't remember when, he had begun to fall, dropping quickly inside himself the way he had sometimes fallen in dreams, unable to tell the momentum of the fall from the gravity inherent in his own flesh. It wasn't a mental thing – he'd had hours, even days at a time, when he'd felt a thick, blind panic, and he had gone through it. No, it was something physical: a long, maybe unending fall along his spine that threatened, sometimes, to open him up and escape through his ribs, the way a bird flutters away from a loosened hand, the wings unfurling, the body a tossed pulse, willing to break or burst. He'd had that sensation for years – before Jamie died, before he'd been laid off, before anything. Maybe it had been there all the time, the one thing that had set him apart as a kid. Maybe other people could feel it too, a tension, a flicker that might have been visible all along, on the surface of his skin. It was the worst burden he could imagine, this sense of falling, because he knew what had caused it, and he knew, too, that there was nothing he could do. The problem, he knew, was pity: he felt sorry for Mary, even when she left him, just as he had felt sorry for his father; he felt sorry for Jamie, too, and for the boys at work, when they had been laid off and they had nowhere else to go. When he took drink, he felt sorry, not only for himself, but for everyone; he had vivid memories of his mother, of going with her on trips to Edinburgh – a wee boy in a blue anorak and a woman in an old raincoat wandering about, looking around the shops, admiring things they couldn't afford, pretending to the assistants that they were considering the clothes or books or furniture, his mother saying she would have to think and the assistants coldly polite, seeing through the whole act, and pitying them. Later they would find a bench in Princes Street Gardens and sit there eating the biscuits and the damp sandwiches his mother had made the night before. What had bothered him most was the way she always tried to make the best of things, wandering the streets or sitting out in a field somewhere, amongst the scrubby gorse bushes and sheep-shit, doling out Wagon Wheels and fish-paste sandwiches.

All of a sudden, the memory was unbearable. Sconnie felt he could hardly contain his anger, that his mother had been made to live like this, that millions of other women, just like her, were sitting in parks with their kids, eating sandwiches, lonely and unhappy in their damp clothes, wandering the streets and looking at things they could never afford to buy, things that other people could have whenever they wanted. He wanted to kill all those people. He wanted to kill the whole world.

Sconnie thought he had seen the girl before, but he didn't know where. It was in the third pub he had gone to, seven or eight drinks into the night; casually, and natural as you like, she had just walked up to his table and sat down; then she'd started asking him all kinds of questions, about who he was, and where he was from, and if he was on his own. Sconnie couldn't help noticing that she was pretty; she had a slender, well-formed figure, and long straight, light-brown hair − and there was something about her eyes, a light, a vividness, that fascinated him. Her body was amazing. She was wearing a tight sweater to accentuate her rounded breasts, and a short skirt, that made her legs look incredibly slender and long. Sconnie felt shy with her, but he didn't want her to go and they sat there for over an hour, drinking, talking rubbish, looking around at the other people in the pub, to see if anyone was watching. Sconnie didn't say much, the girl did all the talking. She had an amazing voice, sweet and haunting, almost too musical, even; he could have sat there and listened to her forever. He bought her a couple of drinks, though she didn't really seem that interested − then, out of the blue, she asked him if he needed a place to stay.

He'd had his doubts, but he had gone with her in the end. There was nothing he could have done to stop himself. Before they left they bought some more cigarettes and a carry-out, then they walked a mile or so through the dark streets to the girl's house. Sconnie reckoned she must be about twenty-two or three, maybe a little younger and, though he could hardly take his eyes off her, he didn't really know what he was doing, going back to a strange house with this beautiful, strange girl. He was in that stage of half-drunkenness where his mind kept flipping back and forth between logic and folly: one moment, he was deciding to make his excuses and get away from her, the next he was asking himself if maybe something wouldn't happen between them, in spite of the girl's age, some incredible moment of pleasure or understanding.

The girl wasn't helping, though. She was talking about some tribe she had read about, somewhere in South America, who made sacrifices to the sun god every so many years. The people would choose one man – someone upright and well-respected, a fitting messenger to carry their prayers to the other side – and they would treat him like a king for a day and a night. He could have anything he wanted – riches, power, the most beautiful woman in the tribe – and the people would revere him, as a god almost, until the time came to send him on his mission. Then, just before sunrise, they would give him a bowl of special drugs, made from the leaves of certain sacred trees, which he would drink, in preparation for his journey. Before long, his body would begin to grow cooler, he would become numb and very still, and he would feel nothing when the priests came to complete the ceremony. The girl smiled. The thought of that man, singled out for a grotesque death, seemed to please her.

'It must be amazing,' she said. 'To be the one who is chosen, the one man in the whole tribe who gets to speak directly to the god.'

'I'm not so sure,' Sconnie answered. 'Still – I suppose if you believe in something enough, it would probably be different. People like us can't really know what's going on in the mind of a person like that man.'

'Oh, I don't know,' the girl said. 'I think I can.'

Sconnie shook his head.

'I'm not so sure,' he said.

They had come to the place where the girl lived: a grey, narrow terraced house, with odd-looking brand-new replacement windows that looked completely out of place there, and a bright blue door. The girl rummaged in her bag for her key.

'Are you sure this is all right?' Sconnie asked her.

'Sure,' the girl said. 'Nobody else is home.'

'Oh.' Sconnie watched as she pulled things out of the bag then let them fall back in – a bottle of red pills, a packet of cigarettes, a pencil case.

'Who else lives here, then?' he asked her.

'Me,' she said, finally retrieving her keys. 'And two girls from college.'

'You go to college?' Sconnie asked.

'Yeah.' The girl opened the door and Sconnie realised then that he didn't know her name. He felt a bit more relaxed, though, knowing that she went to college. That would explain her interest in all that weird stuff about South American sun gods.

'What do you study?' he asked her, as she led him into the dark hallway. She groped her way forward a few steps, her hand flat against the wall, to find the light.

'English,' she said. The light went on and the girl led Sconnie into the front room.

'We can sit in here,' she said. 'It's nicer.'

The room was a tip. In one corner, there was a huge pile of

dirty laundry – socks, knickers, jeans, even shoes. There were piles of books and papers on every available surface, tins of paint, dirty bottles, an old iron kettle with a hole in the side, CDs scattered around the floor, an ashtray full of cigarette butts on the mantelpiece. In amongst all the dirty laundry, in a fancy red costume and a pointed hat, a wooden clown stood grinning at him, with a perplexed, almost embarrassed look on its face. There were dead or dying pot plants by the window; a guitar in the far corner; an empty bird cage; several rolls of toilet paper. In the midst of it all, an island of space amongst all the clutter, there was a small, threadbare two-seater sofa. The girl dropped into one place and slapped the other with her hand.

'Sit down,' she said.

Sconnie sat. Immediately he felt uncomfortable, out of place, perched there amongst the intimate paraphernalia of this young woman's life. It unsettled him, that he was next to her now, close enough to touch her: he could feel her body warmth, he could smell her skin. It was an effort to resist the desire to reach out and hold her.

'Do you want some music?' she asked.

Sconnie looked at her.

'Fine,' he said.

The girl grinned.

'What do you like?'

'Oh. Anything.' He had almost asked her for Trisha Yearwood, or Tammy Wynette, and he'd only just stopped himself in time. He couldn't tell if he was drunker than he had thought, or if it was just this girl who made him confused and a bit crazy. Right now, he couldn't get his mind straight.

She put on some music – something with strings and an odd, metallic-sounding piano, and no vocal – and they sat there, listening, not talking. At one point, Sconnie opened his carry-out, and the girl went to fetch glasses; later, she brought out the bottle of pills from her bag and they took some. As she handed them over to him, tipping them out of the bottle into her hand, then passing them to him, one by one, she said something he couldn't quite make out, something about how everything would change. Sconnie wasn't so sure about it, but when she took the first couple, he decided it was all right. For a while he sat there, waiting for something to happen, but they didn't seem to be having any effect on either of them, and he wondered if it was just some game she was playing, to test him out. He couldn't see why this girl was there with him: she was too beautiful, too young. He looked at her. The side of her face was glowing, she looked soft and lit up from within and, involuntarily, he lifted his hand, his finger extended, as if to touch her. At that very moment, the girl turned to him and smiled.

That was when it began. Her face began to cloud, as if he was seeing her through fog. When she spoke he could hear the words, but he couldn't make out what they meant and he realised he was floating, his mind turning to vapour, his body filling with a warm, sweet light, becoming weightless, empty, insubstantial. For a moment, before he slipped away alto-gether, he felt an urgent, desperate wish to know the girl's name and he tried to ask her, but for long moments his mind couldn't frame the question, and when he did speak his voice sounded distant and fuzzed, like some noise you might hear out in the woods, from far away, coming through leaves and rain, a bird-call, perhaps, though you wouldn't be completely sure, it could as easily have been a child's voice, or an animal, or something falling. Then he was losing consciousness – or rather, it was him that was falling, or not even him, just something, not a body any more, not a person, but a space, in which a fall was happening, though if anyone had asked him what it was, he wouldn't have been able to answer. The last thing he saw, or thought he saw, as the fall began, was the girl, slipping off her sweater and tossing it on to the floor and, as he slipped back and away, she moved over and lay down beside him, her hand on his face, warm and soft and perfect.

When he woke, the girl had gone. The music was still playing, but it was different now – a slow, mournful sound, like a long, empty passage, an endless dim tunnel of string sounds and muted piano. Sconnie tried to sit up, to look for the girl, but the effort was too much, and he remembered the pills she had given him. What was it she had said? If he took the pills, it would turn him into someone new – something like that – but all they had done was fuzz up his brain, so he could feel it, every inch, every fissure, inside the empty space of his skull. He tried to remember what they had looked like, but he couldn't picture them. His body felt weightless still, completely insubstantial, and he knew it would be a while before he could get control of himself and stand up. He felt a surge of fear then. Maybe the girl really was crazy. Maybe she was one of those women you read about, who want to get revenge on men and go around picking up strangers in pubs and poisoning them. He didn't think so, but you could never tell. People did strange things, sometimes.

He was drifting. At one moment, he was sure he remembered the tablets as blue and lozenge-shaped; then, a moment or minutes later, he could see them quite clearly in his mind's eye, four, or maybe six pink, round things, not even pink exactly, just off-white, like that toilet paper or paint you could get, with just a hint of rose in it. Then he remembered how large they had felt in his mouth, large and dry, like walnuts, when he'd tried to swallow, and he'd had to wash them down with something – whisky, he thought. They had been warm, he thought, from the girl's fingers. He moved his head to one side; then, minutes later, he tried to move again. As his eyes focused, he could see, by the pile of laundry on the far side of the room, the clown he had noticed earlier. It was still watching him, with the same puzzled, almost embarrassed smile on its face, and he thought, for a moment, that it really was alive, that it really was looking at him – alert, slightly scared, waiting for something to happen. Sconnie felt a sudden rush of fear, and he desperately wanted to know where the girl had gone. If there was danger, he thought, she would protect him. If he could only find her, everything would be all right again, the way it had been the night before, when he had looked into her eyes and he had seen himself, tiny, contained, perfected.

He made one last effort and managed to lift his head and shoulders off the sofa. What he really wanted, he knew, was to be on his feet, to be ready, to see things from what now seemed an impossible height. He felt the impulses moving along his body towards his feet – instructions, the way they told you the body worked in school, that little control box in the brain sending out its orders to the hands and feet and taste buds, exchanging communiqués like a general at HQ guiding the troops at the front. He felt the messages running out in waves of electrical impulses, and he waited for them to take effect, for his feet to swing down to the floor and push him upward, but nothing happened. For a moment, he thought he really was standing, then he heard a noise, a soft rustling behind him somewhere, and he realised he was still lying on the sofa. He realised that someone had taken off his shoes and loosened his belt. At the same time, the door creaked somewhere behind him, and he heard people moving, coming into the room, quickly, quietly.

For the first few seconds, he couldn't see them. He turned his head to look up, because he thought he could feel someone above him, leaning over, but there was nobody there. He knew it was more than one person -- two, maybe three, maybe more -- and it was this that alarmed him; this, and the fact of their silence, their quick scampering movements, like the movements of hunting animals, quick and precise and directed towards some end. He tried desperately now to sit up, but his legs were completely dead. Then he felt a warm, firm pressure on his arm and he saw the first boy, kneeling on the floor by the sofa, his face blurred and sticky-looking.

'It's all right. It's all right. It's all right.'

The voice came through a thick fog, and Sconnie thought he'd lost consciousness for a moment, that he was probably dreaming all this. Then he saw the second boy, standing above him, dressed entirely in black. He had dark hair and a very white face, and Sconnie realised he was wearing some kind of make-up, like that boy who used to be in the Alex Harvey Band, the one with the white face and a very red mouth, like a clown's.

'How are you doing?' the second boy asked him, with a smile.

Sconnie tried to raise himself up, but the first boy pushed him back down. To Sconnie, this pressure felt light, even as it held and controlled him, light and somehow just, like a bird coming to rest, something indisputably correct, almost immaculate – a gentle pressure, then a gradual, pleasant settling of weight.

'What did you say your name was?' The dark-haired boy asked, leaning over, grinning into Sconnie's face.

'Sconnie.'

The dark boy turned to the other one.

'Did you hear that, Paul? He says his name's Sconnie.' When they talked to one another, their voices sounded odd, like when a tape slows down, and the words come out too deep and slow and blurred.

'Yes, Tom, I did,' the other boy replied, with a smile. 'It's an odd name, isn't it?'

'It is,' said Tom. 'Very odd indeed.'

Sconnie laughed. He could see now that the boys really were clowns, with their white make-up and their funny slowed-down voices, even if their clothes weren't right. They kept coming into focus and fading again, as if he was watching them on a bad television set, and he looked around for the girl, with the vague notion that she could make sense of all this, that she would just adjust something and it would all come back into focus. When he couldn't see her, he lay back and closed his eyes again. All of a sudden, he wasn't worried any more. He felt so warm now, all he wanted to do was sleep.

The dark boy called Tom leaned in close to his face.

'Hey! Sconnie!' His voice was louder than before. Sconnie opened his eyes and tried hard to get him into focus.

'You're not going to sleep, are you?'

The boy called Paul was still on his knees by the sofa, one hand on Sconnie's arm, the other trailing, out of sight – holding something, Sconnie thought; and he felt again the vague, reluctant desire to pull himself up and see what it was. There had been something in the boy's voice – a faint note, the vaguest suggestion – that made him wonder what it was. Now Tom was leaning over him, and he could see the girl, standing by the door, an odd, questioning look on her face, as if she wasn't really sure what was going on. To Sconnie she looked very far away.

And then, suddenly, as if he were remembering something from years ago, he recalled what the girl had said, the night before – that story she had told him about the Brazilian tribe, and what they did to the chosen one. That was why she had undressed and lain down beside him – he could see it now, in her face – and these boys, who looked so much like clowns, were really the priests who would open his veins and draw out his soul, as an offering to some tawdry god they kept hidden somewhere, in this damp, chill room, amongst the debris and soiled laundry. He opened his mouth to shout – not for help, not so someone else might hear, but in protest at the stupidity of it all. But no sound came and the first boy, the one called Paul, quickly slapped his hand over Sconnie's face, as he raised the knife he had been hiding and, quickly, deftly, he made the first cut.

part two

argyll

The first evening, they found a track into the woods, just wide enough to take the car out of sight of the road, and started getting ready to camp out till bedtime. It was still just light, the time when the day animals started to find places to hide, and the night creatures came out to hunt, and they could hear noises through the trees, small shifts and rustling sounds amongst the undergrowth, or the odd bird call, far into the shadows, but there was nothing to suggest a human presence, and Alan felt they were as safe here as anywhere, probably safer. He wanted to toss a coin to see who would get to sleep in the car, but Rob said it was all right, he didn't mind sleeping on the ground – he'd done it often enough, he said, when he was younger. They debated a while about whether to make a fire – they'd stopped on the way to buy some food, some pot noodles and pies and a few tins of things, then, as an afterthought, Alan had picked up a bag of potatoes, and some apples, in those little pre-packed trays wrapped in cling film, and they'd got plenty of drink with the money Rob had taken from Malcolm's pockets. Alan thought they ought to wait, but Rob said he was hungry; he needed something hot if he was going to sleep out all night. They were sitting in the car, drinking the beer they had brought and passing a half-bottle of whisky back and forth, and Alan was beginning to feel a bit better about the whole thing when he remembered they didn't have a tin opener, or even anything to cook the stuff in, or water for the pot noodles, or anything like that.

'Maybe we should leave the car here,' he said. 'There's bound to be a pub or something, further down the road.'

'What for?' Rob's voice sounded a little slurry, and Alan realised he'd already had four cans and about half the whisky on any empty stomach. He remembered that time in the pub about a week ago, when Rob had almost passed out and he wondered again if maybe there was something seriously wrong with him.

'We don't have stuff to cook with,' he said, after a moment. 'We'll have to get it tomorrow.'

'What stuff?' Rob sounded belligerent now, as if he thought Alan was playing a joke on him.

'Pots. A tin opener. That kind of stuff.'

Rob snorted.

'Don't need it,' he said. He reached into his pocket and pulled out a knife. It was the kind of knife people have for fishing: a six-inch blade in a folding clasp, with a brown wooden handle. Rob opened it out and held it up to the light.

'We can use this,' he said, waving it back and forth so it caught the last of the daylight, like a character in a murder film, the crazy one, that you know from the start is going to cause trouble.

'Okay,' Alan answered, a little too quietly. 'What about pots?'

Rob turned suddenly, the knife still in his hand. Alan realised he was already half-cut.

'We can use the tins,' Rob said. 'We just need to get the tops off. And we can bake the potatoes in the fire. We used to do it all the time, when we were kids.'

'Okay.'

Alan had begun to feel uncomfortable; part of him wanted to just get up and go, to just leave Rob there for a while, to just get away from him, but he was scared to leave him alone for too long, in case he started thinking about driving again. On the way over, as they were passing the far end of Loch Earn, Rob had decided the road looked empty enough for him to have a go at driving – just for a while, to get a feel for it. He said he reckoned if Cathy could drive, it couldn't be that difficult, and he'd driven before, off the road, so what difference would it make, with these roads around here being so empty and quiet, he would just take it slow and get a feel for the steering. It had taken some work to make him see that the road was too narrow and winding for him to be practising his driving; even after he'd stopped going on about it, he'd sulked for the next twenty miles, till they stopped at the shops and he'd filled a couple of boxes with beer and whisky, and cigarettes for their camping expedition, while Alan went around with the basket, picking up food. Still, he didn't think Rob would get very far, even if he did have a go at driving the car: to get back to the road he'd have to reverse it up the sloping dirt track and, besides, he was probably ready to stay put, with the box of beer in the back seat of the car, and the whisky and plenty of fags to keep him going. The only thing was, Alan felt unhappy about the knife, and he wanted to get away for a while, till Rob calmed down a bit. He didn't mind letting him have all the beer, all the whisky even, if he thought it would keep him quiet. Later, when he had a bit of peace, he would have a good think. He had to clear his head, to try and figure out what they were going to do.

'Okay,' he said. 'If we're going to make a fire, we'll need some wood.' He took the keys out of the ignition casually, hoping Rob wouldn't notice, and fetched one of the boxes out of the back. It was already half-empty; Alan took out the remaining cans of beer, handed one to Rob, and left the others on the back seat.

'I'll fill this with twigs and stuff,' he said. 'I won't be long.'

Rob snapped his can open and took a long swig. He didn't say anything.

As soon as he was away from Rob, Alan felt better. He hadn't gone twenty paces when the darkness and the quiet began to get to him: he had grown up in places like these, in woods and open ground and wastelands at the edge of little towns, hiding in dens and hollows all summer long, shifting from boy to animal to hunter as the mood took him, becoming part of the bracken and the shadows between the trees, becoming a spy, trying to make himself invisible so he could stay wherever he liked, and never have to go home, or back to school, or become a man like his father. It wasn't that he'd been so unhappy at home, or no more or less unhappy than anyone else he knew, it was just that he'd known, deep-down, without even having to think about it, what his future would be – how he would become a man like his father, a man who would have to work, stuck in some pit or mill all day, or in some factory amongst the roaring and screaming of machines, then come home to a house that wasn't really his, an alien space that others had occupied all day and made their own, a place with secrets and special codes, fragments of mystery and magic that he wouldn't understand. He knew it would make him angry the way it had made his father angry – but it would make him sad, too, because he would have wanted more, just as his father did, and he wouldn't be able to have it. Being in the woods was the one thing he knew that took him away from all that – from that future of noise and invisibility and from the guilt he felt when his father came home, dirty and clumsy and bewildered, angry that the home his work was paying for didn't welcome him, or even give him any space that he didn't take for himself, almost by force.

It was also out in the woods where Alan had first discovered sex. He'd seen people kissing in the films, at Saturday matinees, where all the kids went, and you could sometimes get in with just a packet of tea, or the money you got from collecting empty bottles, but he'd always known that there was more to it than that, always known there was something they were keeping from him. He'd overheard things people had said, men and women when they were drunk, making jokes, and he'd guessed what people did with their bodies, what the parts were that went together, and the mechanics of it all, but he knew there was something beyond that too, and it was this, this mystery that had nothing to do with love scenes or jokes or people making babies, that he discovered in the woods, by accident, when he was invisible, moving slowly through the trees, silent and invisible as the wind, on a late summer's afternoon, as the light was just beginning to fade.

He had recognised the couple right away, though he was confused by seeing them together. The man was Jack Patterson. He worked at the pit, as an office person. Everybody said he could have done better, if he'd had a mind to, but he seemed happy enough. He was always joking with people, and whenever he went some place, into the paper shop or Reekie's, or wherever, people were always smiling to themselves by the time he left, or laughing at some remark he'd made. The woman was somebody he'd only seen a couple of times before, in church, or around the town. Her name was Carole; she had come from Australia to stay with the Pattersons, because Janet Patterson was supposed to be her auntie, though she wasn't really, she was just a friend of her mother's, somebody she hadn't seen for twenty years or more, since before Carole was even born. Carole was just visiting for a little while before she moved on to London – she had a job there and some friends to stay with; she had already travelled all over Europe, to France and Italy and even to a kibbutz in Israel, a place which was really called Palestine, or at least it was the place they showed as Palestine on all the school maps. Somebody had told him that it had changed, that it wasn't Palestine any more, it was Israel now, but he couldn't see how a country could just change like that, and become something completely different, from one day to the next. Carole said that, on the kibbutz, people had lived as one big family, and they shared everything. Nobody had any personal possessions, but they got free cigarettes – as much as they wanted – and nobody told anybody else what to do. People would do any kind of work that needed doing, and they worked really hard because the kibbutz belonged to all of them. Everyone took a part in bringing up the children, even the people who didn't have any of their own, so the kids didn't just have one mother and father, they had lots. That was what Carole had told everyone in Reekie's one day, when she was out shopping for her Auntie Janet. They had all wanted to know about Australia, but she'd told them about Venice and Paris and Israel instead, and some of them wondered if maybe Australia wasn't all it was cracked up to be, if she couldn't think of anything to say about it, and had to talk about all those other places.

Alan had just stepped out of the woods, at the edge of the clearing, when he saw them there, Carole and Jack Patterson together, with their arms around one another, kissing. He'd ducked back immediately and hunkered down amongst the bracken, not looking at them, as if he thought they would know he was there just because he was looking. When he looked up, spying through the gaps amongst the ferns, they were already sitting down, and Jack was touching Carole's leg, just above the knee, at the hem of her mini-skirt. They started to kiss again, and Jack's hand moved up, under the skirt, drawing it up so the tops of Carole's stockings showed. Alan could see that she wasn't wearing anything else, and he crept forward as quietly as he could, to try to get a closer look. For a moment, he was out in the open almost, only half-hidden, then he had ducked down and slithered forward, in amongst the bracken; by the time he looked up again, Carole was lying on her back, her knees up, her legs wide open, and Jack was lying on top of her, with his trousers pulled down to his feet, moving up and down and making small gasping noises. In some ways, it all happened in just the way he had always imagined it would; yet there was something missing, some mystery that had to do with the woman, which had been rendered invisible. At first he hadn't realised what that was, but later, when Jack rolled over and they both sat up, adjusting their clothes and turning away from one another, suddenly shy, he saw that the mystery had been stolen from him by Jack, by the very presence of the other man. What he wanted to see was Carole, alone, in some special attitude, like the women he'd seen in magazines, watchful, naked, waiting to be touched.

As soon as he had gathered enough wood for a small fire, enough to cook on, at least, he started back. When he got there, Rob was still sitting in the car. He had something wrapped around his hand – a piece of paper, or a tissue – Alan couldn't see what it was in the half-light; he was sitting in the passenger seat where Alan had left him, smoking a cigarette and staring into space.

'What is it?' Alan asked, as he came up alongside the car and set the box of twigs down on the ground. He could see there was a tin there, amongst the carpet of needles and fallen leaves, and the knife lay next to it. He turned and gave Rob a look. Rob took one last draw on the cigarette, then flicked it out of the window, past Alan's face, and into the dark undergrowth.

'It's nothing,' Rob said. 'I just cut my hand.'

He turned away and reached over into the back seat for another beer.

'It doesn't matter,' he said, as he balanced the can between his knees and pulled it open with his good hand. 'I'm not hungry now, anyway.'

The farmer woke early, as always. It was still only half-light outside, but he could hear birds, and he wanted to be up and about, working, doing things. His new wife lay asleep beside him, and he tried to be careful getting up, so as not to disturb her, but she woke just as he was about to slip out of the room, as if no amount of noise or movement could disturb her as much as his impending absence. As he opened the door – carefully, quietly – she sat up with a rapt look on her face, as if she had just been wakened from a vivid and beautiful dream. Looking at her, in the white shirt she wore to bed, the first light threading her butter-coloured hair, he was struck, once again, by how beautiful she was – or rather, by the idea of her beauty, an idea that had kept him going for some months now, through difficult times, when his sisters had first objected to, and then refused to attend the wedding. He couldn't understand it: there could be good reasons for not wanting someone you loved to marry, if it was the wrong person, if it was somebody you knew to be dishonest or faithless, but that wasn't true in this case. The only reason his sisters gave was that she was too old for him: eight years too old, in fact – the same age as they were. For weeks he had waited for them to relent and come to the wedding, but the more time passed, the more determined they became to oppose what they saw as a disastrous match. The farmer didn't mind for himself so much – he had become accustomed to his older sisters meddling in his affairs – but he did mind for his wife's sake.

'What is it?'

Her voice was soft, musical, a sound that belonged to this time of the morning.

'Nothing,' he said. 'I just want to get started. Go back to sleep.'

She sat upright a moment longer, gazing at him, as if she wanted to fix his image in her mind and carry it back to the dream she had been having. Then she lay down and, in a matter of seconds, went back to sleep.

In the kitchen, he fed the dog, then made himself a cup of tea. He didn't like to eat first thing in the morning; he enjoyed waiting a while, then coming in hungry, after a couple of hours of good work, with a pleasurable ache in his arms and back. It was something he had learned from his father, to get some good work in when it was first light, and so earn his breakfast. This morning, going out into the yard, he ran through the list he had built up in his mind of things to do, odd bits of maintenance, fixing and cleaning, the jobs he liked best, for some reason. Some people liked to start something new, they minded having to do the ordinary, everyday jobs; but that was what most of life was about, he thought, and if there was any grace in working, any sense of pride, it surely resided in this – in cleaning, keeping, maintaining, oiling, repairing. Now that he was married, he felt more keenly than ever how important it was to keep the place just right. At some level, deep in his being, he was glad of the opportunity his sisters had given him, by rejecting his new wife. It would be his task, his happiness, to make her happy. It would be his job, his only satisfaction, to defend her from the world, to make sure, day after day after day, that nothing would ever harm her.

Alan woke early. He'd slept badly, unused to the narrow back seat of the car; he'd been worrying, too, about Cathy, and Jennifer, and about what would happen to Rob when the police caught up with him. Because the police would catch up with him, for sure. When Rob had turned up the night before last, banging on the door and shouting for him to come, Alan had known it was something serious, but he wasn't even remotely prepared for what his friend had to tell him. He'd thought maybe Rob needed money, or he'd had a row with Cathy and done something stupid, but when Rob said he'd attacked that boy Malcolm with a hammer, and maybe he had even killed him, Alan's mind went blank. He'd been sitting there, thinking about Jennifer, and wondering if she would ever come and see him again, but now, he knew, he had to do something, to help Rob get himself sorted out at least, and maybe get him out of the country. Or maybe the two of them could go and find somewhere new and start again. It would be better for Alan, anyway, if he made himself scarce for a while: if he saw Jennifer again, he didn't know what he would say, or worse, what he might do. He wanted to touch her again so badly, it hurt him, in his stomach and chest, and at the back of his neck. He told Rob he would get the car out, and they would get away somewhere, to begin with at least, so the police wouldn't find him. Then he asked about Cathy.

Rob didn't answer.

'You'll have to let her know you're going,' Alan said. 'Does she know what's happened?'

Rob stared at him. He looked desperate.

'Rob?'

Rob shook his head.

'Malcolm's her cousin,' he said, looking away.

That was when Alan guessed. He hadn't asked any more questions, but he knew, whatever had happened, Cathy had been involved. The thought came to him that Rob could have killed them both – he was probably capable of that, when his temper was up. Because Alan had seen Rob's tempers. When he lost the heid, Rob had no sense of himself, he just saw red. Usually it was over something stupid, too. Some trivial little thing would get him started, and he wouldn't know when to stop. Still, Rob was his pal, and he had a duty to help him, any way he could. If you couldn't be responsible for your pals, who could you be responsible for?

So he'd got the car out and asked Rob where he wanted to go.

'Argyll.'

Alan shook his head.

'We should go somewhere else,' he said. 'Maybe out of the country.'

'No, Alan. The police will expect that.'

'How come?'

'They just will.'

'But if you get away now, before they put two and two together, you could be outside their jurisdiction.'

'No. I want to go to Argyll.'

'But why? Why Argyll?'

'Because. I like it.' Rob looked awkward, he didn't really have a reason for going there, it was probably just the first place he'd thought of.

'I went there once, on my holidays,' he added, at last. 'It was nice.'

So Alan had given in. They'd stopped off at the bank and Alan had drawn out two hundred, and Rob had some money in his pocket, money he'd taken off Malcolm – and then they'd set off for Argyll, early on the Monday morning, before much traffic was about. Alan didn't ask any more questions – he reckoned if Rob wanted to talk about it, he would – and most of the way they just drove along, looking at the scenery and listening to Alan's music tapes. It was weird, though, because a lot of the songs didn't sound right, they were all about love, or wanting to kill somebody, or revenge, or whatever, all dying and crying and lying songs, and Alan would wince, now and again, at the lyrics. Rob didn't seem to mind it though. It was like he'd done something terrible, but that was in the past, so he wasn't that bothered about it now – which wasn't a very nice idea, if you included Cathy in whatever it was he had done. The only thing to think about now was the present, and whatever consequences the past might bring, now, or in the immediate future. It wasn't a question of guilt, or regret. It was a question of trying to get away with what you had done.

Now, Alan got up and stepped out of the car. It was cold. He looked over to where Rob was lying. It seemed like he was still asleep, so Alan left him, and started gathering more wood to make another fire. As he wandered about under the trees, he realised how quiet it was, quieter now than it had been in the night, and he could feel the silence sinking into him, making him calm, detaching him, somehow, from the person he had been the day before, and the day before that. If you could stay out here just for a little while, he thought, you could become a different person. And wasn't that what everybody wanted to be, in the end: a different person, someone other than the body and the mind and the limited personality you received at birth, and had to carry throughout your life, till you laid it down in the grave? Didn't everybody want to be somebody else, deep down? To be who you really were, instead of the person everybody expected you to be? Maybe, if you stayed out here long enough, that could happen. Maybe that – and maybe more than that. Who knows?

'What if you had your life to live over again?'

They were sitting on the ground, on opposite sides of the fire, having a breakfast of pot noodles and bread. Rob was in a bad mood: he kept shaking his hand, and looking at it under the makeshift bandage that Alan had rigged up for him. It was obvious that he didn't want to be starting this conversation, but Alan wanted to make him talk. He wanted to know, not so much what had happened, as how Rob felt about it. He wanted to see, if not remorse, then at least regret.

'What about it?' Rob said.

'Well. Would you do it any different?'

Rob shook his head.

'I don't know. I suppose so.'

'What would you do?'

Rob shook his head.

'What's the point,' he said. He sounded almost sad – though he might just have been tired. 'It's no use thinking about stuff like that. You don't get your life to live over again, so what's the point talking about it?'

'Well – maybe you do. You don't know for sure.' Alan looked at him. 'Some people think you have more than one life. You get to live over and over again—'

'Till you get it right—'

'Or maybe there's an infinite number of possible worlds,' Alan continued, ignoring the interruption, 'each with one tiny difference from this one.'

Rob tossed his pot noodle into the weeds, pulled the half-empty bottle of Teacher's from his pocket and treated himself to a first-of-the-morning swig, then he lit a cigarette.

'I'll tell you one thing,' he said.

'What?'

'If I had my life to live over again, I wouldn't marry Cathy.' He laughed softly. 'That's one thing I wouldn't do again in any possible world.' He stood up and started walking away through the trees.

'Where are you going?' Alan called after him.

'Where do you think?'

Alone, Alan thought about his own life. If he could live it over again, he thought, he would change just one thing, one tiny detail, way back somewhere, something that seemed almost insignificant, but which would have a far-reaching effect on everything that happened later. For example, he would have lived in one place when he was a kid, instead of moving every couple of years. At the time, he hadn't thought he minded: it seemed an adventure, of sorts, to move from place to place, finding new short-cuts, learning different street names and landmarks, becoming accustomed to the smell of raw timber or pig-iron, to the noise of traffic or the wind, or people running in the dark outside his bedroom window. He had gone to five different schools before he was in seniors, and he'd learned to answer to five different nicknames, as if it was really him each time – when you move about, he soon realised, you do everything you can not to stand out, so people don't think you want to be different, or special. So by the time he left school, he had acquired a practised neutrality, a blankness that had become second nature to him. No one ever knew what he was thinking. Meeting him for the first time, people found him stupid, or foolish; he couldn't connect with the lives they had chosen to lead, or the questions they had decided were important. At the same time, they couldn't talk about anything that really mattered to him. So it appeared that he was always failing to connect with other people, and to them, it would often seem deliberate. When someone asked him where he came from, for instance, he had to stop and think: there were several possibilities, or there were none. When people asked that question, he realised that he couldn't say where he came from.

Yet he had a home, of sorts, a composite of different houses and gardens and people, a working assemblage of things he had chosen not to forget. Once, for example, they had stayed in a prefab, on the edge of Cowdenbeath, next to a poultry farm. His father had a job for the summer, working on building sites in Glenrothes and for a time, they were better off than usual, with new clothes, and food, and occasional trips to the pictures. Of course, it hadn't lasted long. Soon his dad had started betting again, and drinking all weekend; there were weeks when he didn't bring home his wage packet, and all they had to live on were the supplies of dried peas and tins that Alan's mother had accumulated for what she called 'emergencies'. Once or twice, in desperation, she had sent Alan to wait at the door of the Woodside Hotel, so people going in and out would see him, and maybe shame his father into going home. It was a risky strategy, of course, and she probably knew it. When he felt he'd been shown up in front of his pals, the old man would become enraged, and it didn't matter that, later, when the drama was over, he repented whatever it was he had done. It had been about this time that

Alan had taught himself – quite consciously, quite deliberately – to become indifferent to his father, and he had succeeded, over an alarmingly short span, in erasing him from his mind, like a street on a map that was no longer occupied, the houses long demolished, the factories closed, or like one of those signs you saw on shop walls, advertising some product that was no longer available, some brand of cigarettes, or cycle parts, or electrical goods that nobody used any more.

That year – less than a year, really – was the year of the egg farm. As his father disappeared from sight, Alan began spending all his time over there, helping Mr Robertson with his chores, going from coop to coop collecting eggs, or scattering feed, or standing over the incubator, waiting for a glimpse of the newly hatched birds. He liked the thought that these birds were born like that – his mother had told him, once, that he had been kept in an incubator, just after he was born, and it made him think he was half-bird, half-boy, born from an egg, connected to nothing but the smell of yolk and broken shell. The birds lived in wide runs – free-range, of course. When Mr Robertson let Alan into a run and he walked about, scattering the grain in all directions, they would rush up to him and cluster around his feet, till he felt they would absorb him, drawing him, ounce by ounce, from the gravity of his body, and making him one of their weightless flock. Most of all, he loved the smell of the place, that rich earth-scent, mingled with body warmth and old chicken lime. If he had a home anywhere, it would be in that smell. There had been times when he had even thought of it as a privilege: people who had fixed places to belong to didn't have the chance to invent their homes, whereas for him, it had always been a matter of choice.

Alan looked up. He could see Rob coming towards him

through the trees and, for the first time, he thought about Cathy. He could see her, all of a sudden, in his mind's eye, falling, over and over again; it was as if he had been there, as if he had seen it all on television, on the news, say. He studied his friend's face. Rob looked vacant, absent in an almost practised way: a man out for a walk in the woods, with nothing on his mind. Yet, when he saw Alan looking at him, his face changed and he stopped walking, just as he reached the remains of the previous night's fire.

'You know what?' he said. It was as if he had read Alan's mind. 'I've been thinking about what you said.'

He waited, as if he wanted leave to go on speaking. Alan nodded, just enough to show he was listening.

'I think it wouldn't have happened,' Rob said, 'if it hadn't been for the dogs.'

He kicked at the cinders and a cloud of grey ash rose around his legs.

'So if I could live my life over again,' he said, 'I would never have moved in there, next to the dogs.'

Alan didn't say anything. He couldn't tell, now, if Rob was serious, or if he was just talking for the sake of it. Rob shook his head, and kicked at the ashes again.

'It's amazing how things happen,' he said.

By the middle of the morning, Rob was fed up with being in the woods. They hadn't set out with any specific plan, but Alan was happy enough to just knock about in the open, the way he had always done when he was a kid, camping and making fires and living out of tins. On the other hand, he realised that they couldn't go on like that forever. So when Rob suggested they go down to the town, Alan agreed.

'But we'll leave the car here,' he said.

'What for?'

'Well, the police might be looking for it,' Alan said.

'The police will be looking for me,' Rob shot back. 'Not the car.'

'They might be,' Alan replied, not really sure why he wanted to leave the car behind. 'But they could still be looking for the car.'

Rob wasn't happy with the idea, but in the end they had walked. When they'd got to the top of the dirt road, Alan had glanced back at the car, locked and oddly still, parked in amongst trees – and he remembered seeing something like it in an old gangster film, though he wasn't sure which one. All he knew was, it was a colour film, though the colour seemed pale and washed out, as if the memory of what had happened in the story was already beginning to fade. It was a different kind of car in the film, of course, but there was something familiar in the scene, something that made him think of people on the run in America. It was some notion of early colour, of people sleeping in a car under the trees, the trees dripping dark water, the light finding them out like some detective, finding them and exposing them to the inevitable conclusion, the shots fired, the bodies lying amongst the larch litter, the faces blank, the bodies twisted into odd shapes.

It wasn't a bad day, not sunny exactly, but at least it wasn't raining. And when they'd got out of the woods, and down the road a bit, they had come to a turn, and suddenly it had all opened out before them: a wide stretch of water, with little wooded islands here and there, and low, brown hills rising up behind. Just below them, stretched out along a flat, glittering stretch of silt and mud, was the town: a row of houses and a church, a couple of pubs, some boats sitting in the water just offshore. That was what Alan liked about places like this, that it was all so clean and simple, no clutter, no mess. As they descended the long sloping road, the sun started to poke through the clouds, and Alan felt almost happy, at ease with himself and the world. He'd realised that before, and it had surprised him every time: things could be bad, you could have no sense of direction in your life generally, no prospects, no hope, even, but for moments, or even hours at a time, when the sun came out, or you found a good pub and went in and sat down, on your own at a table by the window, before the crowd got there, you could be happy. Not just happy, even; it was more than that, it was like a sense of the grace of things, a sense of being filled with joy.

The pub at the near end of town looked a bit swanky, more a hotel than a pub, and Alan hadn't wanted to go in. As soon as they had reached the town itself, as soon as they started walking on pavements, he'd become painfully aware of how out of place they were, two strange men who looked like they'd slept in the woods – which they had – walking into this neat, almost silent place, not sure of where they were going, with strange accents, strange clothes, probably strange looks on their faces. They'd walked the length of the town – it wasn't a town, though, more a village – to the other pub, and that had looked a bit more basic, a bit like the Mercy, if you could have lifted it off the Perth Road and set it down beside a sea loch, or whatever this water was that they could see through the window, as they sat, drinking the first real pint of the day, and a couple of whiskies. Rob lit a cigarette.

'This is more like it,' he said.

Alan wasn't so sure. The barman had given them a bit of a look, as if to say look what the cat's dragged in, but he hadn't said anything, he'd just poured the drinks and taken their money, his mind half on the radio that was playing through the back. Which was another thing, of course, Alan thought. Usually, in places like this, they would have a bit chat, try and find out where you were from, if you were on holiday, that kind of thing. But this boy hadn't said a word.

Still, after a couple more drinks, and with the sun coming out over the water, making it sparkle and glitter, he felt a bit better. The radio was still playing through the back, though it was quieter now; some people had come in, a couple of local boys sitting at the bar, making the odd crack to the barman, and there was an old couple on the other side of the room, sitting upright, all closed in and neat, still in their coats and hats, having lunch. Things were just getting good, when the boy at the bar rang a bell and called last orders.

Rob looked at Alan in disbelief.

'What?'

Alan looked around at the barman.

'Are you closing now?'

The barman nodded. 'That's right,' he said.

'What for?' Rob wanted to know. He couldn't get his head round this one, obviously.

'Because it's time,' the man answered, simply. 'We only stay open in the season,' he added, grudgingly.

'Oh.' Alan gave Rob a warning look, so he wouldn't say or do anything daft. 'When's the season?'

'That depends,' the barman said.

They were almost back at the car, just at the edge of the woods, when they met the tramp. Alan was carrying the box of carry-out and bits of food they'd picked up in the village, and it was getting heavy now. He would be glad to put it down, and let the tiredness seep out of his arms. He could do with a bath, too, he thought; a bath, or a swim, in some cool woodland pool or burn. All the way up the hill, he'd been wondering if, maybe later, or the next morning, he could go back down and find a quiet place and go for a swim in the loch. He could imagine the taste of the salt water, the feel of the weed on his skin, the crunch of sand under his feet.

As soon as he saw him, Alan knew the boy was off his head. He was standing in the middle of the track, halfway between them and the car, with a big walking stick in his hand, swaying back and forth like he was drunk. Only he wasn't. He was dressed in an old raincoat, tied around his waist with a bit string, and big heavy boots; his face was almost completely hidden by a thick, grey-white beard – all except for his eyes which, even at this distance, looked buggy and swollen, like the man was part-fish or something. Alan wondered if he'd found the car.

'What the fuck now,' Rob muttered, to himself mostly.

As they got closer, the man barred their way.

'Who are you?' He called out the words in a kind of singsong, his voice rising and falling as he spoke.

'None of your business,' Rob had answered immediately. 'Get out of the way, you stupid old bastard.'

'You can't come here,' the old man shouted, squaring up and stationing himself. 'You're not allowed here. This is private.'

'Aw, fuck off!' Rob shot Alan an incredulous look; still, Alan couldn't help noticing something in his face, a kind of grim pleasure, as if he was glad of what was about to happen.

'You fuck off!' the old boy shouted back. 'You fucking well get away from here. I'm telling you.' He was like a big kid now, and Alan couldn't help feeling sorry for him.

'Get out of our way, you old cunt,' Rob said, mock-wearily now.

The old man had raised his stick then. He was just a pathetic old man, no danger to anybody; he was obviously crazy, and he thought this bit of the woods was his special place, like a kid who had built a den in some hidden neuk, and didn't want anybody to find it. But Rob was ready for a fight; he was just as keen to start something as the old man was.

'All right. Put that down,' Rob shouted, suddenly loud in his turn. 'And get out of the fucking way.'

The old man made a decision, then. In his state of mind, he probably thought he was invincible; he was obviously far too out of it to know when to be scared. He took a couple of steps forward, jabbing and feinting with the walking stick, then he charged straight at Rob, the stick raised above his head. Alan stepped to one side, trying to balance the box of cans and bottles, as the man hurtled towards them; at the same time, Rob made his move – one step up and one to the side, so he

240

was close enough to the old man as he charged to trip him, putting him down on the ground with a neat turning movement. The old man went sprawling, the stick clattering against the ground and flying out of his hand. Which was too bad for him, Alan thought. He remembered the conversation he'd had with Rob once, about how you should always finish an opponent quickly, so he couldn't come back at you, ever. They'd been talking about some film where, as usual, the hero had beaten the bad guy fair and square, then let him go, showing mercy, the way heroes were supposed to. Rob had said that was stupid: the boy in the film was supposed to be an ex-soldier or something, which would have meant that he had enough training to know you immobilise your opponent, and you don't relax till he poses no further threat. Which was the only sensible thing to do. As far as Rob was concerned, films like that were a stupid lie: he'd seen boys get hurt for being like that, being all noble and shit, fighting Marquess of Queensberry, letting people walk away, turning their back on somebody who was dangerous. What you did was, if anybody came up against you, you fucked them, any way you could, and you didn't stop till it was over. Now, as the tramp rolled over and tried to get to his feet, Rob stepped up and put the boot in, the side of the head first, and then the arms, the ribs, the back. Alan moved in.

'Come on, Rob,' he said. 'Leave him.'

Rob gave the crazy old bastard a few more hard, decisive kicks. The old boy had been cursing when he got up, but now he was silent, curled up like a hedgehog almost, trying to defend himself.

'No,' Rob said. 'It's too late. He's seen us.'

'He's nobody,' Alan said. 'He's just a harmless old tramp.'

'Fuck off, Alan!'

Rob stood over the old man, watching him, breathing a little hard. He looked pale again, and Alan wondered if he was still sick. Maybe he'd been sick all the time. Maybe that was why he had done what he'd done, because he wasn't in his right mind.

'You go on,' Rob said then, 'and I'll get rid of this.'

Alan shook his head.

'No, Rob,' he said. 'It's not worth it.'

Rob sighed.

'He'll only go down into the town and tell people about us,' he said. 'And then where will we be?'

He gave Alan a sidelong look, to show he was decided, then he reached into his pocket and took out his knife.

'No, Rob,' Alan shouted. But it was already too late. Rob was dipping down, the knife in his hand, and Alan turned around quickly and started walking away, so he didn't have to see – or so he wouldn't be a part of it. He wouldn't have that blood on his hands, at least. There was a noise behind him, like a scuffle, then he heard a kind of half-shout, and more scuffling. Then it was still.

Rob caught up with him after a minute. The knife was gone out of his hands, and he looked the same as usual, except that he was breathing hard still, like a man who's run to catch a bus, or hurried up a flight of steps. That didn't stop him from taking his fags out and lighting up, though. And when they got back to base camp, he had hardly waited for Alan to put down the box before he fished out a can and sat, half-leaning on the car, pouring it down his neck. Alan noticed how much he was enjoying it, and the thought passed through his mind that Rob had really enjoyed the thing with the old man. There had been no need to get involved in the first place, and certainly no need to use the knife on him, but it was just in Rob's nature, to hit out and to hell with the consequences. It wasn't because he lost the heid so much, though. It was because he liked it, Alan thought. The thing was, he enjoyed hurting people. He'd probably enjoyed doing what he'd done to Malcolm. Maybe even to Cathy. He'd been storing it up for a long time, nurturing it, keeping his rage and hate alive till it was ready to blossom, and then he'd struck out, just like that. Without a second thought.

By eight o'clock, half the beer was gone. Alan was pretty tired now, and he felt a bit sick, maybe even a bit scared after what had happened with the old man earlier on. In the pub, he'd been watching Rob all the time, afraid he would do something stupid, and get them both in trouble. Which Alan probably was now, come to think of it, since he had driven Rob here, and helped him cover his tracks. Which made him an accomplice. Which meant he would probably go to prison too. He'd read about people being arrested as accomplice to murder, just for putting somebody up for the night, and giving him towels to wash the blood off his hands, or for burning some old clothes or bits of carpet, or dumping a car in a lake. What he had done was just as serious, and even if Rob hadn't told him about Malcolm, even though he still hadn't said anything about Cathy, that wouldn't make Alan innocent in the eyes of the law.

But tonight, after everything that happened, Rob wanted to sit up, and have a drink, and talk about how shitty the world was. He'd gone on about work for about an hour, then had a big go at women. Now it was men's turn. Meanwhile, he was putting away the beer and whisky like there was no tomorrow. Which, of course, there might not be.

'Look at men,' he was saying. 'I mean. Look at us. The whole world is about men being fucked up. I'm not talking feminism crap here, or anything like that. I'm talking about us. Look at us. I saw a sticker on somebody's car.' He held his hands up, framing the words on the sticker.

'Give It To Him TONIGHT
– Scottish Beef.'

Rob pulled another can off the six-pack, and tore the top off. 'Something like that. I mean – who's giving what to who? When was it ever a present that somebody was supposed to give you?'

Alan didn't say anything. When somebody was in this sort of mood, he thought, the best thing to do was just let him get on with it.

'See them boys we saw today? Down the pub?' Rob gave Alan an accusing look, as if he was somehow responsible for the existence of such people. 'They've all got homes, and wives and kids, and stuff they own, stuff they're paying for. If there was even a remote chance of going home and feeling they belonged there, they'd be out of there quick as anything. But they don't belong there. That's the wife's place, her and the kids. You can't go there unless you play by her rules.'

He snorted.

'Men are supposed to have the power. Have they fuck. What power do I have? What power do any of these boys have? They don't even know who they are, or where they come from.'

A pause. Alan glanced across at something that he'd almost seen, moving amongst the trees.

'And you know the worst thing?' Rob was spitting the words out now. 'The worst thing is, they don't even know how fucking miserable they are.'

He laughed.

'They think they're well off.'

He looked up.

'Are you listening? Or what?'

Alan nodded.

'Yeah,' he said. 'I know what you mean. Most men live lives of quiet desperation.'

'What?'

'Most men live lives of quiet desperation. Thoreau said that.'

'Oh.' Rob looked pissed off, like he'd just wasted his time for the last half-hour. 'And who the fuck is Thoreau?'

Alan had gone to bed early, leaving Rob there by the fire with the whisky and what was left of the beer. He'd had enough. He'd driven out here, to the middle of nowhere, to help Rob, but Rob didn't care about that. Alan had sat watching him all night, listening to the crap he was talking and watching the flickers of hate pass across his face, and he'd realised Rob really was sick. Sick in his body, and sick in his mind, but most of all, sick in his soul. People didn't believe in that kind of thing so much any more, but Alan knew there was something there, a soul, a spirit, something that made you who you were, something original, something that couldn't be changed by the ordinary events of a life. Rob was sick in his soul, and nothing else mattered. He was condemned, by some accident of biology, in the same way as somebody born blind, or without hands and feet, or with two heads, was condemned, only this was worse, because it was a sickness right at the core of his being. Rob was what people used to call a sinner – not just because he sinned, but because he wanted to sin.

But maybe they were both sinners. He thought about Jennifer and he wondered, for maybe the hundredth time that day, where she was at that moment: where she was, what she was doing, who she might have told about him, what she might have said. It had been stupid of him to run; she didn't hate him for what he had done, she didn't even know what he'd been thinking, she'd just reached out to somebody for a bit of human warmth. Probably she was unhappy at home – or at school maybe. She was too different, which was always a problem when you were a kid. As he lay there, thinking he would never get to sleep, he pictured her in his mind's eye: her face, her eyes, her mouth, her hair, her body. Then he was half-asleep, with the sounds of the woods all around him, moving in slowly to fill his mind; then he was dreaming, somewhere far away, in woods like this only different, looking for Jennifer.

Some time towards morning, he woke with a start and sat up in the still darkness. The fire had burnt down but it wasn't out and he could just see Rob's sleeping form on the far side. There was a glint of something shiny in the reddish glow of the fire; Alan realised it was the last whisky bottle, empty now, lying beside Rob's blanket. He must have sat up – no surprise – till all the whisky was gone; then he'd bedded down, still in his clothes, next to the fire. He'd probably had the last of the beer, too. Which, Alan realised, meant he would be dead drunk by now, and wouldn't get up in the morning at all, no matter what – or, if he did, he would be in a bad mood and no doubt about it, things would get nasty again. The thought passed through his mind again that it really wasn't worth it, all this looking after Rob and listening to him and trying to keep him happy. It was just too much trouble. The problem with Rob was, he would never be happy. He would always be looking for trouble, no matter where he was.

He wasn't conscious of making decisions, probably because he wasn't. Everything had been decided already, while he was sleeping, maybe, or during the farce of the previous day. Or maybe it had been decided from the first: maybe some things really were inevitable. People talked about free will, and about individual human beings having a choice of how to live their lives; they forgot that, as soon as you were born, things were starting to happen to you; things happened when you were small and powerless, and things went on happening, while you tried to cope as best you could. Your character was formed, right from the start, by forces beyond your control. Nobody really had much of a choice. You were who you were. Nobody could really blame anybody for anything. You just had to decide what was possible, and what wasn't.

He shifted forward into the passenger seat, fished the gun George had given him out of the glove compartment and put it into his pocket just in case. Rob didn't move when he switched on the engine; but to be safe, he left the lights off. If Rob woke and caught him, he could say he just had the engine on to get the heater going and get warm, and Rob wouldn't know any better. He left the choke out, so it would run warm quick, and he locked all the doors, so when he started away, Rob wouldn't be able to get in. He felt a bit bad about it, about leaving his pal out there in the woods, but an idea had formed in his head, some time while he'd been sleeping, that the best thing that could happen to Rob now was to be caught, or to go off and fend for himself for a while, and not have someone else to look after him, giving him money and driving him about all over the country, because he couldn't keep the heid. Alan's responsibility was to Jennifer now, he knew; the best thing he could do was to go back and fetch her, and take her away some place, and look after her. Because during the night, while he'd been dreaming, he'd made another decision; from now on, Jennifer would never be unhappy or lonely again, not if he had anything to do with it.

Rob woke as the car began to reverse up the track, but he

didn't move. He felt lost, feverish and too hot, his mouth dry, his body raked with shivers. He was sick, was what he was. He'd been sick for days. He could see that it was still dark, and he thought Alan must be going for a doctor, or why would he be driving away like that, in the middle of the night. Alan must have checked on him in the night and seen he was sick, and now he was going for help. Which was stupid, really, but Rob was beyond caring. At that moment, he couldn't have stood up, couldn't even have got out of the sleeping bag, no matter what was going on. There could be police swarming all over the woods, and he wouldn't be able to move.

As the car reversed on up the track, the wheels turning a little on the damp larch-litter, he lay as still as he could, to try and keep from shivering. Alan was going for help, and that was that; Rob had decided he would wait till help came, and they gave him something to take away the pain, to stop the fever, to rest his mind and then, when he felt better, he would decide what to do. The lights came on, and he looked out through the gap in the sleeping bag at the trees beyond. For a moment, he thought something was there, some figure of a deer or some other animal, standing amongst the trees, watchful, listening, but when his eyes adjusted to the light, there was nothing, just the space between the trees, then light, and then, when the light had gone, darkness.

As soon as he was out of the woods, Alan fished out a tape and slid it into the cassette player. It was a copy he had made of the Heather Myles album, *Untamed*; and he drove off down the road, past the village, past the haze of the loch, past the woods on the far side, listening to 'Indigo Moon', 'Until I Couldn't Have You', 'It Ain't Over', 'Coming Back To Me', 'And It Hurts' – beautiful songs about love and roads and about doing what you had to do, because you had no choice. Day was just breaking, there was nobody about, and he wondered why he couldn't always live like this, driving in the grey light, with Heather's voice, so close to him, like it was in his own soul, in his own heart. He remembered something Sconnie had said, how these singers, singers like Heather Myles and Trisha Yearwood and Reba and the others, had something special in their voices, something redemptive. If you listened to them every day, he'd said, you'd know what to do in your life, no matter what happened, and when you made mistakes, you wouldn't regret it, you'd know what you'd done was the right thing to do, even if it got you into trouble. Now he knew that the right thing to do was to go back and get Jennifer and take her away with him. If he explained to her she would understand how he was, and they would go somewhere where nobody knew them, and get jobs and save a bit of money.

250

Then they would go to America and drive all the way across on Highway 50, starting from the east coast and ending up in California, travelling across the country, hardly seeing a big city, just passing through the real land. It wouldn't last forever, but then, nothing does. The main thing was, they would be alive for a while, on their own terms, and that was the best you could ask for.

It was light now: that moment when it was suddenly day-time – it was never really as gradual as it ought to have been, considering the dawn, and the way it always promised to come slowly, the light seeping in through trees, or across water, or the sun rising in a gold-red glow, soft and molten at first, then harder and cooler, behind a car park or a row of houses. It always promised to come slowly yet, whether it really happened that way, or whether it had something to do with attention, there would be a moment when it was suddenly day, sometimes before the sun had fully risen, sometimes after but, curiously enough, it was never the same moment from one day to the next. It was like that game people played, where you spilled sand on to some flat surface; at one point it's just grains of sand, and the next, it's a pile of sand – only you never knew where it began, you never knew which grain changed it into an organised pile, instead of just some sand on a table. Or it was like when you were lying in bed, trying to get to sleep, and the last thought you'd have, or the last that you could remember the next morning, was the absolute conviction that you weren't tired, that you'd never get to sleep, no matter how hard you tried. That was the best thing about life – how one thing, one state, one impression, changed into another, and those changes were happening all the time, but mostly, they were going unnoticed, from all the other distractions and business and noise that went on. If people could only get the chance to stop and listen and watch for those tiny, subtle changes, everything would be much better; they would see how rich life was, and how much better it could be. That was what Alan thought, anyway.

When the car came off the road, he had no idea why it was happening. He had reached the foot of a steep brae, where the woods met the loch, and the road was turning, dipping and then coming up again, and he had been fine, alert, awake, no trace of the drink in his body. Then, suddenly, he'd lost control and he was swerving across the road, towards the trees, trying to steer, trying to brake, and feeling nothing – no response, no control. There was a moment, then, when he could see it all; he could see that there was going to be an accident, but he felt safe, he felt guarded somehow, and he knew nothing bad would happen. He could see everything, but it wasn't slow motion, the way people said it sometimes was when accidents happened. Everything was happening in real-time around him – it was just that his awareness seemed faster now, more awake, more alert to detail. He saw the tree coming, flaring out of the half-light to meet him, and he thought he should have been able to do something, to pull away at the last minute – but he didn't; almost wilfully, he sat frozen behind the wheel and let it all go. It was as if something had been planned and no matter what he did, nothing could change that plan. He knew, still, that he was safe from all harm. There was a sudden, vivid light, an astonishing whiteness, then everything was just as it had been: car, tree, grass, ferns, rocks. He pushed the door open and slid out on to the damp grass. It felt to him now as if all of this had been rehearsed, many times before, and he was following a deeply

253

engrained pattern, each movement prearranged, each thought preordained. The car looked useless, all of a sudden, as if it had never been a machine at all, as if it had always been destined to be wreckage. It was only now that he heard, in memory, the noise of the impact: impossibly loud and quite beautiful, like a vivid segment of some bizarre music. He was struck again by the idea that nothing mattered: not his life, not his memory, nor the things he had done. All those wasted months that he'd sat in the pub, poisoning himself systematically with the drink. All those afternoons and early evenings, hanging around in the close, half-cut, waiting for Jennifer. All the years of his childhood, his dad hammering him so he would do better, his mother pleading and crying, while something had just hardened in his mind, the way the soft growth of a hedging tree encloses and hardens around a strand of barbed wire. All the bad mornings, slipping into the half-light of madness. It didn't matter now – it never had, really – because he didn't matter, he could be changed, he could wake up, any day, any morning, and become someone else, if he chose to do it. That was the other side of the predestination thing: there was another person, his real self, waiting to be assumed, waiting to come true, if he only recognised it. As soon as he did, the wheels would be set in motion, and nothing would be able to halt the process. It was all a game – and it was life itself that mattered, the fact of it, the game it was playing with itself, that had nothing to do with him, or with any other single individual. You just had to notice that game and everything would be different. You could become anyone, do anything, go anywhere. He was surprised to realise that he had always known this.

The farmer walked to the middle of the slope, where it evened out into a slight ridge, before it dropped again, down to the road. He had come out early, with his gun, to see if he could pick up a couple of rabbits for the pot, and he'd ended up going for a walk in the woods, just to enjoy the morning light and the cool, sweet air you always got in the woods, at that time of day. There was a gap in the trees below, and he could see the loch there, about eight hundred yards away, the low sunlight playing across the surface, making a soft, glittering mirror of the still water. There had been a noise, a loud crash, somewhere close, just off to his right, and he knew exactly what it was. Someone had come off that corner, just below, where the road twisted down and in, away from the water – someone who had been driving too fast, or not paying enough attention, half-asleep probably, this early in the day. Accidents happened there all the time: there had been a girl killed, just last year, when her car came off the road and hit a tree, late at night, when she was on her way home from a party. She had been on her own, for some reason, though she had gone out with friends to begin with – or maybe it was her boyfriend, he couldn't remember the details exactly. People had said she was drunk, but it wasn't so, she'd had a few glasses of wine, earlier in the evening, but she'd been more or less sober, they thought, when she set out for home. She had just come off at that corner, not paying enough attention, and she'd run into the woods. The car had travelled quite far, after she lost control and, whether it was because she wasn't visible from the road, or because there hadn't been anybody else on the road that night, the girl had been lying there for hours, trapped in the wreckage, till just after dawn. So when they finally did find her, she was dead. The farmer hated the thought of that more than anything: to know where you were and what was happening, and not be able to do anything, to be trapped and helpless, and to have to wait, while the life seeped out of you. It was like that story he'd heard on the news, just that morning, about the boy in America who had gone around his school with a hand-gun, shooting other kids at random, walking around and firing and then reloading when the gun was empty – he'd even brought a rucksack full of ammunition and a spare gun, and worn it on his back, like he was out on a hill-walk or a picnic or something – completely insane and yet totally efficient, almost rational, even. What it must have been like for those others, helpless and trapped in their classrooms, or sitting in the school canteen, watching their friends die – in familiar places, places where they had imagined they would be safe. Like Dunblane. Or Hillsborough. Ordinary places, ordinary lives, and then suddenly everything turned into a nightmare. But then, the worst things happened in the most ordinary surroundings: accidents in the home, accidents on the road, accidents at work, happening to ordinary people with wrist-watches and memories and underwear. People like him.

He thought the noise had come from the right, just below – which would make sense, if the crash had been on that tight little corner – and he started walking diagonally across the slope, holding the gun carefully out and away, just in case. He was used to guns, like he was used to chainsaws, or tractor machinery, but that was what you always noticed about people who had accidents – they were the ones who were used to what they were doing, and they got careless, they didn't pay attention. There had been this friend of his dad's one time, who had come out to clear away some trees and scrub on the edge of his dad's bit ground, and he'd cut into this tree trunk – no big deal, standard stuff, except that there had been something in the tree, something embedded in the wood, and the chainsaw had come back on him; it had opened his neck up and he had lain there, bleeding to death, while his mates tried to do what they could. It was all over in a matter of minutes. He hadn't been wearing a helmet, or a face guard, or any safety stuff. It was just a routine job, and he knew what he was doing – he'd been doing this kind of work since he was a kid. That was what happened, if you didn't remember the risks; life was a series of infinite possibilities, some of them bad, some good, and you had to prepare yourself for every eventuality. There were no guarantees, of course, you could be careful as anything, and something bad could still happen – still, there was no sense inviting the devil to sit down at your table, as his dad always used to say. The thing about accidents was, they were almost always banal and avoidable, when they did happen. That was what really bothered him – that, and the fact that, once something had happened, you couldn't go back. It was irreversible.

He saw the man before he saw the car and he called out, to ask if he was all right. The man was standing near the road, holding something; he didn't look too badly hurt, but he must have been dazed, or in a state of shock, because he didn't seem to hear, or maybe he had heard, and was ignoring him – and then the farmer had seen what was in the man's hand. It was a pistol, a hand-gun, probably just like the one that boy had used in America the day before, a small gun, neat and clean and efficient – and now the man was turning, raising his arm, the arm with the gun, bringing it round to take aim. The farmer saw his face – the face of a madman, his eyes staring, his lips moving slightly, like somebody talking to himself. The hand was moving slowly, but it was moving upwards, coming up to take aim, the man saying something, but quietly, to himself – to himself or to one of the voices in his head, maybe the voice of the devil who controlled people like that, telling them what to do, explaining the world to them in a new, insane light, a voice from hell, with its own inner logic, its own morality, its own beauty, almost. The farmer raised his own gun then, and fired, quickly, without thinking, just to stop that movement, to stop the gun hand rising. The man looked surprised then, and he staggered back, almost falling but somehow managing to stay on his feet. His movements were jerky and disjointed, like the movements of a puppet, but he stayed up, miraculously; a moment later he had dropped the gun and he was turning, walking towards the road in short, slow steps. The farmer stayed where he was. He could see the gun on the ground, where the man had dropped it; he was safe, unharmed, and suddenly that was a surprise, because the idea had passed through his mind that he would be a victim, that no matter what he did, the man would shoot back at him, and he would be left there, by the side of the road, with a complete stranger, in his own blood, and his wife back home, sitting in the kitchen, having breakfast, or reading a magazine, fading away from him, and not even knowing it.

After a long time, Alan reached the water. A moment ago, it had been moving, the waves greying and darkening as they turned on the shore, but now it was still, calm, almost glassy in the morning sunlight. He walked down to the edge of the water and stood with his back to the woods, looking out at that space above the water where the sky began. The morning breeze was blowing almost straight into his face; he could feel the salt spray clinging to his skin and hair, and he remembered that phrase he had heard in school – something about a sea change, how everything that was alive would be changed by the sea, renewed, redeemed, by the taste of salt and the cold water. He'd had this moment before, this sense of a life that was waiting to touch him, not just at the surface of his skin, but deeper, as deep and as far as the bone, as far as whatever it was the soul might be, buried in its house of flesh. Whatever it was, this life had nothing to do with the god he had learned about in school, or the god he had prayed to, sometimes, in moments of panic or despair. It had nothing to do with Jesus, or the Holy Ghost. You could say it was something cold and impersonal, yet even that wasn't quite right, because cold could mean hard or cruel, and impersonal could mean indifference, and even they were feelings, human qualities that you could describe or name, whereas that life, the life that belonged most completely to the sea, was nothing you could talk about at all. It was itself, and it was beyond telling.

He remembered the time he had been staying with his auntie, down in Anstruther. His mum had just gone into the hospital again, and his dad had sent him over there, to give them both a bit of a rest from each other, as he put it. It was early April, but the weather was bad for the time of year: it had been a mild winter, and now all hell was breaking loose: howling winds, sidewise rain flying down the streets, people bent double, trying to get home before the wind blew them away. As soon as you stepped outside, it hit you: the rain and spray were like tiny, freezing pellets on your face and hands, the wind made you stagger and reel like a drunk, and after a few minutes you would be chilled to the bone. It went on like that for days, and what made things worse was, it was the school holidays, so he had nowhere to go except out into the rain, or upstairs, in his narrow little room, high up in the roof of the house, where he could see the Isle of May across the water, and the waves pouring over the harbour bar, huge white walls of water rising twenty feet into the air then breaking up and vanishing, leaving behind a visible absence, like the space that remains when a tree is felled: a specific gap, something unto itself.

Alan thought the storm was the most beautiful thing he had ever seen. He wondered why nobody else seemed to appreciate it, but whenever he went to the shops with his auntie – who insisted on using her umbrella, though it twisted and turned inside out and every which way, making her stop every few yards to straighten it out – whenever they went into a shop, the people would be standing in little huddles, dripping water and complaining, in that grim, satisfied way they had, about the rain and the wind, and the damage it could do if things got worse. They had a kind of faith in things getting worse, or maybe they felt if they talked about it enough, the worse wouldn't happen but, as far as Alan was concerned, there was nothing he could think of that was better than to be out in it, and he would search for excuses to leave the house, saying he wouldn't be long, and wrapping up well to run little errands or to go down to the harbour and watch the big waves crashing over the wall.

One morning, he took the little camera his dad had given him, an old Voigtlander 35 mm he'd had for years that seemed more object than machine, something to be looked at for its own sake, rather than used, and he decided to take some photographs of the sea. With his pocket money and some of the other money he'd been given, he'd saved enough to buy a roll of film – whenever he was farmed out to other people, when his mother was ill, and his dad wanted the house to himself, he was always given more, odd sums of money and little, spontaneous presents – and he went out into the storm with the camera under his coat so he could get a picture of the waves. He wasn't quite sure what he wanted. He'd pretended it was for a school project, but it wasn't really; it was something for himself, a moment he wanted to experience and fix: some fragment of grace, some image he would recognise if he managed to capture it on the film, something that would make sense of everything, of all life, all time and space.

He knew people thought he was unhappy when they sent him away from home, and he had to live in a spare room somewhere, with relatives or family friends, but he wasn't really. He traded on that sometimes, without really knowing what he was doing, but he didn't really mind where he lived. The people he lived with were virtual strangers, but they were just as interesting as his parents, or the other people he was used to seeing: in fact, whenever he stayed away from home, he felt oddly liberated, detached from the concerns of others, free to concentrate on the things that really mattered – things like the storm, or the way one bird would build its nest on the ground, while another built it halfway up a may bush, in amongst all the thorns, or the way people acted when they didn't know they were being watched. It didn't bother him, staying in strange houses, mainly because they *were* strange: people who only seemed familiar and unmysterious when they came to visit were entirely different when they were at home, in their own houses. For one thing, they paid him less attention: they got on with their lives, and that left gaps here and there, spaces where he could slip through unnoticed. The other thing was, they were much less alert at home than they were outside their own houses, so he could watch them easily, without undue interruption, sometimes for hours at a time. He could see their bonds and their sins, the promises they made to themselves and to one another, the small redemptions they hoped for, the moments of revelation or realisation they most feared, and he would go for days thinking about them, figuring out the gestures they might have offered one another, the moments of kindness or understanding of which they could have been capable, had things been different. Most of the time, he thought, they were just too involved, too close to one another. Or they had learned to rely on so little, like those birds with their nests, unable to see any other way to take things.

He knew they thought he was unhappy, and he didn't do or say anything much to make them think otherwise, but the truth was, that day, as he walked about in the freezing rain, far from home, he was as happy as he could imagine being. From the outside, no doubt, people would have seen a lonely boy, a bit shy, a little bit withdrawn, even, who missed his mum and his friends, but the fact of the matter was, he was completely engrossed in what he was doing, and if someone had said he could stay that way forever, he would almost certainly have agreed without a second thought. By the time he had run through the whole roll of film – thirty-six exposures – his fingers were red and completely numb, and his jacket was sopping wet. He'd had a hard time taking any pictures at all: it was a dull day and whenever he pointed the camera at the water, the lens quickly blurred with the rain and spray. To begin with, he'd tried walking on the little strip of beach opposite the lighthouse, but the wind was so strong there he could hardly stand still long enough to get the camera in focus. Finally, he had taken shelter in the lee of a wall, at one end of the harbour, and he'd managed to get a few shots of the really big waves, as they struck the bar and cascaded across the road. It was the best he could do: he had no idea how well the pictures would turn out but, in some way, by the time the film had run out, he had begun to understand that that didn't really matter. It was being there that counted. Being cold and wet, letting the water soak him, letting the wind chill him to the bone – that was what mattered.

Weeks later, when he'd saved enough money to have the film developed, the pictures he'd hoped for weren't there. He wasn't really surprised, when it came down to it; he'd almost expected it, in fact. Whatever it was he had been looking for, he knew it couldn't be captured like that: it couldn't be seen or fixed or even talked about, and if it could have been, it wouldn't have been the thing he had been looking for. Now, standing on the shore, with the same wind in his face – because it was the same wind, the same wind and the same life – he knew, as he had then, that nothing really mattered:

nothing except that life, which was infinite and eternal, if anything was, no matter how it shifted and slipped past you, teasing you with the promise of something that could never be grasped.

But this wasn't the sea. It was a sea loch, or a firth – he wasn't sure which – and the water was still and calm, cold water, full of weeds and fishes and all the rubbish and treasure and clues that had been thrown in, or lost, or left there for safe-keeping. He heard a voice call out behind him, but he didn't turn around – and then he saw Jennifer, standing at the water's edge, her legs bare, her skirt hitched up, as if she was just out for a paddle, looking down at her feet and taking tiny steps up and down in the slow surf. The light was on her hair, half-hiding her face, but he knew it was her. After a moment, she turned and saw him; she smiled then, and waved, then she turned and started walking, taking small, careful steps, towards the light where the sky began, halfway across the water. She didn't look back, she just kept on walking, but Alan knew she wanted him to come with her, and he followed, slowly, carefully, keeping her back in sight, walking into the light. Someone was calling out behind him, some warning, maybe, to let him know he had made a mistake. The voice was urgent, concerned and, for a moment, it seemed beautiful, like the voice he had been waiting to hear for the longest time, a reminder of something that had happened long ago, some childhood happiness, some loved one. There was a moment, even, when he wanted to turn back, to see what it was the voice wanted – but he pulled himself away, and the sound faded, the way the voices fade at the end of a record, the way the piano recedes into the distance and the voices hang for a moment, as if they wanted to go on singing forever. He took another step and the water reached his knees, then he went on, ignoring the warning that came again, out of the fade of things. With every step he took, he felt lighter and cleaner, as if his body was dissolving, leaving him only spirit and light. He could see Jennifer, walking away towards that space where the sky happened, and he went on, the lightness growing in his body, bright and cool and perfectly balanced, the weight he had carried for so long dissolving between his shoulder blades, in the pit of his stomach, in the ache of his groin. The water came up to his waist, and then to his chest. He couldn't see Jennifer any more, but he knew she was there, and he kept on walking, stumbling over the rocks, but moving on, moving on, emptying, becoming weightless. One more step, and he would be there. Spirit and light. Spirit and light. The words ran through his head, like the words of an old song, and he smiled. The voice behind him rang out one more time, but he ignored it because, now, for the first time, the first time ever, he was certain that he knew exactly where he was going.